# DOMINATING MR. DARLING

## SCANDALOUS BALLROOM ENCOUNTERS BOOK 5

## VICTORIA VALE

# PROLOGUE

*L*ady Amelia Fitzwilliam had never been like other young ladies—of this, she was well aware. Not just because she enjoyed what might be considered masculine pursuits such as hunting, shooting, and fencing—all while wearing breeches. There existed a restlessness inside of her, as if her very soul vibrated from a need to be in constant motion. It had driven her governess absolutely mad when she'd been a girl. It had gotten her into no end of trouble with her uncle—the man tasked with raising her and her brother, Simon, after the death of both their parents.

As she grew older and transformed from a girl to a young lady, it also became obvious that she did not relish following the dictates of the men responsible for her future. She *hated* being told what she must do, how she should act or speak, or where she could not go, simply because she'd been born with a pair of breasts and a quim. Simon had warned her that no man would want to wed her, but had given up trying to reform her once he'd realized she could not be changed.

Not that Simon was a bad person. As elder brothers went, he proved better than those of her other female acquaintances. Generously allowing her access to a portion of her massive inheritance, he gave her carte blanche to purchase whatever she might want, to do whatever she pleased. Perhaps that was because of their strict upbringing at the hands of their uncle, and the unspeakable horrors that had been committed by a man she knew now suffered eternal damnation.

One thing was certain, Simon's assertion that no man would want her had been proven wrong the moment she'd arrived in London for her first Season. Despite being spotted riding while wearing breeches in Hyde Park, and her penchant for saying whatever might be on her mind—even if it could be construed as rude or insulting—the gentlemen of the *ton* fawned over her, tripping over themselves to secure her notice. Younger women whispered about her behind her back, while wanting to emulate her. The matrons turned their noses up at her and pulled their precious debutante daughters, granddaughters, and nieces out of her path as if she might sully them. Not that she cared—the last people she would have wanted for friends would be those stuffy old windbags.

Only Simon's reputation as a cold brute with the power to ruin anyone who spoke against her had saved her from being cast out of society altogether. In fact, her brother's status as the Marquis of Ashton and one of the wealthiest peers in the realm had given her the freedom to do as she pleased—and she liked things this way.

While her suitors seemed perfectly *nice*, and she enjoyed the attention that being named The Incomparable had brought, she found the notion of marrying any of them unappealing. She'd spent her entire childhood hiding from her uncle, afraid to move or speak or simply *be*. From the moment of Gregory Fitzwilliam's death, she had decided the time had come to live life on her own terms. Her brother had done it … why couldn't she?

She still remembered her first lover quite fondly—a stable groom at Ashton House, who had openly admired the way Simon's old breeches had clung to her legs and hips. She had flirted with him whenever she walked back to the mews to retrieve her horse, and wondered what it might be like to sit upon his cock.

In order to keep her from being easily seduced, Simon had sat her down before her first Season and very frankly explained relations between men and women to her. So frankly, in fact, that as she had raked her gaze over the well-built groom, her stare settling on the outline of the erection pressed against the front of his breeches, she could picture exactly how she would fuck him. The idea grew more enticing by the day, until she could hardly think of the groom without growing moist between her thighs.

Deciding that there was no reason she should not do exactly what she wanted, Amelia had marched straight to the mews and imperiously dismissed the other grooms except for him.

"You," she'd said, bracing her hands on her hips. "What is your name?"

His eyes had lowered, his attention fixated upon the breeches hugging her hips. "James, m'lady."

His common accent had sent a thrill through her, as had the way he'd gazed upon her with naked hunger. The men of the *ton* treated her like a porcelain doll, an object to be admired like some priceless painting. This stable groom looked at her as if he wished to devour her whole.

"James, I want you to fuck me," she had declared.

The way his eyes had widened while his jaw fell slack might have been amusing, if not for the frustration his hesitation caused her.

"Are you hard of hearing?" she'd snapped.

"N-no, m'lady," he'd replied quickly. "It's just ... well, I weren't certain I heard y' right."

Biting her lower lip, she had edged closer to him. She reached up to the buttons running down the front of her shirt—another castoff from Simon's youth. Loosening the buttons from their holes, she revealed the valley between her breasts. They were small, fitting her almost boyish frame, but she'd once overheard one of the footmen saying that the nipple was the best part. If that proved true, no man would care that the mounds were small when they were tipped with plump, pink nipples just waiting to be touched and suckled.

"You heard correctly," she replied, her voice dropping into a husky purr. "You want me, do you not?"

His Adam's apple bobbed in his throat as he swallowed, his hands clenching and flexing at his sides. "Yes."

Advancing on him again, she reached out to take his hand, pulling him into an empty, clean stall. Anyone approaching the mews might see or hear them, but that only added to the excitement of what she was about to do.

"Open your breeches," she commanded, standing back and gesturing toward the organ between his hips.

He quickly obliged, his breath quickening as he fumbled to open the fall of his breeches.

Amelia's mouth went dry as she caught sight of his cock, thrusting out from beneath his dirty linen shirt. Jutting from a nest of coarse-looking, dark hair, it was quite large, thick, curving up toward his belly. A pearlescent bead of moisture seeped from the slit in his flared head—the seed, she remembered. The substance that came from the man into the woman was the seed, which produced offspring. That, she could not allow.

"Do not impregnate me," she warned.

He nodded, the movement jerky. "No, m'lady. I won't, m'lady."

*M'lady* … he was calling her that, even though they were about to have intercourse. A tiny thrill went through her as she realized she liked it—his deference and respect, even before he would pierce her maidenhead.

Striding forward, she knelt before him, reaching out to grasp his cock. James gasped, his eyes sliding closed as she squeezed him, testing the hard yet soft rod filling her palm. Curious, how more of the wetness came from him as she rubbed him, closing her hand and stroking up and down.

"Bloody 'ell," he muttered, knees buckling when she leaned forward to lick him—to taste the substance smeared over the tip.

It was salty, with an unfamiliar tang. Masculine. Primitive. With a groan, she closed her lips around him, hungry for more.

James gasped, his hips thrusting to shove more of his cock between her lips. He gripped her head and attempted to push it down, to force more of his length into her mouth—to control her.

She reached up to cup his bollocks, giving them a vicious squeeze in retaliation. He yelped, releasing her hair and falling to his knees.

"What the 'ell did you do that for?" he bellowed, his face reddening.

Interestingly enough, the pain did not seem to have affected his state of arousal.

"Do not do that again," she warned him. "Do what I say, and nothing more. Understood?"

Nodding, he didn't fight her when she threw him to his back and bowed her head to kiss his tortured balls—remorse for the pain she'd dealt them. She sucked and lapped at his cock while he thrashed and moaned beneath her. Then, grasping his shoulders, she turned onto her back and pulled him on top of her.

She ordered him to take off her breeches and boots, which he accomplished with clumsy, shaking hands. Then, she wrapped her legs around his waist, dug in her heels, and urged his hips toward hers.

"Fuck me," she whispered in his ear, tangling her fingers in his hair. "Now."

The initial pain of his invasion had only lasted a moment, and James had followed her every command—moving slowly at first until the pain faded and she stretched to accommodate him, then faster when the tension coiling in her pelvis became unbearable.

It had been the single most glorious moment of her life, climaxing with the stable groom's big body on top of her.

Afterward, she had placed a kiss upon his brow and murmured, 'Well done.' The grin he'd given her had spoken in a way words never could. He'd liked hearing her praise afterward, knowing he had pleased her.

She'd conducted an affair with him through the rest of the Season, learning more about what she enjoyed, about how shamelessly she could demand anything she wanted as long as James became aroused enough.

This, she realized, was another one of those things men did that were supposed to be unnatural when women attempted them. Dominance. Commanding another person to serve them, to give them what they wanted. A lady was supposed to be demure, quiet, a vessel for her husband to fill with his seed and flaunt on his arm.

If marriage meant she must give up the heady feeling of lust and control she'd felt with her stable groom, then she would never marry.

As the Season came to an end, seeing more than half her friends wed, Amelia had wondered if she'd made the right decision.

But that had been before an unlikely encounter with a guest of her brother's. One that would change her life, and solidify her decision never to wed.

Her name was Lady Millicent Dane, and she was one of the most ravishing women Amelia had ever seen. Tall, statuesque, with a body made of sin—large breasts, a slender waist, and flaring hips. Even Amelia, who had never looked upon another woman and felt lust, found herself thinking of sex the moment she laid eyes upon the notorious widow. She had married an elderly earl after her first Season, becoming a dowager countess mere months after the wedding. The generous settlement he'd left her in his will would see her taken care of for the rest of her days. And so, the Widow Dane—as she was known amongst the *ton*—did as she pleased with whomever she pleased.

Sure, she had become shunned in many circles, but it never seemed to bother Millicent. Amelia envied the woman, and often pondered the merits of marrying a man old enough to be her grandfather. Of course, with her luck, the bleeder would live to see one hundred, and she'd never be free of him.

The sudden appearance of the widow at Ashton House had not

surprised her. Shunning eligible chits, her brother liked nothing more than a widow or actress—some bit of skirt he could carry on with, free of obligation. That he should choose the Widow Dane as his latest conquest made perfect sense.

Seated in the rose drawing room with a book, she glanced up just as the butler admitted Millicent. Standing, she set her book aside and moved to the door, watching through the crack as Simon emerged from his study to greet her.

"My lady," he said in that brusque, clipped tone of his. "If you are ready to begin, we can adjourn to the dungeon."

Millicent smiled and inclined her head in acquiescence. "After you, my lord."

Dungeon? Did Simon refer to the basement he never allowed anyone to go into? She had often walked past the locked door, detecting the moans and groans that accompanied intercourse, assuming that it must be another bedroom for the purposes of illicit affairs. Her brother's eccentric tendencies—not allowing anyone to touch him, for one—no longer surprised her. However, the mention of this *dungeon* struck her as odd. Who referred to a room set aside for intercourse as a dungeon?

Peering around the corner and watching as they disappeared through the now unlocked door, she became gripped by an insatiable curiosity. While she was not averse to watching others copulate, she found the idea of spying on her own kin repugnant.

However, Simon did not remain in this so-called dungeon for long. Moments after escorting Millicent into the room, he reappeared, turning the corner to return to his study.

Odd, that.

If Millicent hadn't come for a night with Simon, why was she here?

Creeping past her brother's study on bare feet, Amelia made her way swiftly to the door. Pulling it open slowly, she then slipped into the dungeon—aptly named, she soon realized, due to the chill and the darkness. Crouching on the wooden steps, she peered down into the dimly lit room.

As her eyes adjusted to the dark, she found the room filled with ropes and what looked to be bridles and straps hanging from a beam overhead, as well as a wall with various riding crops and whips hanging from nails. She also noticed a table spread with odd instruments she could not name. A wooden structure leaned against the wall, in the shape of a diagonal cross.

Standing in the midst of it all, she found Millicent. She had undressed, and now wore only a black silk corset trimmed with red ribbons, with matching stockings. The red ribbons on her garters sat just below the plump cheeks of her buttocks, left bare by the absence of drawers. Most intriguing of all, a pair of black boots reached up to mid-thigh, their surface polished and gleaming in the light of the torches mounted on the wall.

A man knelt at her feet, hands captured behind his back and bound with rough rope. Completely nude, he grew aroused at the sight of Millicent, who stood with her legs spread, a long, black object coiled in one hand.

Amelia's mouth fell open as the black thing unraveled and fell to the floor, cracking ominously with a flick of the Widow Dane's wrist.

A whip.

"What are you staring at, my pet?" she purred, circling the man with a feral glint in her eyes.

The man—who had been captivated by the thatch of curls blanketing Millicent's mons—quickly lowered his gaze.

"I apologize, Mistress," he murmured.

She laughed, a deep, throaty sound that even made Amelia squirm. The woman was absolutely divine … everything she wanted to be.

"It's quite all right," Millicent said to the man. "You were looking at my cunt, weren't you, my pet? Thinking of pleasuring me … tasting me … touching me. Admit it."

The man's breath hitched, a tremor shaking his body. "Yes, Mistress … I want all those things. Let me pleasure you."

Amelia's mouth went dry as she looked over the man at Millicent's feet. He was no milksop—even on his knees, he was tall, with broad shoulders and a bulging chest, his arms appearing strong enough that he could snap the ropes holding him if he wished.

Then, why did he submit to Millicent?

*Because she's too tempting to resist,* she told herself.

Bold. Daring. Beautiful. Millicent commanded his attention, his respect … his deference. He knelt because it was the only way to reach that coveted valley between her thighs.

"You shall have the chance to earn it," Millicent promised him. "But first, a punishment for your wandering eyes."

Pausing behind the man, she looped the whip around his neck, pulling it taut. He gasped, as she knelt behind him, giving him a rough jerk and tipping his head back to rest against her breasts.

"Yes, Mistress," he croaked, his voice strained by the bite of the whip against his throat. "Punish me."

Releasing him, she untied his hands and circled to stand in front of him. "On your hands and knees, my pet."

Amelia clung to the balustrade, forgetting the hardness of the step she rested on, the discomfort of sitting for so long with her knees bent up toward her chest. She lost herself in the seductive dance of pain and pleasure, watching as Millicent whipped the man, alternating blows with strokes of her hands, and kisses to soothe the pain. He groaned in pleasure and bellowed in pain, enduring it all and thanking her—for the pleasure or the pain, Amelia was not certain.

And then, finally, the man received his reward. One word from Millicent, and he lunged for her, lifting her off her feet, throwing her onto an empty table, and plunging deep into her. Amelia left the room then, certain that if she continued watching, she would go up in flames.

She retreated to her drawing room, but found she could not return to her book. Her mind whirled dizzily from all that she had seen and heard. Meanwhile, she lamented the loss of James, who had found a better position at another house in London. The way her breasts tingled and her channel throbbed for want of a cock, she knew her own efforts would not be enough.

After what felt like ages, voices sounded in the corridor once more. Dashing to the door, she peered out through the crack, watching as Millicent's lover took his leave. Then, the widow knocked upon the door to Simon's study. Her brother appeared, and the two spoke in hushed tones for a while before he took her arm to escort her to the door.

"I do thank you for your generosity, my lord," Millicent said, accepting her hat and spencer from the butler. "I hope it isn't too much an imposition."

"Of course not, my lady," Simon replied, helping the woman into her spencer.

"Next week … Same day and time?"

He nodded, standing back while the butler opened the door for her. "Naturally. For as long as you need … think nothing of it."

Amelia frowned, watching as she disappeared and Simon retreated back to his study. The room of sin that Millicent had just occupied with her lover must have been created by her brother. Did what she'd just witnessed occur at Ashton House regularly? Did *Simon* enjoy being whipped and ordered about by women?

No … her brother would never allow that. Too controlling.

Perhaps he was the one wielding the whip with his lovers. That seemed far more likely.

However, Simon's predilections did not interest her so much as Millicent's. As she slid her feet into her slippers before dashing from the drawing room and through the front door, she realized that those urges were also her own. Thinking of James, of all the times they'd been together, she realized that her pleasure had come more from his willingness to do anything she commanded than from the act of intercourse itself. She must learn what she did not know, understand the power she could wield with the right tutelage.

She spotted Millicent walking just ahead of her and broke into a run, not caring about how unladylike it might make her appear.

"Lady Dane!" she called out, coming up short as the woman turned to face her.

Millicent smiled—a catlike motion of her lips that Amelia envied, just as she coveted this woman's secrets. How did she do it—command a man twice her size with the flick of her wrist?

"Enjoyed the spectacle, did you?" she murmured, giving Amelia a knowing glance.

Instead of being embarrassed that the widow had been aware of her presence the entire time, she nodded.

"Very much," she admitted. "I had been ignorant to such practices, but now that I've seen what you can do—what you can get a man to do—I must know how."

Arching an eyebrow at her, Millicent glanced about to ensure no one came close enough to overhear them. "Ashton will not like it. Your other exploits about town have frustrated him enough as it is."

"I do not care," she declared. "I have never cared what anyone thinks of me."

"Yes, I know," Millicent replied. "You remind me so much of myself when I was a young debutante—or rather, you remind me of the girl I would have wanted to be. You see, I did not obtain my freedom until the earl passed away. Only then did I become bold enough to start demanding what I want, and neglecting to take 'no' for an answer."

Amelia nodded, her heart swelling in her chest at the promise of what Millicent stood to offer her. "Please, my lady. This isn't about what Simon wants … it is about what *I* want. He never has to know."

Falling silent for a moment, the widow studied her intently. After a moment, she bowed her head in acquiescence.

"I will teach you, on one condition," she said.

"Anything," Amelia blurted, too desperate to wonder what Millicent might require.

"Ashton must know that I am training you," she said. "He trained me, you see … and while I own many of the implements for practicing at domination, his dungeon is the best to be found in London, and he allows me to use it from time to time. It is the only place I can give you the full education you would require to become a true Mistress."

Her palms broke out in a sweat as she thought of her brother.

Simon allowed her to do what she pleased, but this, he would not permit. He would fight her at every turn, she felt certain of it.

"Come, darling," Millicent said, taking her arm and looping it through her own. "We shall browbeat him together. This shall be your first lesson as a dominant … the art of demanding what you want. Of course, with a man like your brother, it is best that you let him *think* it is a negotiation."

A tremor rolled down her spine as she turned wide eyes up to the woman leading her back to Ashton house.

"Oh, Lady Dane … I do like you."

Millicent gave her a sly smirk. "Likewise, my dear. I can see the two of us will get along quite famously."

# CHAPTER 1

"Simon, do sit down … you'll wear a hole through the rug at this rate."

Glancing up from her novel, Amelia found that her elder brother, Lord Simon Fitzwilliam IV, Marquis of Ashton, had failed to heed her directive. Raking a hand through his midnight-black hair, he continued down the corridor, spinning on his heel and pacing back toward her. His pale gray eyes—silver, her sister-in-law would insist—darted about, while his mouth had pinched into a straight line.

Seated in a high-backed armchair, she sighed. "Simon, sit."

Her commanding tone might not have affected him on any other day, but today, her brother obeyed. Plopping into the chair beside hers, he rested his head against the wall and closed his eyes. Despite this, his posture remained rigid—back erect, both hands resting upon his thighs. One would think the man awaited the executioner.

"Do relax," she murmured, giving him a small smile. "She isn't dying, she is only—"

A woman's bloodcurdling scream emitted from across the corridor, echoing through the entire house. Simon leapt to his feet again, crossing the hallway to the closed door in one long stride.

"Sophie! Sophie, darling … are you all right?" he called out, both hands braced upon the wooden panel.

"Of course I'm not all right, you bloody idiot!" came Sophie's enraged howl from the other side. "I vow, if you come into this room, I shall disembowel you … and I doubt it would hurt as much as this!"

"Giving birth," Amelia murmured under her breath, completing her sentence.

Though neither of them heard her.

Simon pressed his forehead to the wood and sighed.

"I'm sorry," he replied. "Just get through this, and you'll never have to do it again, darling. I promise you."

Turning away from the door, he gritted his teeth. "God, please let it be a boy so we never have to do this again."

She quirked up an eyebrow at him. "The heir must have his spare, dear brother."

He scoffed. "Like hell. I shall keep the lad in a padded room—I'll pay to have the sidewalks of Grosvenor Square redone in velvet cushioning if I have to in order to protect the boy from harm. Anything to keep from having to sire another child on that … that unholy demon shrieking in there."

Hiding a smirk behind her book, Amelia silently mused over how much life at Ashton House had changed. If, last year, someone had told her that Simon Fitzwilliam IV would work himself into a state of worry over his childbearing wife, Amelia might have laughed in their faces. After all, her brother had always been a man who never flinched in the face of anything—not since he'd been a lad.

Yet, marriage to Lady Sophie had transformed him in a way Amelia might have never imagined. While still stoic and reserved most of the time, Simon could often be found smiling or laughing—usually due to some magical thing his wife did. He seemed less burdened, less angry … no longer broken.

Another scream came, followed by a string of curses, all of which sounded quite comical in Sophie's lyrical voice. The woman who had captured Simon's heart with her sunny disposition had been transformed by her delicate condition. While Amelia had no notion of how it felt to carry and birth a babe, she found it perfectly reasonable to blame the man who had caused said condition. She found it reasonable to blame the male sex for most things.

A moment later, the door swung open, and Sophie's lady's maid, Frances, appeared. With a wide smile, she stepped out into the hall to meet Simon, who had stood and ambled toward the doorway.

"'Tis a boy, my lord," she said with a radiant smile.

Amelia closed her book and stood, grinning as Simon digested the news. With wide eyes, he ran both hands through his hopelessly disheveled hair.

"A boy," he whispered. "My God, she did it."

"And," Frances added, her smile widening. "A girl!"

Amelia's eyes grew wide as she glanced from her brother to the maid. "What? What did you say?"

"Her Ladyship has given birth to twins, my lady," Frances replied, chin lifted proudly as if she'd helped carry and birth said twins. "One of each—a boy *and* a girl."

A surprised huff left Simon, and for a long moment, he stood staring at the door hanging ajar.

The flurry of movement and sharp cries of two infants drew Amelia forward, and she peered inside to find two maids washing the babes over basins of water, while the physician tended to Sophie.

"Oh, well done, Simon," she quipped. "Two in one go on your first try … never let it be said that you lack ambition."

Opening and closing his mouth several times as if trying to express a thought—any thought—her brother appeared like a fish out of water.

"Breathe, Simon," she commanded.

He obeyed, suddenly exhaling as if he'd been holding his breath. Then, he turned to face her with a smile.

"Twins," he murmured, seeming unable to say or think of much else.

She stood back and watched as Frances ushered him into the room. She would wait to be invited inside—giving her brother and his wife their privacy for such an intimate moment. She sat and took up her book again, but could not concentrate.

After realizing she'd read the same line four times, she closed the tome and rested it in her lap.

As her gaze traced the pattern of the wallpaper, she mulled over the future—her own future, specifically. With so many things changing so quickly at Ashton House, she'd begun to feel like an intruder. Not that Sophie or Simon would allow her to call herself a burden. Both her brother and sister-in-law insisted that they enjoyed her presence. However, it had stopped feeling like her home, and more like the home of her brother and his wife—and now, their children.

This was the way things should be, and she couldn't be happier for Simon. For so long, she'd worried that their horrible uncle had beaten the love and affection out of her brother, leaving him a hollow shell.

"Well, he certainly showed you, didn't he, Uncle Gregory?"

Rubbing the nose of a dead man into her brother's triumph felt better than it ought. She took comfort in the knowledge that Lord Gregory Fitzwilliam was neither mourned nor missed. The day he'd left this world had been the day both Simon and Amelia had been set free.

Perhaps the time had come to expand the bounds of her freedom. Leaving Ashton House had always been inevitable, but now, it had become imperative. Her brother and his wife did not need her underfoot; not when he often joked that having her about was akin to looking after a child. He meant it in jest, but it was how she'd come to feel.

The bedroom door swung open, and Simon reappeared, holding one of the swaddled infants in the crook of his arm.

"Amelia, come and see," he murmured, his voice holding a gentleness she'd have never thought him capable of.

Rising, she set her book on the chair and joined him in the doorway, gazing at the red-faced babe he held. A headful of inky black hair covered its head, while matching lashes rested over closed eyes in the same shade.

"This is the girl," he whispered, as if afraid to wake her. "Her name is Joanna Ruth Fitzwilliam."

Her eyes stung as she tore her gaze from the beautiful baby and looked up at Simon. "You named her after Mother."

He nodded. "Sophie's idea."

A beautiful name, and a fitting tribute to a woman Amelia had never known. Lady Joanna had died giving birth to her, during Simon's sixth year. He remembered her fondly, and now, his daughter would carry her name.

Stepping further into the room, she found Sophie resting in bed, propped up by several pillows, a clean, white chemise covering her, along with a mountain of blankets. Strands of dark brown hair clung to her damp forehead, but her vibrant green eyes twinkled with joy. She held the other twin against her chest, the top of his dark head visible atop the swaddling.

"Come closer," Sophie urged. "Meet your nephew."

Amelia approached the bed and smiled down at the lad as he smacked hungrily, attempting to fit his fist into his mouth.

"Did you name him Simon?" she asked.

"I wanted to, but your brother wished for him to have his own name," Sophie replied. "So, he is Phineas Samuel Fitzwilliam."

Amelia nodded in approval. "Wonderful names, Phineas and Joanna … As their aunt, I reserve the right to refer to them as Phin and Jo."

Sophie giggled. "I like the sound of that."

"Congratulations to you both," she said, reaching out to stroke little Phineas' head. "I am so proud."

"As are we," Simon replied, though he did not meet her gaze. He had eyes only for baby Joanna.

Edging away from the bed, Amelia cleared her throat. "Well, I shall leave you to become acquainted with the little loves. Sophie, send Frances for me when you are ready for company."

"Of course," Sophie replied.

Turning to leave the room, she paused beside Simon. She reached out and took his shoulder in an affectionate gesture—something that did not come easy between them.

She found tears gleaming in his eyes when he met her stare, and she shared both his joy and his fear.

"You will not botch this," she whispered. "Do you hear me? You are a *good* husband, Simon, and I know you'll be a wonderful father. Those children are fortunate to have you."

Nodding, he blinked, containing the tears. "Thank you, Amelia."

Standing on tiptoe, she kissed his cheek. Then, stepping out into the corridor, she closed the door and set off for the stairs. Today marked a new beginning for Simon and Sophie, and for that, she was grateful.

But what was there for her?

The Season had reached its halfway point, and she had yet to find a man she wished to wed. As she had promised her brother she would at least try to secure a proposal, Amelia had set out at the onset of the Season with marriage on her mind. He'd allowed her a stipend for new clothing, and the moment she mentioned being ready to dispense with her status of spinster by summer, the men had converged upon her like a pack of ravenous dogs after a juicy steak.

She'd tried to like them—she really had. She had allowed herself to be courted by several men, and not a single one had met her requirements for a mate. At least, not one that could be considered suitable. As the sister of a marquis and the recipient of a large inheritance, she attracted the most influential men of the *ton*. Even those with empty pockets in need of her fortune came with pedigrees as impressive as any royal's. Her reputation as a bit of an oddity among the peerage only made her more desirable—or so she'd been told. There didn't exist an unmarried lord in all of England who did not want to claim the most elusive prize of all. Her.

The problem did not lie in quantity, but in quality. The sort of men who pursued her lacked the bollocks to match her. Pampered, perfumed, and catered to, there didn't seem to be a real man in the lot. Hair artfully tousled in the style of Byron, bodies trussed up in flamboyant clothing, and feigning the sort of affected boredom that had become fashionable ... there could be no type of man designed to cause her cunt to dry up faster than that.

The sorts of men she *did* like also happened to be the unsuitable sort. Stable hands. Footmen. Merchants. Men who went by 'mister' instead of 'my lord'. Aside from that, many were not interested in marriage to a wealthy heiress as much as they enjoyed being dominated by one.

And therein lay her conundrum. If only she could find a titled man of the peerage, who might think of her as his equal, but who would also enjoy submitting to her ... she'd marry such a man in an eye's blink!

However, as there seemed to be no such man in London, Amelia had begun to resign herself to a life of eternal spinsterhood.

Reaching her bedchamber, she opened the door to find Kate, her lady's maid, laying a gown across her bed.

"Good evening, my lady," she murmured, straightening to curtsy. "How fairs Her Ladyship?"

"My sister-in-law has given birth to twins. Can you believe it, Kate? A boy *and* a girl. They named the boy Phineas and the girl Joanna."

Kate smiled, clapping her hands together in glee. "Oh, my lady ... what wonderful news! I am certain His Lordship is quite pleased."

Thinking of Simon's tear-filled gaze and the look of awe he'd worn while gazing upon his daughter, Amelia nodded. "He is."

Crossing the room to her vanity, she sat on the cushioned bench and faced her reflection. While she and Simon had both inherited their mother's black hair and grey eyes, she carried many of her father's features. She'd been told that his spirit lived on in her—that he'd been the sort of man who smiled often. Not that she would know. He'd perished in a terrible accident not long after Lady Joanna had died birthing her.

She ran a hand across her forehead, marveling at the youthful appearance of her face. She'd been led to believe that her impending age of thirty put her near death. Or, perhaps it was only her unmarried state that caused people to respond with shock when they learned her age.

Her brother had even told her that he worried at the prospect of her dying alone. He wanted a happy future for her, the sort of life he shared with Sophie.

"Yes, but he loves her," she whispered to her reflection. "And that is the difference."

"Beg your pardon, my lady?" Kate called out from across the room.

Sighing, she shook her head. "Nothing, Kate."

Simon and Sophie had not been in love at the time of their marriage, but had been fortunate enough to find it together after they'd wed. Amelia was not brave enough to risk that. Perhaps because to marry a man meant placing everything she held dear into his hands—her life, her freedom, her body. What if she chose wrong and ended up regretting the decision for the rest of her days? What if her husband turned out to be cruel, the sort of man who would treat her the way Uncle Gregory had? Or worse … what if he did to their children what their uncle had done to her and Simon? Just the thought made her ill.

"My lady, I took the liberty of laying out the rose satin for tonight's fête," Kate called out from where she stood in Amelia's dressing room.

Turning to face Kate, she shook her head. "No … I do not believe I'll be attending. Ready my buff breeches and the blue brocade waistcoat instead. Do not forget my boots."

"Of course, my lady," Kate replied.

The maid never batted an eyelash anymore when Amelia

requested the men's clothing—her collection of waistcoats and cravats proving larger than the number of gowns she owned. Tonight, she had no desire to attend some dull party and pretend to be interested in the inane prattling of the debutantes or the overtures of the men tripping over themselves to impress her.

Tonight, she would celebrate the birth of her niece and nephew by visiting one of her favorite haunts in London. A few hours of beating a room full of men at Hazard ought to do the trick.

<h1 style="text-align:center">CHAPTER 2</h1>

Michael Darling lingered outside the unassuming façade of the building he'd been told housed one of London's most disreputable gaming hells. Having only journeyed to the city a handful of times in his life, he supposed he must take the word of the man who had directed him here. It was, he'd been informed, one of only a few gambling houses in London that permitted women—and unlike all the other men gathered to squander their money over dice and cards, he had not come to get away from a woman, but to find one. Not just any chit, however. Michael had come here for the express purpose of finding a particular woman.

Lady Amelia Fitzwilliam.

Giving himself a cursory glance, he decided he looked decent enough. His ensemble might be a bit behind the current style, but that was to be expected of a man who resided primarily in the country—where news of the latest fashion took a bit longer to reach. However, these were his best boots, and the only coat he owned that hadn't been mended to hell. His breeches proved a bit worn, but fit well and were clean. Besides, in the darkened interior of the club, he hoped she would not notice his outmoded attire.

Nothing screamed 'fortune-hunter' like shabby clothing.

And, truth be told, he had now reached some place *beyond* desperate. Desperate had passed him by months ago, and now, he had committed to the one thing he'd always hoped to avoid: rushing off to London in search of a bride.

Having lived most of his life in Norfolk, it had seemed reasonable to assume he would eventually take one of his neighbor's daughters as a wife. A simple gentleman farmer wedding the daughter of a simple gentleman farmer, and breeding future gentleman farmers. It was the sort of life his forebears had lived, and it had been good enough for him.

Until he had been forced to face a most harsh reality: if he did not find and marry a wealthy heiress, and soon, he risked financial ruin. Thus his position outside a gaming den in London. While the eligible women of his acquaintance all came with dowries, none proved enough to save Oakmoor. Year by year, his debt mounted, while the income generated by his farmlands dwindled. He needed a large sum of money, quickly, or everything he loved, everything his father and his father's father had ever worked to build, would be lost.

If he was going to rely on his last resort—marriage to an heiress— he could not marry just any heiress. She must come with heavy pockets.

Upon arriving in London, he'd pored over the gossip columns, hoping to learn which eligible chits came with the largest dowries. It hadn't taken him long to find her, a woman the gossipmongers referred to as *The Incomparable Lady A* in their writings. It had been said that her reemergence on the Marriage Mart had thrown the *ton* into a frenzy—especially when it got around that her brother and guardian had tripled her already obscene dowry. Having been twenty thousand pounds at the start of her first Season, it now sat at a whopping sixty thousand—enough to set all his debts right and breathe new life into the now dilapidated Oakmoor Manor.

It hadn't taken long to discover who 'The Incomparable Lady A' might be, as she held a certain reputation in London. A bold and brash woman, she inexplicably did what she wished without facing many consequences. Shunned by few—lest they face the wrath of her brother—and adored by many, she had become a spectacle, the sort people craned their necks to stare at whenever in her presence.

Not that it mattered to him. Gossip like that rarely ever reached Norfolk, and it wasn't as if he had some precious, titled bloodline to safeguard. A woman to breed with and refill his depleted coffers—that would be all he needed.

Entering the establishment, Michael vowed to do whatever it took to secure her. Though he doubted it would be very hard. After all, the woman had reached her thirtieth year without nabbing a husband—surely, the increased dowry proved desperation on her brother's part. If the men of the *ton* wanted nothing to do with her, he would gladly whisk her away along with her generous inheritance.

As he stepped into the first large, open gaming room, he craned his neck to take in his surroundings. A massive chandelier hanging over-head, along with the thick Oriental rugs, marked the establishment as the sort of place catering to wealthy clientele—despite its unfortunate location in the seedier part of London. Two large Hazard tables took up the middle of the room, where the people gathered around kept their rapt attention upon the dice being rolled by a young man in snappy, fashionable attire. Their mingled cheers and groans of disap-pointment followed him from the room as he moved on, certain he had not seen her among them. He passed several other rooms of similar design—tables covered in green baize where the underbelly of London mingled with members of the *ton* not too high in the instep to descend into the gutter, together trying their luck at dice and cards.

It was in the fourth room that he found her—The Incomparable Lady A. He did not have to initiate an introduction to know she was the woman he sought when the gossip rags had described her perfectly. Slender, with an almost boyish figure, shining black hair, and a wide mouth that appeared to hold a ready smirk at its left corner. Dressed in men's attire, she pulled off the tailcoat and breeches with flair, her cravat tied in a whimsical fashion that would have been over the top on a male, but softened her feminine features. An expensive-looking cameo brooch rested at her throat where a man would place a tiepin, and her waistcoat seemed tailored to fit her lean frame.

Piquet was their game, Michael realized as he came further into the room. Edging toward their table along the wall, he recognized the exchange of cards. Piquet being a game he excelled at, he found himself confident in his strategy. Lady Amelia had refused every man who had offered for her, which did not intimidate him in the least. He was not some dandified, perfumed milksop of a lord. This might have been considered a disadvantage with any other London chit … but not this one.

Glancing up at him, she met and held his gaze, even while her lips moved in conversation with her opponent. She grinned, though Michael felt certain it was not because of something the man had said. It almost seemed as if she found his bold assessment amusing. He could see how she might intimidate other men; her expression would leave a less confident fellow wondering if she laughed at him. He could not care less if she did … all that mattered was securing her promise to marry him. As it happened, he knew exactly how to accomplish such an aim.

He continued watching her as she finished with her opponent, trouncing him quite efficiently. The man rose from the table, bid her good night, and disappeared into the cigar-smoke clouded room.

Michael took the opening quickly. As he pulled out the chair across from her and sank into it, he became lost in her stare. Merry grey eyes possessing the gleam of silver held his gaze. They were the color of storm clouds, but held the fluidity of silk. Surrounded by a fan of sooty lashes, they were beautiful, though not her most remarkable feature.

His cock twitched in his breeches as he lowered his gaze to her mouth. Wide, lush, and curved into a smirk at one corner, those lips tempted him with unspoken promises—of what it would be like to plunder that mouth, to bite the lower lip, to fist her hair and have her wrap those beautiful lips around his cock.

"Is it Piquet you've come for, or an audience with The Incomparable Lady A?" she asked when he merely sat there staring at her like an idiot.

Clearing his throat, he gave her a smile. "Both, if I may be so bold."

Gathering the cards, she shuffled them into a neat deck with expert flair. "I do like a bold man. Though I feel a bit disadvantaged. You know who I am, but I do not believe I've had the honor … or the pleasure."

The back of his neck grew hot at the way she purred those last words—*or the pleasure*. Thus far, the little hoyden had more than lived up to her reputation.

"Mr. Michael Darling, at your service," he replied, inclining his head. "It is an honor to meet you, Lady Amelia."

Lifting the small sherry glass at her elbow, she downed what remained of the red-brown liquid and grinned. "Join me for a sherry? I find I cannot keep my wits about me while playing Piquet unless I'm good and foxed."

A dimple appeared in her left cheek, drawing his eye and overwhelming him with the urge to sink his tongue into the little hollow.

*One thing is for certain,* he thought. *I needn't worry that I won't want to bed the chit.*

In fact, it was all he could think about at the moment.

She waved down a passing waiter and imperiously called for two measures of sherry. As they waited, she placed the cards in front of them.

"Shall we cut to see who deals first?" she offered.

He glanced down at the cards—a standard 32-card Piquet deck. Gesturing toward them, he raised an eyebrow. "Ladies first."

He drew the high card, making him the dealer for the first *partie*, so as their sherry was served, he took up the entire deck and began dealing. Once they each held twelve cards, he placed the remainders in the center of the table.

"What brings you to London, Mr. Darling?" Amelia asked as she studied her cards.

"How do you know I am not a resident of the city, my lady?" he asked.

"I've lived exclusively in London since my coming out," she replied, glancing at him over her hand. "Though I did spend my childhood at Ashton Abbey, and it has not been so long that I do not know a country bumpkin when I see one."

Before he had a chance to be annoyed or insulted, she grinned and laughed, the sound stroking at the base of his spine.

"I happen to *like* country bumpkins," she added, shifting the cards around in her hand.

He began sorting his own cards, taking a moment to think on his first move. "You've got me pegged, my lady. I own land in Norfolk and have resided there since birth."

"There's such an honesty about people who aren't tainted by the evils of London," she said.

Smirking at her, he raised one eyebrow. "Who said I was untainted?"

"Oh, la!" she said with another laugh. "And here I was hoping I could be the one to corrupt you. What a shame."

"Oh, my lady," he replied, finding that he enjoyed matching wits with her. "While I am not pure as the driven snow, I am certain there are many ways The Incomparable Lady A could … corrupt me."

If he was not mistaken—and he was generally good at noticing such things—heat flared in her gaze in response to his teasing. So, she was not unaffected then, either. This heat … this *spark* he'd felt the moment he'd clapped eyes on her, was apparently mutual.

Excellent.

"You have yet to answer my question," she said, laying five cards face down on the table beside her and keeping the other seven. "What brings you to London, Mr. Darling?"

Pulling aside six of his own cards and placing them on the green baize, he met her stare and declared his intentions boldly.

"I am here to find a wife, my lady."

# CHAPTER 3

$\mathcal{A}$melia fought to keep her composure as she studied Michael Darling. Her gaze met his over the top of her cards while she reached out to the pile resting between them to replace the ones she'd set aside. His answer to her question had hardly surprised her. The landed gentry tended to have slimmer pickings when it came to selecting mates. And a man like him would not be satisfied with marrying some freckle-faced country girl from the estate neighboring his.

No, a man like Michael Darling would want a woman who could offer him the excitement of a challenge.

It was in his eyes—so blue, she had a difficult time looking away from them. They suggested a good humor, yet, experience had taught her to look deeper, to discern just what it was that the men in her company wanted.

Yes, there, behind the soft sky blue of his irises, concealed within its prisms, Amelia saw what he wanted.

Adventure, a thrill … something perhaps he was not even aware he craved.

She had learned how to spot the signs of such desires, and at the moment found herself grateful to be able to see it in Mr. Darling. It had been weeks since she'd last taken a lover into her bed, and just now, the man seated across from her proved a most tantalizing prospect.

No, he did not fit in with the other men in this room—but it was this aspect that appealed to her most. His plain clothing concealed a body honed by labor, the white shade of his linen contrasting sharply with his sun-darkened skin. The width and breadth of his shoulders, along with large, rough, calloused hands told her that though he belonged to the landed gentry, he proved no stranger to hard work. A gentleman farmer who often toiled alongside his tenants—not the sort of man she typically became involved with.

That only made him more appealing. Additionally, his chiseled features, strong chin, and the rough shadow of a few days' worth of golden-blond stubble combined in a mingling of classic handsomeness and rakish appeal to make her pulse flutter. She wanted to kiss the line of his jaw and nip at his chin … to rake her fingers through the carefully combed blond hair curling at the nape of his neck … to tear his clothing off and bind him with ropes, forcing him to his knees and commanding him to do her wicked bidding.

Just the thought of that powerful body knelt in submission before her made her shiver.

He had come to London searching for a wife. But, who was to say the man did not wish to indulge in a bit of fun while he was about his search?

As she drew cards to replace the ones she'd discarded, she smiled at him. "Deuced boring business, that. I gave up the search long ago, as I'm certain you've heard."

"Hmm … so I did," he replied while taking his turn pulling from the deck between them. "A dagger in the heart of every eligible bachelor in London, I am sure."

"For certain," she quipped.

He smiled at that, though he kept his eyes on his cards. "I do envy you … to be able to enjoy city life without the pressing concerns of marriage. Alas, my circumstances have left me with no other choice."

Ah, an impoverished gent. Mr. Darling's presence in London now made even more sense. Here, one could not throw a stone in Hyde Park without striking a debutante with a large dowry.

"Poor Mr. Darling," she crooned. "Such a tedious process. I am certain you will find yourself in need of a reprieve from time to time during your search. How long will you remain?"

He fell silent for a moment while they exchanged cards, his brow furrowed in concentration. Once he'd finished taking his turn, he met her gaze once more. Yet again, Amelia found herself drowning in their depths, intrigued by the hint of danger she found lurking in the otherwise unassuming depths. A thrill shot down her spine, making her shiver.

"As long as it takes, I suppose," he replied, shrugging one shoulder. "My lady, as you are a longtime resident of London, I do wonder if you might be amenable to enlightening me on the ways I might find … relief from such tedium. Being a country gentleman, I am accustomed to filling my days with vigorous activity. I must admit that the prospect of slipping into the indolent habits of the London gentleman do not appeal to me."

A flutter began between her thighs, and she squeezed her legs together to stifle it.

*I could ride you until you pass out from fatigue, Mr. Darling,* she thought. *Vigorous activity, indeed.*

Raising an eyebrow at him, she pursed her lips. "I understand your dilemma, Mr. Darling, as it is the same problem I often face. Perhaps we could be of help to each other in this regard."

Heat flared in his eyes, the soft blue darkening as his pupils widened in response to her innuendo. Amelia had often been accused of being too bold, too overt in making her wants and desires known. But she had spent far too much of her life afraid to speak, to move, to simply exist. She had vowed long ago that any man who could not abide her boldness did not deserve her attention.

Michael Darling, she could see, appreciated that she did not hedge around the subject at hand. Yes, he would be the perfect bedmate … especially if she could teach him to submit to the sort of pleasure she could unlock for him with the use of dominance and pain.

She took the last of her sherry in one quick swallow, but found it did nothing to temper the urges causing her breasts to tingle and her cunt to throb. The sooner she coaxed this man into her bed, the better. He proved just the sort of diversion she needed to take her mind off her own troubles.

His voice intruded upon her thoughts, drawing her gaze back to his. The cards seemed to have been forgotten for now—by them both.

"It has occurred to me that we have not yet placed a wager upon our game," he said. "We have not yet declared hands … it isn't too late."

Taking in his clothing—well-made and clean, but worn and several years out of fashion—Amelia knew he could never hope to match any bet she might place with money. However, as his gaze burned intently into hers, she saw what he did not say.

It was not money he spoke of, thank heavens.

She slid her foot forward, finding his beneath the table. Nudging it with her own, she bit her lower lip and allowed the toe of her boot to caress his ankle.

"What did you have in mind, Mr. Darling?" she purred.

"One night with me," he said, leaning toward her across the green baize table and lowering his voice. "If I win, that is the payment I require."

She inclined her head. "Do you think you must win this game in order to tempt me to your bed?"

He chuckled. "No … but I do believe I would have to win it in order to coerce you to not only come to my bed, but allow me free liberty with your body."

Her blood ran cold, and her desire tempered a bit at his challenge. He could not know how his words sent a frisson of stark dread through her. Yet, they did … causing her to consider refusing the offer. She had *never* allowed a man free reign with her body and did not intend to begin now.

Clearing her throat, she forced a smile and donned the mask of The Incomparable Lady A once again. She wanted him badly enough to risk it. With a hand as good as hers, she could afford to call his bluff.

"Agreed," she said. "If I win, I wish for the same liberty. Anything I demand of you, I want done without question."

His smirk was mocking, almost as if he thought himself humoring her. Most likely, he did not expect for her to demand anything more than the things he'd done with previous bedmates.

Michael Darling was in for one hell of a shock, and Amelia could not wait to deliver … to see the look upon his face when she tied his hands behind his back and did what she wanted to him.

"Done," he replied.

They fell silent as the match continued, exchanging lingering glances as they moved through the various phases of the game. Amelia tallied their points, reminding herself how imperative it was for her to win. They remained neck and neck for most of the match, Michael proving to be as good as her at Piquet.

However, the final deal of the *partie* resulted in a win for her, bringing their wager to a satisfactory conclusion.

She could not help a grin as she glanced up to meet his gaze, triumph raising her chin.

Leaning back in his chair, he nodded in admission of his defeat.

"Well done, my lady," he said. "I am yours for the night, as promised."

As she gathered the cards to arrange them back into a neat deck, the familiar thrum of anticipation began at her pulse points and between her thighs. Nothing excited her more than initiating a man into her world—showing him what she was capable of as a Mistress.

Rising to her feet, she raked her gaze over his body as he did the same, revealing that he towered over her by several inches. The promise of the power concealed by his clothes—of the body she could not wait to unwrap and reveal—caused moisture to pool between her thighs.

"Mr. Darling, no words could prove to entice me more than those you just uttered."


Michael glanced at the woman walking confidently beside him down the darkened London street. Despite being several inches shorter than him, Amelia proved tall for a woman, her long legs keeping pace with his easily. The man's coat she wore had been tailored to fit her shoulders and waist, but fell to her ankles, fluttering behind her as she walked with long, self-assured strides. She had donned a beaver hat before leaving the gaming hell with him, and twirled an ornate walking stick in one hand. Not once did she attempt to take his arm or let on that being in the slums of London in the middle of the night rattled her.

Lady Amelia Fitzwilliam was unlike any woman he'd ever known, and damn if that did not send the blood to his cock swifter than ever before. The organ pressed greedily against the fall of his breeches, pulsating with the need to be buried between her beautiful legs.

He could make out their shape with each step she took, the breeches molding to sinewy thighs, the supple leather of her boots displaying strong calves. If only her coat did not conceal the flare of her hips and the swell of her arse. Bending her over as he snatched down her breeches appealed to him in a way he'd never have thought possible. Fucking her while she wore boots and breeches … bloody hell, just the thought almost made him spend in his smallclothes.

But, no, he could take no such liberties. He had promised to allow her full control for this evening's encounter—had purposely thrown their Piquet game in her favor in order to give her what she clearly wanted. If he was going to tempt Amelia to the altar, he would need to employ a bit of strategy. Allowing her to think she was in charge would go a long way toward earning her trust, as well as assuring she would not simply toss him aside after this one encounter. He intended to do everything he could to make sure she came back to him for more.

"Here we are," he said as they neared the inn he'd taken up residence in. "I do apologize if the accommodations are a bit Spartan for your tastes."

Pausing just in front of the inn, she turned and pierced him with her intuitive gaze. "Do your accommodations include a bed, Mr. Darling?"

"Of course," he replied, avoiding her stare now. It caused him to feel far too vulnerable and exposed, as if she could ferret out his every secret with little effort.

The flash of her teeth in the dark drew his eyes back to her, and he found her grinning at him.

"Then it is good enough for me," she declared, gesturing for him to lead the way.

They remained silent as he guided her to the two-room suite he had rented for himself and his valet. Thankfully, he had instructed Oliver not to wait up for him, and the door connecting his room to the valet's remained closed with no light coming through the crack.

He made quick work of lighting a few tapers, illuminating the small, efficient space with yellow light.

Removing her hat, she set it upon the escritoire situated in the corner of the room, then leaned her walking stick against its side.

The urge to cross the room, sweep her against him, and explore the contours and planes of her body with his hands seized him in a tight grip. But he clenched his hands at his sides and forced himself to remain where he stood near the bed and allow her to come to him. Something told him she would not take kindly to him assuming control.

She met his gaze as she grasped the lapels of her coat and began peeling the garment away from her shoulders.

"Have you ever fucked a woman who wore men's clothing?" she asked.

He smirked. "You will be the first, and I must admit the notion did not appeal to me until I saw you in those breeches. Upon you, they are positively wicked."

Her mouth curved at one corner as she tossed her coat carelessly aside and reached for the buttons of her waistcoat. He followed suit, taking hold of his coat to remove it, but was stilled by the shake of her head.

"No, Mr. Darling," she murmured. "I get the pleasure of doing that."

As she removed her waistcoat and threw it to lie on top of her jacket, he lowered his hands to his sides. Another first for him—allowing a woman to undress him as opposed to tearing off his clothes in his haste to get his prick inside a warm cunt.

Once free of the waistcoat, she approached him, her steps swift and sure as she crossed the room. He noticed the pink shadows of her nipples showing through her shirt just before she took hold of his coat and pulled him down toward her, raising up on tiptoe to claim his mouth.

He groaned against her lips as they kissed, the knowledge that she wore nothing beneath the shirt causing him to want to press his mouth to the fabric, sucking one of the little nubs through the linen. She mashed her body up against him, and her tongue engaged his in a sultry dance, frustration flaring in him at not being able to feel her the way he wanted with so many layers between them.

His fingers itched to touch her, to fill his palms with her breasts and ply her nipples until they grew stiff between his fingers—to cup her mons and coax the wetness from her core before slipping his fingers inside.

Unable to stifle the urge any longer, he cupped her buttocks, bending his knees to grind his stiff cock against the mound between her legs. She gasped, and he made a low sound against her mouth, nipping at her lower lip as he caressed his way up the front of her body toward her breasts. Her nipples tickled his palms through the shirt, and for a brief moment, she arched her back as if to settle them more fully into his grasp.

But then, as quickly as she seemed to bend to his will, she placed both hands against his chest and shoved him hard enough to dislodge his hold. He stumbled back, and had barely regained his footing when her palm cracked against his cheek. The blow barely stung, but rippled through his entire being as his eyes grew wide and his mouth fell open. Instinctively, he touched his jaw, the skin tingling where she'd struck him.

It surprised him that the blow had not done a thing to temper his desire … if anything, it seemed to have increased, his cock growing longer and harder as she chastised him with a click of her tongue.

"Bad form, Mr. Darling," she said sharply, like a governess admonishing an errant pupil. "I am in charge tonight, remember? You will keep your hands to yourself until I instruct otherwise. Understood?"

In the far reaches of his mind, rational thought fought to intrude upon the moment. What on Earth could he be thinking becoming involved with such a woman—considering her for marriage? However, the instinct to follow her every command, to see just where this night could lead, won out, proving louder than his rationale.

"Yes, my lady," he replied.

Something he could not name sparked in her eyes, and she licked her lips as if being reminded of her superiority over him had appealed to her. Not typically one to bow and scrape to the nobility when he owned as much, and often more, land than most of them, Michael found his pride falling to the wayside. This woman *was* superior to him, with her delicate hands and soft skin. Nothing would satisfy him more than sullying her, touching her with his work-roughened fingers and filling her with his ignoble seed.

But first, he must earn the privilege, a thought that only served to make their differences more apparent, and therefore, even more appealing.

"Mistress," she snapped, reaching out for him again. "This evening, you will refer to me as Mistress."

He lowered his gaze to watch her deft hands work to unbutton his waistcoat. "As you wish … Mistress."

The word fell easily off his tongue, and as she divested him of his waistcoat and coat at the same time, he decided that the title fit her.

Her hands rested against his chest, and she hummed in appreciation as she smoothed her palms over the muscles, then down his stomach. His cravat fell away with an expert flick of her wrist, and once she'd set it upon his bedside table, she began attacking the buttons of his shirt. She didn't seem opposed to his assistance in removing the garment, and allowed him to pull it off over his head once she'd undone the final button.

She released a long, low sigh as she reached out with one hand to touch him, her fingernails tickling his skin through the coils of hair smattering his chest. He sucked in a sharp breath as she traced a fingertip through the grooves in his stomach, then lower over the bulge in his breeches. His chest heaved, and he shook from the willpower it took not to pick her up, throw her onto the bed, and fuck her senseless. Instead, he remained as still as he could while she cupped him through his breeches, testing the length and breadth of him. A hoarse groan tore from his chest when she fondled his bollocks, then slid her hand back up the length of his prick, causing the evidence of his need to seep from his head.

Opening his breeches, she freed him from his smallclothes, dropping both garments until they rested around his knees, impeded by his boots. His cock strained toward her, dripping with wetness at its tip and engorged to its limit. God's teeth, he'd never been so aroused, and she had barely even touched him.

Her gaze fixated upon his member, she sank to her knees before him. He hissed when she flicked out her tongue to taste him, smearing the flared head in the fluid that had escaped from the slit. She glanced up at him as she opened her mouth wide and began to take him in inch by slow inch.

His gut clenched, his breath coming in erratic spurts as he found himself unable to look away, entranced by the sight of her beautiful lips wrapping around him. It was what he'd wanted from the moment he'd laid eyes on her, from the first time she'd smirked at him with her plump, perfect mouth.

She paused once she'd taken half his cock, and he felt certain she could manage no more than that. None of the women he'd bedded had proven capable of swallowing his entire length. Desperate for friction, for the suction of her lips and tongue, he drew back and prepared to plunge back in, but faltered when her hands slid up his thighs and gripped his buttocks. Digging her fingers in, she urged him closer, farther into her mouth.

"Fuck," he muttered as he slid past the back of her throat, a shudder ripping through him as her tongue caressed the underside of his prick.

His knees buckled when she withdrew, sliding her lips all the way back up to his tip before enveloping him again, taking him in as deep as before. Eyes sliding closed, he clenched his hands and fought not to take her hair into his grasp and fuck her mouth. He had never wanted anything more in his life.

Eventually, she found a steady rhythm, sucking him with more skill than any tavern whore he'd ever fucked, each pass of her lips and tongue over him wringing a sound of pleasure from him. Within minutes, he found himself shaking and battling against the inevitable climax nipping at his heels. Opening his eyes and trying to focus on anything other than the mouth sucking him toward completion did not help; it only drew his gaze downward, where he found her watching him, her gaze intent as if she studied his every expression and reaction. It only threw him toward the edge faster.

"Mistress," he moaned, his hips bucking at her with a wild abandon he could not control. "You must ... ah ... goddamn it, I'm going to spend!"

Release loomed near, the tension in his groin reaching an almost unbearable limit. He did not want to shame himself by coming so soon, and in her mouth, no less. Yet, he could not stop thrusting against her tongue, seeking the exquisite pleasure unlike anything he'd ever known.

Then, as suddenly as she'd taken him in, she released him, her nose nuzzling the patch of hair at his groin before her tongue flicked against his bollocks. He gasped when she drew one between her lips, suckling so hard that the bliss of her wet mouth became mingled with the pain of her roughness.

Releasing his bollocks, she turned her head and bit him, sinking her teeth into his inner thigh. The sting of her bite shocked him away from the precipice of climax, and the tension eased enough that he felt confident he wouldn't spew his seed all over her face.

Though, the idea did have merit. Perhaps another time.

Still dazed from the torrent of pleasure, pain, confusion, and intrigue she'd just wrapped him in, Michael did not fight her when she pushed him to sit upon the bed. He remained passive while she removed his boots, stockings, and then at last, his breeches and small-clothes. She urged him to lie back on the bed once he had been undressed, and he obliged, far too curious about where this encounter might lead next to refuse her.

Straddling his hips, she sank down until her mons pressed against him through the fabric of her breeches. He shifted his hips against hers, silently begging her for the friction and pressure he needed to reach the height of his pleasure. She seemed content to take her time, reaching up to unpin the cameo from her cravat before removing it, as well. He traced the beautiful lines of her long neck, his gaze fixing upon the pulse thumping near her collarbone as she stashed her cameo on the bedside table and retrieved his own cravat.

So intent was he on studying that thrumming vein in her neck and imagining teasing it with his tongue, he did not realize her intent until she had already bound one of his wrists to a bed post. Glancing in bewilderment at the efficient knot she'd used, he felt her treating his other wrist the same. She sat back on his lap and studied her handi-work, her eyes gleaming silver with mischief.

"What an enticing sight you make, helpless at my fingertips, Mr. Darling," she teased with a smirk.

Bucking his hips up at her, he ground his erection against her mound. "Not completely helpless, Mistress."

Her eyes darkened at his declaration, and she mimicked him, surging her hips so that her pelvis ground against his. "If you want your hands freed, you will obey my every command."

As she left him to remove her boots, he turned his head to stare at the soft flare of her hips and curves of her taut buttocks.

"Whatever you please, Mistress," he murmured.

Turning to glance at him over her shoulder, she grinned. "Oh, I do like you, Mr. Darling … such a quick study."

Before he could think to ask her what she meant, she stood and dropped her breeches, bending at the waist and giving him a view of her arse and the soft mahogany hair blanketing her mons. She bent even lower, and he caught sight of the pink flesh of her cunt, slick and beckoning.

He stifled a disappointed groan once she righted herself and came back to the bed to climb back over him. Not only had she taken away the marvelous view of her quim, she had not removed her shirt. However, once she had straddled his chest, she began to loosen the buttons until the lapels fell open enough to reveal her breasts. Her nipples were the ripest he'd ever seen, succulent and begging to be licked and toyed with.

His breathing grew harsh again as he followed her hands down her body, his mouth going dry as she grasped the bottom of the shirt and lifted it just enough to expose her hips and the warm haven she concealed between them.

"Bloody hell," he grunted when she kept a hold on her shirt with one hand, but slipped the other between her legs.

Her fingers parted her lower lips, exposing the inner flesh. She shuddered as she found her clit and began to massage it in slow circles.

"Do you like what you see, Mr. Darling?" she murmured, opening her eyes and staring down at him.

He could feel her gaze upon him, but couldn't tear his attention away from the slender fingers petting the cunt he wanted to fuck.

"God, yes," he rasped.

"Would you like a taste?" she asked, sliding her fingers back and into her channel.

They groaned in unison as she pumped two fingers in and out of her sheath, the digits growing slick with her essence. Michael's mouth watered at what she offered, her scent and the sight of her juices soaking her knuckles making him want to nibble and suck on her sensitive flesh until she screamed.

"Yes," he replied, his voice a rough bark exacerbated by the strength of his desire.

Poking out her lower lip, she gave him an exaggerated pout. "Bad form, Mr. Darling … you did not say please. Now I'm afraid you're going to have to beg."

Beg? Him?

The suggestion might have repulsed him just a few hours ago. He might have laughed in her face and told her to leave and not let the door hit her in the arse on the way out. But, just now, she held his rapt attention, her fingers still steadily plunging in and out of her channel. Just this once, this night, with this woman, he would beg.

After all, she'd already slapped him, bit him, and tied him to the bed. It did not get more degrading than that.

And, God, how he loved the way this woman degraded him.

"I beg of you, Mistress," he said in his most soothing tone. "Allow me to taste you. You smell so good, and I know you will taste even better. You will not regret it. Please, my lady … I need to taste you."

Their gazes clashed and held, and for a moment, he actually worried she would reject him. And suddenly, pleasing her became the most important thing he could do.

Crawling further up his body, she straddled his head and withdrew her fingers from her channel. "You beg so well, Mr. Darling. Permission granted."

Grunting in satisfaction, he lapped at her, finding her pearl through the seam of her mons. She gasped when he teased it with little lashes, choking on a strangled cry when he exerted more pressure, rubbing the little numb back and forth. Then, closing his mouth around her, he suckled, drawing her clit deep.

"Yes," she whispered breathlessly, reaching down to grasp a handful of his hair. "Yes, Mr. Darling ... just like that."

He moaned in response—to both her encouragement and her taste, sweet and wild, uniquely Amelia.

She surged her hips in time with the strokes of his tongue, riding him and grinding her pelvis down against his face. He closed his eyes and swam in her, his lips slick with her essence, and each caress of his tongue made her grow wetter and wetter. Then, she stiffened above him, crying out as she began to shiver and convulse. He rode out her climax until the end, slowly easing the pressure of his lips until she went limp on top of him with a relieved sigh.

Then, withdrawing from his mouth, she reached down to stroke his hair. "Well done."

The compliment swelled his chest, and he returned her grin. Never had a woman let him know so plainly that she'd enjoyed what he'd done to her. He had grown so used to the games and innuendo of the fairer sex that he'd never imagined one like her existed—one who clearly stated what she wanted, and ensured her lover knew whether he had pleased her.

Bracing her hands against his chest, she began lowering herself onto his cock, once again robbing him of both his breath and all rational thought. Tight, wet heat enveloped him, her bare thighs coming up against his.

"Christ," he groaned when her pelvis rested against him, and she'd taken him in as far as he could go. "You feel so bloody good, Mistress."

She purred in response, shifting her hips and creating the sensation of friction he craved. "Hmm ... shall I fuck you now, Mr. Darling?"

He thrust his hips up to meet her slow downward movements, each stroke coaxing him closer and closer to the edge of madness. She made him want to hurtle over the precipice, the consequences of such careless abandon forgotten.

"Yes, love," he murmured, anchoring his feet to the bed and increasing his pace beneath her. "Fuck me, Mistress."

She threw her head back and groaned, matching his pace and bouncing up and down in his lap. His muscles strained and tightened, his arms pulling at the linen cravats keeping him tied to the bedposts. He had no idea how she'd tied the knots, but no amount of pulling or exertion of his strength could loosen them.

Growling in frustration, he lifted his head as far as he could, his gaze locked on the breast just out of his reach.

"My hands," he murmured as he moved his attention from one breast to the other. "I need them to touch you … give me my hands, Mistress."

His requests had begun to sound more like rough commands, but to his surprise, Amelia did not object. She gave him what he wanted, fumbling with the knots as he bucked his hips, drilling his cock up and into her.

"Touch me," she commanded once she'd gotten one hand free.

But he was already there, lurching upright and using the freed hand to grasp her arse and force her down onto him harder and faster. She screamed, her insides pulsing and clenching around him as he held tight and controlled her pace, moving her hard and fast up and down his shaft. He took her nipple between his teeth and gave it a tug, pulling another scream from her. She shuddered one last time and went still, but he could not stop. He'd become a madman, sweat breaking out over the surface of his skin as he rammed into her at a relentless cadence.

Struggling to draw breath, she fell limp against his chest. He took that as a sign of her acquiescence and took control, gripping her hips and swiftly flipping her onto her back. Falling back between her thighs, he shoved into her, taking up his previous pace, thrusting in and out of her so hard, the bed shook beneath them.

Amelia's arms came around him, her fingernails scoring his bare shoulders. He gritted his teeth and growled when she dragged them over his skin, likely leaving gouge marks. But the pain only urged him on, her heels digging into his back as she wrapped her legs around him, driving him further into the downward spiral of insanity that had gripped him.

Reaching up to grip the headboard with one hand, he snaked an arm beneath her arched back and lifted her, pulling her into each of his rough strokes.

But Amelia did not cry out for him to stop, or pretend maidenly shock over the ferocity of his claiming. She urged him on instead, only crying out louder the harder he pounded her, reveling in her own wantonness.

And then, opening her eyes, she met his gaze and smiled, seeming to sense that the end drew near. The tendons in his neck strained, sweat rolling in beads down his forehead, his jerky movements as he lost his hold on precision … he loomed so close.

"Spend for me, Michael," she murmured. "Now."

Her imperious directive sent a shudder through him, and he did as she commanded, pulling out of her just as he finished, his seed spurting out in hot streams that stained her stomach. He wanted to feel sorry for being so crass, but the sight of his milky white mettle against the bare skin of her belly filled him with a feral sense of satisfaction. She'd held control over him for one night, but he'd marked her. She didn't have to know that he saw it as a permanent branding.

This woman would be his, and now, he had more than her dowry to chase. She'd just ensured that he could not even fathom marrying anyone else. Why pluck a perfect, pampered hothouse rose when he could possess a rare and beautiful wildflower?

Her shirt had ridden up to her chest, so at least he had not soiled it. Reaching for one of the cravats she'd used to bind him, he quickly cleaned the mess off her stomach.

Lowering the shirt past her hips, Amelia lay back against the pillows and reached out to him. His eyelids drooped, and he suddenly felt very drained … as if he would lose consciousness any second and sleep for an entire fortnight. She seemed to understand this, stroking his damp hair as he fell onto her, resting his head on her breast.

"My God … Amelia," he murmured, a warmth suffusing his entire being as her arms came around him. "What is this?"

He had never felt this way after fucking a woman … as if she had just tipped his entire world off its axis. As if he were invincible and could do anything—be anything. This went beyond satisfaction and satiation.

"It is perfectly normal, Michael," she crooned, her voice becoming soft and soothing—a far cry from the sharp commands she'd barked at him earlier. "It will pass."

Nuzzling closer to her, he allowed the fatigue to drag him under, faintly registering her pulling the blanket around him. "I don't want it to."

Truly, it was as if he might take flight at any moment—simply float away on the sensation of feeling lighter than air.

Her lips touched his forehead, and he felt her smile.

"Oh, I do believe I am going to enjoy teaching you."

Before he could ask her what she meant, oblivion claimed him, and he clung to her while surrendering to it.

# CHAPTER 4

$\mathcal{A}$melia woke to Michael's cock nudging its way into her from behind. She smiled, arching her back and wiggling her arse to invite him in. She did not spend the entire night with her lovers, nor did she allow them to initiate sexual intercourse. That right was reserved for her as a Mistress. However, the man had pleased her so thoroughly that she hadn't possessed the strength to leave his bed afterward. And now that his cock was slowly pumping in and out of her channel, the way made slick by the moisture that had begun the moment his head had touched her opening, she wasn't inclined to tell him to stop.

He was so warm and solid behind her, the muscles in his chest and abdomen rippling against her back, one large hand holding her hip and propelling her into each of his thrusts. She practically purred from the pleasure blossoming between her thighs, spreading with each slow thrust of his hips against her derriere.

"Good morning, Mistress," he murmured before taking her earlobe between his lips and giving it a little nip.

"Hmm, good morning, Mr. Darling," she replied, reaching back to touch him.

Her hand found a thick, bulging thigh, the strong cords bunching and rolling with each thrust of his hips. Christ, the man was beautifully built. His calloused hand slipping beneath her shirt to caress an erect nipple drew a moan from deep in her chest, and she closed her eyes, imagining all the other things such deliciously rough fingers could do to her.

She stroked her hand up his thigh and found her way between them, fondling his heavy bollocks and causing his heavy pants to break off on a groan. She couldn't help a satisfied smile as he pumped into her harder, the impact of his pelvis against her buttocks now offering a pleasing chorus in tandem with her breathy moans and his deep grunts.

Amelia splintered first, going limp against him and moaning her pleasure as climax stole the strength from her limbs. He followed closely, slamming into her one last time before pulling away from her to spill his seed.

When she turned over to glance at him, she found him flopped onto his back, the cloudy liquid of his seed staining his lower belly. With a smile, she stood.

"What a mess you've made, Mr. Darling," she chided, going over to a washstand and discovering the basin filled with water gone cold.

Retrieving a clean scrap of linen, she dampened it and crossed the room to give it to him. He accepted it with a grin—which seemed far more impactful in the light of the morning streaming through the window than it had in the dim lighting of the gaming hell. He was even more handsome with sunlight dancing in his hair, accentuating the golden hue.

"One might argue that, as the cause of my pleasure, you are the one who made the mess," he grumbled as he cleaned himself with the linen.

Turning her back to him, she bent to retrieve her breeches, stockings, and boots. She faintly detected Michael's footsteps padding across the wooden floor, and a moment later, he stood behind her, gripping her hips, his now-covered pelvis pressing against hers.

He had donned his breeches, but she still wore nothing but a shirt. A shiver ran down her spine at the feel of his cock, already stirring back to life against her through the fabric.

Coming upright, she giggled, but he did not release her. Using one arm to anchor her to him, he began nibbling the side of her neck.

"Stay," he murmured in her ear. "I've not yet had my fill of you."

Squirming in his hold, she dropped her clothing back to the floor. The offer was a tempting one, but she really ought to return home and at least look in on Sophie and the twins. Besides, his pleas were only caused by the eagerness he now undoubtedly felt to experience more of what she'd taught him.

Oh, he did not *know* he had been taught, but she often found that did not matter when she introduced a man to the sort of pleasure she could offer. Once they received a taste of it, a man with a penchant for submission would find himself unable to get enough.

However, there was much to be said for absence making the heart grow fonder—or rather, making the cock grow longer. If she made him wait, he'd be twice as willing to do whatever she demanded in order to have her again.

So, she pulled at his arm and shook his head. "I really must go."

He sighed as if disappointed, but kept kissing her, working his way down toward her shoulder. His lips felt so good against her skin, she barely realized what he was about to do before the top button of her shirt had come undone, and then another. But then, cold air kissed her shoulders as he attempted to divest her of the garment, dousing her like the splash of frigid water.

Panic flared in her, and she fought his hold, flailing until he released her. Turning to face him, she backpedaled swiftly, yanking the shirt back up over her shoulders and holding it closed. He watched her with a frown, lines appearing between his eyebrows in confusion.

"Amelia—"

"Something you must learn if you wish to have me in your bed again, Mr. Darling," she said in the composed, lofty tone she adopted when acting as Mistress. "I never remove my shirt. You may unbutton it enough to access my breasts, but shall never endeavor to take it off. Do you understand?"

His brow furrowed even more, and he inclined his head, studying her as if attempting to discover her secrets. He would not be the first man to make such an attempt, but she was skilled at deflection, and employed the tactic now.

Coming toward him with a smile, she took his face in her hands and gave him a swift kiss. "Say yes, Michael."

He chuckled and kissed her back. "Yes, Michael."

Ah, he was so witty. She did like that in a man. Oftentimes, she found herself saddled with a man who thought acting as her submissive meant bowing and scraping to her out of bed as well as in it. But she already enjoyed the challenge Michael presented—a clearly self-assured male who would only allow her control while she fucked him. In every other aspect, this man would challenge her ... he would push back when pushed. The idea of sparring with him, both physically and verbally, had her practically salivating.

"You are welcome to call upon me at Ashton House whenever you wish," she said, taking up her breeches and quickly pulling them on. "I go riding most mornings in Hyde Park, and you are welcome to find me, as well. There are also the gaming hells and the theater—both favorite haunts of mine."

"I am certain you will not be too hard to find," he said with a grin. "London often buzzes with bits of gossip about the activities of The Incomparable Lady A."

Sitting down on the bed, she pulled on her stockings, then allowed him to take over with her boots as he sank to one knee before her.

"I will certainly look forward to seeing you again," she murmured, staring down at the top of his golden head.

She wondered what sorts of debauched things she could coax him into next time. A cock ring, perhaps, or a bit of bondage? The thought of tying him to a St. Andrew's cross made her pulse race, but it was most certainly too soon for such extreme practices. She would ease him into the various acts of submission, and by the time she had finished with him, he would beg her for more.

Of course, it would all have to end once he'd found his bride, but by then, Amelia would surely have tired of him—as she eventually did with all her past lovers. Yet another reason she'd avoided marriage for so long.

Once Michael had finished with her boots, she quickly donned the rest of her attire, then managed her hair as best she could without the aid of a lady's maid.

After pulling on a shirt, he walked her to the door of his accommodations.

"I will see you soon, Lady A," he said, lowering his head to kiss her one last time. "*Very* soon."

Tipping her hat to him, she left, glancing back once more to find him lingering in the doorway, watching her. His gaze followed her to the stairs, and once she'd begun to descend, the sound of the door closing echoed down the corridor.

It did not take her long once exiting the hotel to find a hansom cab to carry her home. As the conveyance bounced along the road, she closed her eyes and imagined all the naughty things she would do to Mr. Darling.

She had never anticipated anything more in her life.


Michael dipped his hands into the basin of water resting upon the washstand and splashed his face. The cool liquid did little to temper the heat caused by Lady Amelia's nearness. Typically, when it came to most women, he abided by the philosophy 'out of sight, out of mind.' Yet, Amelia had left his room five minutes ago, and he was hard-pressed to put her out of his thoughts. Her scent still permeated the room—something exotic and spicy, stronger than the floral perfume most women of his acquaintance preferred. It mingled with the lingering aroma of sex, sending a fresh rush of blood to his cock.

He'd need to get himself under control before he saw her again.

Going about his plan would become much harder if he couldn't think of anything other than getting back inside her every time they crossed paths. He needed a level head and a sharp wit, or he'd be swept out of his depth. The woman was every bit the hoyden he'd been led to believe—but she was also more. She possessed the cunning to have him wrapped around her finger and dancing to her tune. What he needed required things to be the other way around. *He* needed to ensnare her, and if necessary, trap her into marriage.

He couldn't afford to let his cock lead him ... though once she became his wife, his cock could lead him often—right into her warm honeypot.

He had just stripped and begun washing with the cold water when the door connecting his room to the one adjoining swung open. He didn't bat an eyelash when Oliver, his valet, appeared, one of Michael's best coats slung over one arm, along with a fresh shirt.

"Good morning," he said, finishing his toilette while the valet went about laying out his attire and making his bed.

He'd planned to make the journey to London on his own, but Oliver had insisted upon being allowed to accompany him. The valet did not wish Michael to be seen in shabby clothing—though that sometimes could not be helped due to the state of his coffers. He'd also gone on and on for at least half an hour reminding Michael of how dangerous London could be. Since Oliver proved a crack shot with a pistol and could be counted upon to watch Michael's back, he'd brought the man along.

"I suppose you were successful in your endeavor last evening," Oliver said as Michael stepped into clean smallclothes, then his breeches.

He arched an eyebrow at the valet and smirked. "Whatever gave you that idea?"

Had he heard them last night? He couldn't find it in himself to feel any shame over it. Oliver understood his mission, and had been informed the lengths Michael might need to go to in order to claim

Amelia. Knowing how dire the situation at Oakmoor had become, he kept any reservations or disapproval he might feel to himself.

"You are different this morning, if you don't mind me saying," Oliver said, effortlessly tying Michael's cravat into the simple style he preferred. "Happier might not be the correct word … but something like it."

He grinned as he thought of the little siren who had just left his bed. Happy, indeed. The feeling of euphoria he'd experienced after fucking her had been unlike anything he'd ever experienced. It could have been the thrill of the hunt ending with the plunder … or it could simply be the woman herself. No wonder the men of London flocked to her in droves. If even half of them had any notion of what it felt like to be with her, it was a wonder she hadn't been kidnapped and chained to some bloke's bed by now.

"Successful, indeed," he replied. "I've gained her notice, and I do believe things are off to a good start. If I play my hand correctly, we should be on our way back to Oakmoor within a week."

Oliver inclined his head, glancing up at him after carefully placing a sapphire tiepin into the white neck cloth—an inheritance along with a few other family jewels he hadn't been able to part with.

"Be careful, Mr. Darling," he chided. "Just because the woman is an oddity does not mean she's devoid of sentiment."

Michael frowned. Of course Amelia was not devoid of feelings—he'd never met a woman who was. However, he had no desire to hurt her. Despite wanting to marry her for her fortune, he could honestly say he could come to enjoy being her husband. She would be protected, provided for, and even if she was not loved—well, he admired the hell out of a woman who strode about in public wearing breeches and knew how to take what she wanted.

Mutual respect had been the foundation of his parents' marriage, and there was no reason his and Amelia's could not be built the same. The Darlings had brought two sons and a daughter into the world, and their progeny now included grandchildren. As the eldest, Michael had inherited when his father succumbed to a bout of pneumonia and died. As the owner of Oakmoor, it was now his responsibility to follow in the footsteps of his sire. He worked the land, cared for his tenants, and ensured his family had everything they needed—when he could afford to, of course.

Now, he would take a wife. Lady Amelia Fitzwilliam would be that wife, and he would accept no other outcome.

"I will," he replied while Oliver helped him shrug into his coat. "Just because our marriage will not be a love match does not mean I will mistreat her."

"Of course not," Oliver agreed.

Once he'd finished off his ensemble with stockings and boots, he left the room with Oliver to seek out breakfast in the taproom downstairs. The fare here was abysmal compared to what his cooks at Oakmoor would lay out for breakfast, even with a limited budget. He took a seat in the crowded room secure in the knowledge that he would not have to suffer through it much longer. Soon, he would be able to return home, bride in tow.

# CHAPTER 5

"Amelia, have you heard a word I said?"

As she flinched at her sister-in-law's sharp tone, Amelia's face grew warm when she realized she had allowed her thoughts to wander during their conversation. It had been two days since her encounter with Michael, and he'd never strayed far from her thoughts.

She cleared her throat and glanced down at the infant lying in the crook of her arm, determined to get a handle on her wandering mind. After all, Sophie spent most of her time confined to her chambers or the nursery while she recovered from birthing the twins. The only contact she had with the world outside those rooms was with her and Simon.

They sat in the nursery now—Sophie in a rocking chair holding Joanna, while Amelia rested on a footstool with Phineas in her arms.

"Of course, dear," she replied with a smile, absently stroking Phineas' plump cheek.

The boy slept against her breast, sparking an odd feeling she'd never before experienced. Could that be maternal instinct? Heavens, she must be falling ill.

"Well?" Sophie prodded, gently rocking baby Joanna when she began to fuss. "What do you think? Blue or pink?"

*Drat.*

She hadn't expected Sophie to call her out on her woolgathering. Hoping to preserve her dignity, she grinned.

"Why, pink, of course."

*Please let pink be the correct answer to whatever question she asked!*

Sophie snorted and chuckled with a shake of her head. "Very well. Pink, it is. I am sure Simon will just *love* wearing a waistcoat of that shade for the twins' christening."

Amelia winced. *Double drat.*

Sighing, she released a sigh, blowing a stream of air upward and ruffling the loose hairs resting on her forehead.

"Do forgive me," she said. "I do not know what's come over me. Blue, of course. The color tricks people into thinking his eyes actually possess some sort of color."

"They do have color," Sophie defended, her tone growing a bit sharp.

Instead of allowing it to ruffle her, Amelia merely smiled. Her sister-in-law would defend Simon with her life if it came to it, so strong was her love for him. She would not tolerate anyone speaking ill of him—not even Amelia. What must it be like to love so fiercely? She doubted she would ever know, since men tended to only give their love to women like Sophie, who bowed to their will in the bedroom as easily as they did out of it.

Not that she thought her sister-in-law weak. On the contrary; it took a rare sort of woman to be able to tolerate her brother's oddities and the darkness that seemed to hang over his head like a cloud. However, she was not naïve enough to believe that such a love could be possible for her. She had never been the submissive type, nor could she ever bear being told what she could do and when or where she could do it. She'd had enough of that living under the tyrannical rule of her uncle. Never again, she'd promised herself. No man would ever rule her the way he had.

"Of course they do," she amended. "But they're rather unique, you know. Not quite grey, not quite silver. The blue waistcoat will cause them to appear a bit grayer, I think. Not quite so disarming."

With a sigh, Sophie rested her head against the back of the chair. "I want this to be perfect. Simon never thought he'd have children, and I'm certain most of the *ton* did not, either. I just … I want it to be a good day, Amelia, a wonderful occasion to mark a new beginning."

Keeping a hold on her nephew with one arm, she reached out and rested a gentle hand on Sophie's knee.

"It will be," she assured her. "You and Simon will be wonderful parents."

"I think you are right," Sophie agreed. "But I do worry for Simon. He'll hold them, but not for long … as if he's frightened to touch them. I wonder if he's afraid he'll fail at being a father before he even tries."

Amelia heart sank at the reminder of their upbringing. Many of Simon's fears were her own. How could they know how to function as good mates to their spouses, or parents to their children, when they'd never seen a good example of either? Yet, Simon had proven that it could be done. He'd found Sophie and learned to let her love him, how to lavish love on her. It stood to reason, then, that he could be a good father.

"Give him time," she replied. "Uncle Gregory is never far from his mind, I'm afraid. He would never admit it, but he's always feared becoming him."

"He could never," Sophia refuted. "He does not have the capacity for such cruelty and violence."

*Not anymore.*

Neither of them said the words, but both remained acutely aware of the sort of man he'd once been. Violence and anger had ruled him, but no longer. He'd learned to control it—something Amelia had discovered came through acting as a dominant. Perhaps it was why she'd so easily gravitated toward being a Mistress herself. When a man put himself at her mercy, she remained in control. She did not take the pain; she dished it out. The heady feeling it gave her chased away every bit of fear and disgust thinking of her childhood inevitably brought.

"Enough about that," Sophie said suddenly. "Tell me about your new lover."

Her mouth fell open in shock. "You haven't been out of this room since you birthed the twins! How on earth could you possibly know I have a new lover?"

Sophie gave her a knowing smirk. "It's all over your face. You have that look … the one you wear when you've found a new piece of flesh to torture."

Thinking of Michael's appealing physique, she smiled and sighed. "Sophie, you have no idea."

Her vibrant green eyes twinkling with mischief, Sophie sat up straighter in her chair. After slowly lowering Joanna into a nearby cradle, she leaned forward and rested her elbows on her knees, staring at Amelia as if waiting for a treat.

"Tell me everything," she urged.

Amelia laughed, rising to place Phineas in the cradle beside his sister. Eventually, the two would find their way to each other, arms and legs tangling as they embraced in their sleep. She found it the most darling thing she'd ever seen.

"There isn't much to tell," she said, shrugging one shoulder. "He's visiting London from Norfolk. We met at a gaming hell."

Sophie snorted. "Simon would love to hear all about that."

Amelia rolled her eyes heavenward. "It is my inheritance. If I wish to gamble it all away, that is my prerogative. Besides, I won more than I lost that night."

"Enough about that," she replied, waving an impatient hand through the air. "Tell me more about the man. Is he tall? Broad? Oh, does he have blue eyes?"

"Yes, actually," she said with a laugh. "He's landed gentry, and he looks as if he's the sort to actually work his own land. Tall, broad … and hard everywhere. Sophie, his body is like a statue's."

Sophie bit her lower lip and groaned. "God, I can only imagine."

Her sister-in-law had evolved quite a bit during her marriage to Simon. Trained to submit to her husband, she no longer discussed carnal matters with a flush staining her cheeks. In fact, she seemed to enjoy hearing about Amelia's latest conquests, and, apparently, having just given birth had done nothing to change that.

"His hair is golden, cut short, and he's got a lovely mouth. And it was not only good for looking at, if you know what I mean."

Sophie grinned. "Did quite a bit with that mouth, did he? Tell me more. Did you whip him? Tie him up? Make him beg?"

"No whips, this time," she replied, sinking back onto her footstool. "He does not yet know he is the submissive sort … but he did let me tie him to the bedposts with cravats and did not seem opposed to me sitting upon his face."

"Oh, dear," Sophie said, reaching for a nearby bell cord—likely to ring for tea. "He sounds absolutely perfect. Perhaps you could marry this one."

She furrowed her brow at Sophie's suggestion, her stomach beginning to churn as she remembered Michael's declaration the night they'd met.

*I am here to find a wife.*

Shaking her head, she dismissed the feeling in her gut and told herself she was being silly. A man did not seek to marry the woman he fucked on his first night in London. He would think of her as a pleasant diversion, just as she would consider him one. The fact that she hadn't stopped thinking about him had nothing to do with marriage and everything to do with the carnal pleasures he seemed capable of. What she needed was the freedom to do with him everything she wished. Once her debauched fantasies had been fulfilled, she'd be ready to part ways with him—just as she had all her previous lovers.

She gave Sophie a teasing glance and forced a giggle. "And crush the heart of every lonely bachelor in London? I think not."

"What was that about crushing hearts?" intruded Simon's voice from the doorway.

Amelia glanced up to find him sauntering into the room, a soft smirk pulling at the corner of his mouth. The sight would still take some getting used to, as her brother had spent decades schooling his face into a mask of apathy. On the rare occasion he smiled wide enough to actually flash his teeth, she often worried that he'd suffered a blow to the head.

She supposed love could change a person. Those changes made themselves apparent now, as Simon nodded at her in greeting before fixating upon his wife. He knelt in front of her chair and took her hand, kissing her knuckles.

"How are you this morning, darling?" he murmured.

Sophie smiled down at him, and the two caught gazes and held. When they looked at one another like that, Amelia felt as if she intruded upon a private moment. So, she stood and began edging toward the door.

"I am well," Sophie replied. "Better now that you are here."

"I only wanted to look in on you and the twins before Parliament sessions," he replied. "They always seem to be asleep when I visit."

Sophie laughed. "The business of being born is quite taxing, it would seem. Stay, Simon. I've just rung for tea. They'll awaken soon to be fed, I'm certain. You can help me get them arranged properly so I can feed them both at the same time if it comes to it."

Amelia fought the urge to laugh at Sophie's attempt to coax Simon into touching the twins. In time, with patience, it would undoubtedly become more natural for him.

"We have a nurse for that, darling," Simon chided.

Amelia paused near the door and smiled. Seeing him so attentive proved another pleasant change. The Simon she'd always known had been aloof and distant.

"They are mine, and I'll feed them whenever I want," Sophie countered. "Now, sit, please … the tea should be here shortly."

Simon found a high-backed armchair nearby and pulled it so he sat near Sophie and the cradle. Amelia left the room, wondering if Simon had even noticed his wife ordering him about. He'd obeyed as easily as a child, something else she'd never seen him do. But then, once she had recovered from childbirth, Amelia had no doubt he'd return to taking charge.

Passing the maids delivering tea to the nursery, she found her way to her own room. The hour proved early enough that she could take a ride to Hyde Park without being forced to interact with half the *ton*.

She quickly traded her morning gown for her favorite riding habit —an olive green, military-style ensemble with a tailored coat and breeches instead of a skirt. After sliding into her boots, she neglected to put on the matching hat—not caring about protection from the sun. Nothing felt better than the warmth on her face and the wind in her hair while she rode. She didn't mind a few freckles here or there, and she certainly did not care about appearances.

As she left home and rounded the house toward the mews, she wondered what Michael could be up to this early. He likely still kept country hours, which meant he would rise with the sun. Perhaps she would ride farther than usual today and venture to the inn. If his response to her the night they'd met proved any indication, he would be happy to see her.

Michael inhaled the crisp morning air, sedately guiding his horse down the winding path leading through Hyde Park. While Amelia had mentioned the park as one of her haunts, he did not expect to find her here this morning. He simply sought to clear his head and indulge in a bit of exercise before going to call upon her at Ashton House that afternoon.

In the days since he'd last seen her, his thoughts had never strayed far from the passion they'd shared. Even as he explored London, purchasing inexpensive gifts for his nieces and nephew and encountering old acquaintances he hadn't seen in ages, he had been unable to put her from his mind. His cock responded predictably each time his thoughts landed on Amelia, and even the stroke of his hand each morning and each night could not rid of him of the persistent desire nagging him every waking hour.

He wanted her—there could be no avoiding that. But, he would not allow her to know just how much. He needed to maintain the upper hand here, and thus far, his plans seemed to be off to a good start. If he'd played his cards right, she had spent the past few days thinking of him. When they met again, he would push for another interlude with her, and then another, and then … he would secure her hand in marriage.

Glancing around the picturesque grounds, he found them beautiful when not overrun with London's elite. The fashionable social hour would see these paths clogged with horses, carriages, and people on foot—out to see and be seen.

The clop of a horse's hooves sounded on the path behind him, and he steered his mount aside to allow the rider to pass. Yet, the horse slowed from a canter to a slow trot as it and its rider came into view.

She took his breath away, faced flushed from the exertion of her ride, hair unbound and hanging down her back, a few wayward strands kissing her forehead and neck.

"Lady Amelia," he said, pulling his mount to a stop while she reined to a halt beside him. "What a coincidence … I was just contemplating coming to visit you at Ashton House this afternoon."

She wore yet another inappropriate ensemble, sitting astride in a pair of olive green breeches and a matching coat—the military style which had become all the rage in women's riding habits. Another frothy, elaborately tied cravat graced her slender throat, the cameo once again in its place among the linen. She held a riding crop beneath one arm, and a pair of supple brown boots hugged her legs all the way up to the thighs.

He clenched his teeth until they ached at the thought of her riding his cock wearing only those boots.

However, her clothing was not the most indecent part of Amelia. No, it was the too-wide grin and the merry eyes practically dancing with glee that caused her to appear far different from any woman he'd ever known. The ladies of his acquaintance had been trained to restrain themselves, school their expressions so that they resembled porcelain dolls, simper like idiots instead of laughing out loud. Christ, it only made her more appealing.

"Good morning, Mr. Darling," she replied breathlessly, still winded from her ride. "It is lovely to see you again. Have you enjoyed London these past few days?"

Reaching out to caress the inky black mane of his mount, he grinned. "I have, though I must say my stay has now been vastly improved."

She returned his smile, giving her a reins a slight tug as her mount huffed and stomped its hooves, seeming restless.

"Flatterer. Surely, you do not have time to miss my company as you go about searching for your bride. How goes the search for the future Mrs. Darling?"

*Quite well, my little hoyden ... I have her right where I want her.*

"Rather dull," he said aloud.

Pushing out her lower lip in a pout, she batted her eyelashes. "Poor Mr. Darling. What might I do to offer relief from the tedium?"

Arching an eyebrow at her, he gestured toward the empty path winding behind them. "How about a race?"

Her eyes glittered as she studied the open space stretching before them—perfect for a horserace. "Oh, splendid. A wonderful idea. Where shall we race to?"

"That tree, there," he replied, pointing toward a large Elm. "But, before we begin ... might I suggest another wager?"

The twinkle in her eyes melted into the molten gleam of desire. "I so enjoyed our last wager, Mr. Darling. Are you suggesting similar stakes?"

He nodded. "If I win, you will give me a night like the last one we shared ... only this time, I will be in control, and you must do whatever I wish."

She chuckled, the deep, throaty sound sending a surge of blood straight to his cock.

"And if I win, you must accompany me somewhere tonight. I will not reveal where, and you must promise to not only come with me, but to observe the event with an open mind."

Amelia grew more intriguing by the second. He doubted he could ever guess where she intended to take him in his wildest dreams.

Good thing he planned to throw the race in her favor.

Extending a hand to her, he nodded in agreement. "Done."

She shook his hand, then gripped her reins. "Ready when you are, Mr. Darling."

Staring back down the path, he tightened his hold on his own reins. "On your mark, Lady Amelia. And … go!"

He snapped his reins at the same time she did, and both horses were off.

Michael kept pace with her as they raced down the winding path, Amelia's laughter and encouragement toward her mount the only sound mingling with that of horses' hooves. He glanced over at her, the sight of her galloping with the wind in her hair causing an unavoidable surge of warmth in his belly. The freedom with which she rode struck him as being in line with the way she lived her life—carefree and without a thought to what others might say if they saw her acting like an ill-mannered strumpet.

No wonder they called her Incomparable. There could be no lady in all of England like her.

The large Elm loomed before them, the finish line in sight. Amelia produced another boisterous laugh and gave her mount a tap with the crop to urge her faster. Michael pulled back on his reins just a bit, slowing his mount at the last second and allowing her to gallop ahead of him to the finish.

He pulled up and halted his gelding, smiling and fighting to catch his breath as she wheeled her mare back around to face him.

"It would seem you've been bested yet again, Mr. Darling," she teased.

Bowing his head in acquiescence, he fought back a smug grin. "So it would seem, my lady. I am yours for the evening, just like before."

Her smile faded, and her eyes radiated seduction as she urged her mount closer to him—so close, her leg brushed his.

"I look forward to it, Mr. Darling," she murmured. "I shall come for you at ten in the evening. Dress for a dinner party."

Dash it all, he hardly owned any attire fit for an evening with the sort of company Amelia might keep. But that was a problem he and Oliver could solve in the hours between now and ten tonight. Yet another obstacle he must overcome to win her in the end.

"Very well," he agreed, reaching out for her hand and bringing it to his mouth. "Until this evening."

He brushed his lips across her knuckles, then released her hand. Urging his mount to continue along the path, he put her behind him and forced himself not to glance back. No matter how badly her disheveled hair and wide smile made him want to look, and keep looking until he'd drank in his fill of her. He doubted he ever would.

# CHAPTER 6

*A*melia arrived promptly at ten that evening to retrieve Michael. Fortunately, Oliver had been able to find evening attire for purchase that did not deplete his limited funds. The coat and waistcoat had been sent back to the tailor when they'd failed to satisfy the lord who had ordered them. It had not taken long to alter the garments to fit him, and along with his best black knee breeches and evening shoes, he managed to appear as if he might actually belong amongst the members of the *ton*.

Of course, he did not know for certain that the dinner party she'd mentioned would include the cream of London high society, but he would be prepared. Oliver had tamed his hair and ensured he was freshly shaved. He'd been told there remained parts of him that always gave him away as genteel as opposed to nobility—such as a body honed by actual work, and hands roughened from farming—but as Amelia alighted from the hansom cab to greet him, she seemed to like what she saw.

Her eyes devoured him from head to toe, though he hardly had time to notice while he inspected her just as closely. For the first time, he had the privilege of seeing her in a gown—which she wore as well as she did her breeches and boots. Black satin clung to her breasts, the small mounds lifted and displayed to their advantage by her low neckline and the corset she undoubtedly wore underneath. The neckline emphasized the length of her neck and supple strength of her shoulders. The satin skirts clung lovingly to her waist and hips before falling to her feet. Matching black gloves covered her arms to the elbow. Her hair had been swept up for a change, in an elaborate coiffure of spiraled curls pinned whimsically on top of her head. Amidst all the black, her lips beckoned to him, painted red with rouge. His cock throbbed as he imagined that rouge rubbing off on his neck and chest as she kissed her way down his body. Stifling a groan, he pushed aside thoughts of her smearing that vibrant red color all over his prick.

"I must say, you clean up nicely, Mr. Darling," she said.

"As do you, my lady," he replied. "Wherever we are going this evening, I am certain to be the envy of every man present."

She allowed him to give her a hand up into the carriage, settling into her seat as he hoisted himself in across from her. Once their driver spurred the conveyance forward, she lifted the small box resting on the seat beside her. Opening it, she revealed two simple masks—one scarlet, and one sky blue. They were plain and without adornment, a far cry from the elaborate things typically worn for masquerade balls.

"The blue one is yours," she declared before taking the red one for herself. "They are required at all of the Widow Dane's dinner parties."

Accepting the blue mask, he wracked his brain for any memory of a widow by the name of Dane. Unable to think of any, he simply donned the disguise. Perhaps the woman was an eccentric like Amelia. A masked dinner party was certainly different than anything he'd ever participated in.

"Now," she said once he'd settled the fabric over the upper half of his face. "As I stated this morning, the event we'll be attending is … special. I'll wager you've never seen anything like the things you will experience this evening. I could explain, but my words would not do it all justice. You must simply find out for yourself."

He pursed his lips, wondering just what he'd gotten himself into. Whatever it was, a sixty-thousand-pound dowry lay on the line. Besides, he had no doubt the evening would end with them in bed together again, which would make whatever preceded it well worth it.

"I am intrigued," he replied, picking a bit of lint off his new coat.

She smiled, the slash of her red lips in the near darkness of the carriage drawing his eye once again. The cab came to a stop a moment later, and he opened the door to alight from the carriage first, then offered Amelia his hand as she exited.

They stood before an elegant townhome on Half Moon Street—not the loftiest neighborhood in London, but still well out of his reach at the moment. Once he wed Amelia, they'd be flush enough to rent or purchase a home in Grosvenor Square, if she desired. Not that they would spend much time here. He preferred the country, and had much to do to set things right at Oakmoor.

The front door swung open, and a properly staunch butler stood in the opening waiting for them to ascend the front steps. Amelia took his arm as they approached the steps, but pulled him up short before he could guide her up.

"One last thing," she said, leaning in close and lowering her voice. "Being invited to one of these parties requires a bit of discretion. Lady Dane does not invite just anyone, and my invitation also extends to the guest of my choice. I do ask that you not speak of this to anyone, nor reveal any person you might recognize here tonight."

Wrinkling his brow, Michael again wondered what on earth could be taking place inside this house that she should feel the need to warn him a second time.

"Of course," he agreed. "You have my word. I will never speak of it."

She gave a satisfied nod, then allowed him to guide her to the door. The butler greeted them, motioning for them to follow the short line of guests who had arrived before them. They trailed up the stairs, men and women all elegantly dressed and each wearing a mask.

He had assumed that the red and blue masks were meant to symbolize male and female—yet, he spotted several other colors among those gathered—yellow, pink, green, and black. Most of the men wore black, leaving him wondering why blue had been chosen for him. And there was no mistaking that the colors meant something —a signal of sorts to those in the room. Some women wore red like Amelia, while most of them wore blue. Several wore pink, though he noticed a few men in the shade, as well. A small number of males wore green, and members of both sexes could be found wearing yellow.

Leaning close to Amelia, he whispered in her ear as they began the walk up the stairs. "What do the colors mean?"

Giving him a coy smile, she clung to his arm and gave him a gentle pat as if to reassure him. "Patience, Michael. You will see."

Once on the third floor of the townhouse, they were ushered into a dining room where a ravishing woman awaited them.

His mouth fell open at the sight of her—all sumptuous curves, red lips, and golden hair. Tall and statuesque, she commanded the attention of everyone in the room as she greeted her guests and urged them to sit at the table. She wore an ensemble of scarlet, her mask the same shade as Amelia's.

She must be Lady Dane, their hostess for the evening. As they approached her, she gave Amelia a wide smile and pulled her into an embrace. Amelia released his arm to hug her friend.

"Amelia, darling!" Lady Dane exclaimed. "How lovely to see you. It has been an age."

"It has," she agreed. "Though, a new aunt's work is never done, I'm afraid."

Their hostess beamed and clapped her hands in delight. "Oh, yes, I had heard the marvelous news. The marquis and marchioness were blessed with a set of twins. How splendid!"

Amelia inclined her head. "It is indeed. They are beautiful and healthy, and my sister-in-law is making a speedy recovery. You will likely receive an invitation to their christening soon."

"I look forward to it," Lady Dane said before shifting her gaze to him. "And who is your guest, dear? I do not believe I've had the pleasure."

Taking hold of his arm once more, Amelia urged him to her side. "This is Michael. Michael, might I introduce Lady Dane?"

Taking the widow's extended, gloved hand, he bowed over it and chastely kissed her knuckles. "I am honored."

"The honor is all mine," Lady Dane insisted. "Please, enjoy yourselves this evening. There will be quite a titillating demonstration following dinner, after which you are free to adjourn to the room of your choice."

"Thank you," Amelia said graciously as she steered him toward the long table adorned with white cloth, silver, and candles.

Before he could even think to ask what sort of 'demonstration' he should expect, the scene at the table stole his ability to speak. He paused in the middle of pulling out Amelia's chair, certain his jaw might just scrape the floor if he did not pull it back up. Yet, he seemed incapable as he stood openmouthed and took in the scene before him.

A man in a black mask sat to his right, but his female companion— wearing a pink mask—knelt at his feet instead of sitting in the chair beside him. She gazed adoringly at the man, allowing him to tip a champagne flute to her lips. Like a babe being fed, she drank from the glass while he held it.

"Not too much, my pet," he chided, pulling the flute away once it was half-empty.

"Yes, Master," she murmured, lowering her eyes.

The man turned to a gentleman seated at his right, and two engaged in conversation, both seeming to ignore the woman. Across the table, a man in a yellow mask sat flanked by two ravishing women, both wearing masks of the same shade. One of the women reached over him to stroke the hair of the other, the two gazing at each other with a hunger that couldn't be mistaken. One of them rested her hand on the chest of the man between them, while the other leaned in and began nibbling on his ear. He grinned, shifting a bit in his seat as the hand on his chest slid down and disappeared beneath the table.

Michael did not have a hard time working out where that hand had gone.

To the left of the trio, two men in green masks sat far closer to each other than would be considered proper in a public setting. In full view of the entire party, they began to kiss, seemingly oblivious to those around them.

His bewilderment grew as he glanced around and realized he was the only one who seemed shocked by such behavior.

"Sit, Michael," Amelia said, the command in her tone clear.

He sank slowly into his chair, hungrily taking in every detail he could.

As the first course was served, he began to notice a pattern among the guests and the colors of their masks. The women in pink acted in a downright childlike manner, much like the one sitting at the man's feet beside her. One sat in the lap of a man wearing a black mask, beaming proudly as he stroked her hair and called her a 'sweet girl.' Another allowed herself to be fed spoonfuls of soup, thanking the black-masked man feeding her between servings.

The men in black appeared to enjoy exerting control and dominance over the women in pink. They also seemed to like flaunting them—touching them with possessive hands, showing them off to be admired by the other males in the room.

The men wearing green masks obviously preferred the company of other men, while those in yellow appeared excessively amorous—preferring multiple partners. They sat in threes and fours, touching, kissing, looking on as the others in their group enjoyed each other.

Which left two mask colors he could not quite figure out. Only women wore red, and only a few men wore blue like him. A handful of women wore blue, but seemed quite a bit like the ones in pink—submissive to the men in black, though to a lesser degree.

Then, he caught sight of the man standing at Lady Dane's shoulder. A large man in a blue mask remained there like a sentinel watching over her, only speaking when spoken to and maintaining his focus on the widow. He ensured her wineglass was never empty, filling it from a silver ice bucket resting on a sideboard nearby. When she reached a hand up to her neck as if it pained her, the man immediately stepped forward and began massaging it.

"Mmm," she moaned as he applied deep pressure to her nape. "That feels marvelous, pet."

Michael stiffened, his spoon halfway to his mouth.

*Pet.*

Was that what Amelia saw him as? A pet ... a plaything to be shown off among her odd circle of friends? The notion had his hand tightening around his spoon until he feared he might bend the utensil in half. He cast an accusing glance at her, but she pointedly kept her eyes focused anywhere but at him. Methodically lifting her spoon to her lips, she seemed to have no problem enjoying her soup. Meanwhile, he could hardly taste what he put in his mouth, his other senses flooded with the sights and sounds of what went on around him.

Part of him wanted to confront Amelia, even if it meant causing a scene. If she thought of him as some sort of slave or pet, he would set her straight. He certainly did not relish being treated like a lap dog.

However, he had promised her he would remain open-minded. She had warned him, had she not? Until her motives had been made clear, he would endure this all in silence.

He managed to get through several courses while engaging in strained conversation with Amelia and the black-masked man to his left—who fed the pink-masked woman kneeling at his feet from his own plate, absently stroking her hair now and then.

But then, during the dessert course, the man opened the fall of his breeches and urged her head into his lap. Thus, Michael was forced to sit and ignore his dessert altogether as the sounds of her sucking his cock made his own blood run hot. Similar acts went on at the table around him, one of the blue-masked men disappearing beneath the table at the behest of his red-masked lady. Her lips parted, and her breath quickened a moment later—a sure indication that the man under the table had made his way beneath her skirts.

By the time Lady Dane announced the promised 'demonstration,' Michael felt as if he would explode, his prick had grown so hard. He stood less than thirty seconds away from throwing Amelia up onto the table, tossing up her skirts, and fucking her in full view of the entire party. Apparently, these sorts of things were allowed. Why should he not indulge?

The moment passed, and he was forced to get a handle on his raging need as he stood and offered Amelia a hand up from the table. Following the others into the adjoining drawing room, he found rows of chairs all pointed at an elevated dais upon which two tables rested. One table sat covered with various instruments he could not identify from this distance. The other table was empty aside from what appeared to be a set of shackles welded to its surface.

Curiosity prompted him to take a seat beside Amelia and wait for the demonstration to begin.

"My friends," said Lady Dane once everyone had sat and fallen silent. "I thank you for joining me this evening. Because our last gathering featured an exhibition by a male master with a female submissive, I thought we could do with a change of pace this evening. Tonight, my pet and I will demonstrate the proper techniques for the application of pain, as well as a proper balance of power between the dominant and submissive."

Michael raised his eyebrows and glanced around at the people surrounding him. So, if he had to wager, he'd say the red and black masks were the marks of the dominants, while blue and pink signaled the submissives. He supposed that after the way he'd allowed Amelia to take charge during their first night together, she thought of him as submissive. A slow smile crept across his face at the absurdity of it all.

For certain, he'd enjoyed fucking her. It had been the single, most explosive sexual encounter of his life. But that did not mean he intended to follow her about like a puppy begging for a scrap, and it certainly did not mean he intended to let her parade him around like some sort of prized horse. The irony, of course, being that he didn't even possess the pedigree of a well-bred horse. He would have laughed if the sight of Lady Dane beginning to disrobe had not captured his rapt attention.

All humor fled as her gown fell away to reveal a black satin corset, black breeches clinging to her hips and legs like a second skin, and a pair of the most sinful boots Michael had ever seen. Black leather hugged her legs, a slight heel making her taller than she would be in slippers or bare feet. Taking up a coiled black whip from the table of instruments, she turned to face the man she had dubbed her 'pet.'

"Peter, you and I both know your safe word," she said in a firm but soothing tone. "But for the benefit of our audience, would you remind me what it is now?"

"My safety word is *silk*, Mistress," he replied.

Mistress. The same name Amelia had insisted he call her when they engaged in intercourse. He gazed at her from the corner of his eye, but her attention remained upon the demonstration.

"Very good, Peter," Lady Dane crooned. "And you can attest that everything you submit to this evening, you do so of your own free will?"

"Yes, Mistress."

"And if you wish for me to stop at any time?"

"I need only utter my safety word, Mistress."

She reached out to stroke his jaw and smiled. "Very good, pet. Please disrobe and assume your position."

"As you wish, Mistress," Peter replied while reaching for the buttons of his coat.

The entire room remained so silent, one might have heard a pin drop as Peter obeyed the wishes of his Mistress. Once he had stripped to nothing, he sank to his knees facing Lady Dane, hands clasped behind his back, head lowered.

The man did not strike Michael as one he would immediately peg as submissive. Large and obviously strong, he possessed all the attributes of any other rake or libertine in London. He could have women crawling at *his* feet, yet he knelt before the widow as if she were the only woman who existed in the world.

Intrigued, Michael remained quiet and still and studied the scene with the open mind Amelia had urged him to attempt.

Lady Dane circled him, touching him, stroking his hair, massaging one large shoulder.

"You may look at me, pet," she commanded.

Peter lifted his head and locked his gaze upon her without wavering. Still holding the whip with one hand, she reached up to free her breasts from the corset.

Michael's mouth went dry at the sight of them—large, round, and tipped in delicate pink nipples. The little buds did not hold a candle to Amelia's succulent nipples, but he couldn't deny Lady Dane's beauty or sexual allure.

The widow cupped one breast and eyed Peter knowingly—as if all-too aware of what the man wanted.

"You love my tits, don't you, Peter?" she murmured, striding closer to him.

"Very much, Mistress," he replied, his voice low and husky.

Grasping his shoulders, she leaned forward until her breasts hovered mere inches from his face.

Michael would have lost control by now, tackling her to the ground and feasting on the offering she presented.

Yet, Peter proved to be made of sterner stuff. He stayed on his knees, his hands remaining clenched behind his back.

Turning her head to address the audience, she smiled. "Notice how he does not act without my directive, even when tempted."

Grasping Peter's head, she thrust her breasts at him, burying his face between them. Still, the man remained utterly still, though his chest did heave as if he fought to hold back.

Finally, the man's patience was rewarded.

"You may use your mouth on them, pet ... but keep your hands behind your back."

Peter's response came out on a low groan as he lurched forward and took a nipple into his mouth. Lady Dane's soft sighs mingled with the man's deep, guttural grunts as he suckled at her as if he'd been starving.

Michael shifted in his chair, the erection he'd fought down at dinner now making a swift resurgence. At his side, Amelia remained still and silent, though she could not be completely unaffected.

The longer this demonstration went on, the more he began to see her predilections—the very same ones she'd hinted at during their first encounter. She'd wanted him to see this—to understand what sort of woman she was, and the things she desired.

As much as he'd like to pretend it all repulsed him, he had to admit that some of it appealed to him. Pleasuring a woman, knowing exactly what she wanted, what she needed … it was something many men would never experience. In a world full of innuendo and guessing games, he would prefer for things to be straightforward. And it did not get more straightforward than the scene playing out before them.

Peter seemed to forget himself for a moment, lifting both hands and using them to cup Lady Dane's breasts as he switched his mouth from one to the other. He'd just captured her nipple between his lips when the widow moved out of his reach, swiftly reprimanding him with a palm across his cheek.

Michael's face burned as he remembered Amelia treating him the same way. His cock was hard as stone now as he pondered what had followed.

"You're being naughty again, pet," Lady Dane warned, circling her prey and finally uncoiling the whip held in one hand. "What do you suppose I should do about that?"

Several people in the room flinched when she gave the whip a crack, the sound echoing ominously. Beside him, Amelia smirked, while on the dais, Peter lowered his head and appeared outwardly contrite. However, Michael could not help but wonder if the man had not purposely broken Lady Dane's rule.

"I suppose you must punish me, Mistress," Peter murmured. "I am a deviant and a lecher, and I must be disciplined until I have learned my lesson."

No doubt about it … he sounded so incredibly pleased with himself that Michael just knew the man was exactly where he wanted to be.

Lady Dane paused behind him, looping the leather whip around his neck and giving it a swift tug. He leaned back against her naked breasts, closing his eyes and taking a deep breath as if fighting for control. The Mistress had, apparently, begun pushing him toward his breaking point. His entire body had gone rigid, and he appeared as if he might explode at any moment.

"Punish you, I shall," Lady Dane declared, leaning down to nibble on the shell of his ear. "Rise, my pet, and position yourself upon the table the way I prefer."

"As you wish, Mistress."

The man rose and did as the widow commanded, approaching the empty table which Michael now realized was intended for restraining the submissive partner.

Peter stood at its head and bent at the waist, resting up upper body on its surface. Lady Dane laid her whip upon the instrument table and approached to strap him down, securing padded shackles around each of his wrists. With his arms stretched in front of him, he appeared vulnerable, completely at his Mistress' mercy.

Glancing out at her rapt audience, Lady Dane smirked. "Punishment is a powerful tool for a dominant. It ensures your submissive knows that obedience is paramount. And, when followed by pleasure, it can provide them with the sort of release they cannot experience any other way."

Was this why his night with Amelia had been so extraordinary? Granted, she had not inflicted much pain, but her domination, the way she'd led him through the encounter … it had all been unlike anything he'd ever experienced. He now grew curious about how more pain could exacerbate his need, resulting in an even more explosive ending. If it were possible for him to experience even greater pleasure with Amelia, he'd gladly submit to it. Within reason, of course.

"Fleshier areas are best for punishing," Lady Dane continued, turning back to her prey, who remained passively bent over the table where she'd left him. "For a male submissive, this means mostly his flanks … though many enjoy taking their lashes upon their muscular backs. With a lady, the breasts can also become a target for both pleasure and pain, as well as the buttocks and thighs. Now, proper techniques for spanking, flogging, and whipping vary depending upon your instrument of choice, and following this demonstration, I will be available to assist those of you who are new to the practice. Myself … I prefer the whip above all others."

Then, reaching toward the instrument table, she retrieved her whip, giving it another crack through the air.

Michael tensed, his every muscle coiled tight, his lungs beginning to burn as he held his breath in anticipation.

With a flick of her wrist, Lady Dane snapped the whip, this time toward the helpless man before her. The whip made impact, and Peter flinched, grunting as if the blow had been no more than a minor annoyance.

But Lady Dane wasn't finished yet. She flaunted her skill proudly, flicking the whip at her 'pet' from different directions, striking his buttocks and thighs at perfectly timed intervals. Peter endured it all, flinching with each blow, grunting or groaning after each one. Yet, even from here, it became clear the abuse had only heightened his arousal. He squirmed in his bonds, appearing desperate to be free. As Lady Dane dropped her whip and began loosening the shackles, Peter watched her with an unmistakable heat in his eyes. Yes, he'd been punished and made to suffer, but the hard expression on his face spoke volumes.

The moment he was allowed, he was going to fuck Lady Dane into oblivion.

Once his wrists were free, he straightened and folded his hands behind his back to await further instruction. Lady Dane circled behind him, reaching out to soothe his buttocks with her hand. Peter sucked in a sharp breath and closed his eyes, the touch seeming to bring both bliss and discomfort.

"Well done, pet," she said, now standing in front of him. "You endured your punishment admirably … and for that, I will reward you."

As she sank to her knees before him, Peter heaved a relieved sigh. "Thank you, Mistress."

Lady Dane did not reply with words; she simply grabbed hold of Peter's cock and took it into her mouth. The man's knees buckled, but he righted himself, gritting his teeth as she began sucking him. The sounds of her pleasuring him with her mouth stirred Michael's lust even more—a feat he hadn't thought possible—and no amount of shifting his position in the chair could hide the erection pressing against the front of his breeches.

Sneaking a glance at Amelia, he found her sitting as rigid and still as him, though her breasts heaved beneath her gown while she seemed to fight to breathe properly. So, she was not as unaffected by this display as she'd have him think. Did her mind wander back to their night together? Was she remembering the feel of his cock in her mouth, the sounds he'd made as she'd sucked him better than any whore before her ever had? God knew it was all he could think of.

It did not take long for Peter to reach his end, his hips bucking wildly at Lady Dane's mouth, his hoarse groans becoming louder.

Still, the urge to obey was not forgotten. Opening his eyes and glancing down at the woman tormenting him in front of a room full of guests, he managed to speak between shudders that seemed to wrack his entire body.

"Permission to spend … Mistress."

Releasing him from her mouth, Lady Dane continued stroking his cock with one hand. "Granted."

She enveloped him once more, and Peter thrust into her mouth a few more times before going still, and spilling inside of her with a guttural roar.

# CHAPTER 7

$\mathcal{A}$melia took her time pouring herself a liberal measure of sherry, careful to keep her back turned to Michael. The demonstration Lady Dane had put on for her guests had left her yearning. They had been dismissed by the widow at the conclusion—free to seek privacy in any empty room on the third floor.

They'd found a drawing room with a stocked sideboard—along with a table holding a collection of the implements dominants often used with their submissives. The urge to wield the whip herself, to drive Michael to the limits of his control and teach him the pleasures of submission, pounded through her bloodstream, hot and fast.

Yet, she remained uncertain of how he felt about what he'd just seen. Being a Mistress often meant exercising patience, and she would require a bit of that now. Because, even if he'd liked what he'd seen, she would still be faced with the responsibility of initiating him properly—of teaching him before allowing herself free reign to play with him the way she wished.

Pouring another glass, she turned and extended the second one to her companion for the evening. It was hard to decipher his expression through the blue mask, but the hard set of his jaw told her he at least felt conflicted, if nothing else.

Accepting the drink, he downed it in two quick gulps. As she took a leisurely sip of her own sherry, she studied him from head to toe— noting the way his muscles strained against his coat, his cock still thick and hard, creating an enticing outline against the fabric of his breeches.

Apparently, the exhibition had affected him much the same way it had her. The only question remained whether Michael would be the sort of man who became afraid, because he did not know why he'd reacted so strongly to the stimuli, or the sort who would grow curious enough to discover what a Mistress like Amelia could offer him.

Once he'd finished his drink, he set the glass aside and then reached up to remove his mask. Holding up the blue material, he scowled.

"Is this what you think of me?" he asked, the accusation in his tone clear. "That I am some weak-minded fop who will tolerate being led about by the balls?"

Removing her own mask, she set it aside, placing her half-finished drink beside it. She folded her hands in front of her and squared her shoulders. Years as a Mistress had prepared her for this reaction. Most men expressed the same outrage and confusion ... until they became enlightened.

"Of course not," she countered. "In fact, I see you as quite the opposite."

He furrowed his brow, still clearly not understanding. "Then why would you bring me here to witness that spectacle? Or give me the same mask as the sorts of men who enjoy being ordered about like errant children?"

She smirked at that, unable to help that he'd amused her with that last question. "Surely, Peter did not feel like an errant child when Millicent was sucking his cock. What you think you saw was a woman controlling a man ... but, in truth, you have no idea what you truly witnessed."

He inclined his head, his expression softening a bit. "Would you care to enlighten me?"

The rushing sensation in her veins increased, as all her blood seemed to race to her most primal organs. Her breasts tingled, and a slow pounding began between her thighs—a yearning for pleasure, for control ... for Michael.

Approaching him, she reached out and rested both hands upon his chest. Beneath his evening clothes lay a body radiating heat, power, and promise. If she could earn his submission, it would be the single most gratifying thing she'd ever done. This man was unlike any of her past lovers, which only made her want him even more.

"Domination and submission are an equal exchange of power," she murmured, gazing up into his eyes. "As a Mistress, I lead the encounter, but as my submissive, you are not obligated to endure anything you do not like. It isn't only about you pleasing me, but about me discovering the boundaries of what you can endure and derive pleasure from. With me, you will find a bedmate willing to indulge your every fantasy ... so long as you earn your rewards through discipline and control."

"Your control of me," he stated, his mouth tightening at the corners as if the idea repulsed him.

"No," she countered. "Your control of yourself and the situation. I cannot act without your acquiescence ... I do not claim my own pleasure unless I have properly given yours."

He fell silent for a moment, his gaze burning into hers. She watched the indecision war with curiosity in his gaze, shades of dark blue swirling among the lighter hue of his irises. She needed to tip him over the edge, help him move from wariness to anticipation and need.

"I asked you to come with me tonight and keep an open mind," she continued. "You have given me both those things, and I am grateful. This is my world, Michael. Lady Dane trained me herself when I was still quite young. Since I discovered the taboo pleasures of domination and submission, I have been a Mistress, and I am not ashamed of that fact. If you find that repugnant, I am sorry to say that our meetings must come to an end. However, if you are intrigued enough to give me a chance, I will show you exactly how pleasurable submitting to me can be. And once I do that, I can guarantee that you will never want to submit to another woman again."

Dropping her hands back to her sides, she remained standing close, gazing up at him, and waited. Her heart thundered wildly, and for a moment, she feared he would rebuff her.

In the past, the rejection of a man would have meant nothing to her. If the object of her desires did not want her, she would brush him aside and pursue the next willing male in her path. Yet, Michael Darling proved a prize too tempting to walk away from.

Holding her breath, she waited for him to acquiesce or refuse—to accept her or reject her.

Reaching out to grasp her face, he gripped her jaw, his thumb caressing the deep dimple in one cheek.

"One night to convince me," he murmured. "You had better make it count. Additionally, I want to make it clear that I am no weakling. Do not think to manipulate or dominate me outside of these encounters. I submit when I choose, but *I am a man*, Amelia."

She released her breath on a relieved sigh and sank against him, arching her back so that her breasts teased his chest. "Mr. Darling ... that is precisely why I want you. Shall we begin?"

With a silent nod, he took a step away from her. "At your leisure."

Snapping her back straight and squaring her shoulders, she assumed the mantle of Mistress, changing her face from one of amusement to one of cool aloofness.

"Very well, Mr. Darling," she said. "Before we begin, you must choose your safe word ... one that can be recalled in the heat of the moment and would sound out of place during intercourse."

Nodding, he remained silent, his eyes darting as he seemed to think on it for a moment before replying. "Dimple."

She smirked, undoubtedly causing the little cleft to appear in her cheek. "Perfect. Do not be afraid to call it out if you need to, Mr.

Darling. As a Mistress, it is my duty to cease whatever I am doing the moment you utter it."

"Understood," he replied.

"One last thing before we start our session," she said. "I must know beforehand what limits you'd like me to skirt … any activities that you find repugnant. If so, I would like to know them now so I can avoid pushing you to use your safe word if I can."

He cringed, wrinkling his nose. "No buggery."

She chuckled. While she knew Mistresses who utilized dildos to practice buggery with their male submissives, it was not something she enjoyed.

Michael laughed along with her, causing some of the tension between them to ease a bit.

"Agreed," she said with a resolute nod. "No buggery. Anything else?"

He shrugged one shoulder. "You are free to lead me as you please, Mistress."

A shudder raced down her spine at his addressing her as 'Mistress.' She could hardly wait to begin, and had to remind herself that this first encounter would be about teaching him. Patience would serve her well.

"Now that we've gotten that established," she said. "We shall begin. Remove your coat."

He obeyed quickly, peeling the tailored garment away from his large shoulders before tossing it haphazardly over the back of a chair.

"Now what?" he asked.

Approaching him and turning her back, she smiled. "Now … undress me, Mr. Darling."

He began unbuttoning her gown swiftly and without hesitation, a good sign that she'd chosen the right man. While a bit incredulous at first, he'd proved curious and eager to learn thus far.

As he unbuttoned her, she reached up to begin pulling her hair pins free, sending heavy coils of hair falling down her back. By the time she had finished, Michael had loosened her last button and dropped her gown into a pool at her feet.

Stepping out of it, she turned and bent to pick it up, draping it over a chair. Hands braced upon her hips, she faced him, grinning at the expression upon his face in reaction to scintillating attire she'd donned beneath it.

A black chemise draped from her shoulders, falling just to her thighs. Over it, she wore a black leather corset with red ribbons lacing it up the front. Matching stockings covered her legs to mid-thigh, with red satin garters holding them up.

But Michael's gaze fell and remained on her favorite part of the get-up—a pair of boots she wore only while acting as Mistress. Black leather like her corset, they covered her to the knee, the laces efficiently tied. With a heel on the back, they gave her an additional two inches in height.

"Would you like to share your thoughts with me, Mr. Darling?" she asked, adopting the stern voice she affected during sessions with her lovers.

His fiery gaze lifted to meet hers, and he grinned. "I feel like a stallion about to be broken. Are you going to wear those boots while you ride me?"

His little quip amused her, but she must teach him how to behave when submitting to her. Lifting her chin, she smothered the giggle simmering in her throat and shrugged one shoulder.

"If you can earn it," she replied. "Remove the rest of your clothing, and await me upon your knees, Mr. Darling."

Arching an eyebrow at her, he began to do as she commanded, unbuttoning his waistcoat and peeling it from his shoulders.

Amelia stood back, hands still braced upon her hips, enjoying the display of masculinity and strength as he revealed his rough-hewn body inch by incredible inch. The light of the fire danced over his skin and cast his shadow against the wall, large and ominous—hers to control.

Once completely nude, he sank to his knees on the carpet and gazed at her expectantly.

Slowly circling him, she began to touch him, running her fingers through his hair, caressing his shoulders.

"Most dominants wish for their submissives to keep their eyes lowered unless instructed otherwise," she said. "But I prefer a captive audience. You will keep your eyes upon me whenever I am in your line of sight, Mr. Darling."

"Yes, Mistress," he murmured, meeting her gaze.

The low rumble of his voice stroked down her spine and sank into her groin, creating a warming sensation. They'd hardly begun, and already, desire was pushing her to her breaking point.

But she would maintain her composure. Their joining would be all the better after she'd worked him into a frenzy.

Walking back to the table where an array of clamps, rings, and other implements had been neatly arranged, she selected one of her favorites and turned back toward him. He furrowed his eyebrows at the sight of the metal ring in her palm, yet the thick root of his cock remained hard, stretched out toward her as if knowing she could offer it release.

"Stand," she ordered, licking her lips at the sight of the pearlescent bead of moisture gathering at the slit in his engorged head.

He rose, folding his arms behind his back and watching her closely as she approached.

Dropping to her knees before him, she took hold of his cock in one hand. She brought it to her lips and flicked out her tongue, lapping at the drop of wetness. He groaned, his hips bucking toward her instinctively. Deciding to oblige him, she licked him again, this time swirling her tongue over the flared head, then taking it into her mouth. He began to pant, the muscles in his abdomen clenching as he seemed to fight for restraint.

She wondered how long it would take him to lose control if he was already struggling. Giving him one last feel of her tongue, she returned to her original purpose. Still holding his cock in one hand, she used the other to slide the metal ring over the tip. Easing it down the rigid flesh, she settled it at the base.

"A cock ring," she said in response to his questioning gaze as she rose to her feet. "Makes your prick longer and harder, and also ensures you don't spend before I want you to."

Rising, she backed away from him again, angling toward the couch. Plopping down onto it, she leaned back and slouched a bit, making herself comfortable.

"You will stand right there and talk to me, Mr. Darling," she said.

"Talk?"

She heard the frustration in his voice.

"Yes, of course," she replied, as if the urgency of his fully engorged cock did not matter. "I am an inquisitive woman, after all … and I want to hear about all the things you would do to me if I would allow you."

His mouth curved into a devilish grin. "Is that so, Mistress?"

Propping one foot up on the low table before her, she grinned. "I'm waiting."

His eyes seemed darker from this distance, a feral light creeping into them as he raked his gaze over her from head to toe.

"I would snatch down the front of your chemise, for a start," he began. "Pretty little tits like yours shouldn't be hidden away."

Reaching up to the neck of her chemise, she slowly peeled it away, settling it beneath her small breasts. "Like this?"

Michael licked his lips and nodded, his chest heaving as he fought to control his breathing. "So perfect."

Glancing down at her breasts, she sighed. "They are rather small, though … aren't they?"

"The perfect size to fill my hands," he countered. "And your nipples … so pink and plump. If you let me, I'd play with them … pinch them, pluck at them until you moan and thrash beneath me."

"Hmm," she murmured, palming her breasts. "Like this?"

Flutters of pleasure rippled through her as she pinched her nipples lightly, rolling them between her thumbs and forefingers.

Michael grunted, shifting on his feet as his cock seemed to swell even more.

"Yes, just like that," he replied. "I'd taste them, too—like sweet little cherries."

"And then?" she urged.

"That demonstration must have left you in quite a state of agitation," he mused. "Watching Peter being punished."

Squeezing her thighs together, she nodded, the pulsating between them growing more acute. "Yes."

"I could ease that for you," he offered. "You seemed to like me on my knees."

She giggled. "Oh, Mr. Darling, I do."

"Then I'd kneel for you, right between those beautiful legs in those naughty boots."

Spreading her legs, she lifted the bottom of her chemise, revealing the patch of curls between her thighs. "Here?"

He nodded. "Yes, Mistress. Right there. Then, I'd taste you until you spent on my tongue."

Sliding one hand between her legs, she parted her lower lips to expose her hidden flesh.

Michael groaned, taking a step toward her. Seeming to realize his error, he halted … though he did not return to his previous place.

"Where, Mr. Darling?" she urged, slowly massaging herself under his watchful eye. "Where would you put that filthy tongue of yours?"

His gaze slid up her body to meet hers once more as he replied. "You know where."

Biting her lower lip, she circled one finger lightly over her clit. "Here?"

"Yes," he groaned, his lips parting as he watched her stroke herself in slow circles. "I'd lick you and suck you until you scream, Mistress— your sweet juices all over my lips."

Her core clenched at his words, the yearning for something inside stronger than ever. She'd played this game with many of her submissives before, but never had it aroused her so much as it did with

Michael. It was as if he knew exactly what to say and how to say it to drive her mad with lust.

"Stroke yourself," she commanded. "But do not spend."

"Yes, Mistress," he said with a relieved sigh.

He took his cock into his hand and hissed, closing his fist around it and pumping in one long stroke. By now, the cock ring would have made him far more sensitive than usual—something that made itself apparent with each pass of his fist over his shaft.

"Christ," he muttered, seeming to struggle with himself over how fast to pump his hand. He seemed to want to go slow so as not to disobey her, but with the cock ring making him more sensitive, it would feel too good to slow down or stop.

She increased the pressure on her clit, her hips moving in time with his strokes, a low groan spilling from her lips. "And once I'd spent in your mouth?"

He groaned, hips jerking as he steadily stroked himself, his thumb caressing his head—now turned purple from so much blood rushing to the organ.

"I'd fuck you, hard and fast," he grunted between strokes. "I'd drill my cock into you until you begged me to stop."

She whimpered, her eyes sliding closed at the thought of allowing it—of unleashing every ounce of pent-up desire roiling inside of him. But, it was not time yet.

"Come to me, Mr. Darling," she commanded.

He crossed the room in three quick strides, dropping to his knees in front of her and bracing his hands on the edge of the sofa. Looming over her, he waited, every muscle in his body coiled and ready to spring. Yet, he did not move, did not touch her, did nothing other than wait for her next instruction.

"You may taste me," she said. "But you may not touch yourself while you do so."

Before the words had even finished coming out of her mouth, he was on her. He started with her breasts, dragging his tongue over one, then the other, pulling a sharp cry from her. She arched her back as he nibbled on her nipples, tasting them as if they proved as sweet as the cherries he'd compared them to. Sucking one of her breasts deep into his mouth, he used his hands to shove her legs apart as wide as they could go.

Then, releasing the breast, he kissed his way down her corset, nuzzling her belly through the leather and making his way lower. She moaned at the first touch of his open mouth on her tender flesh, her hips bucking as he closed his lips around her clit.

"Bloody hell," she ground out, clenching her teeth as he sucked at her with a relentlessness that left her breathless.

He made an answering sound, but did not reply, his head bobbing between her thighs as he applied his lips and tongue, sucking and lapping at her just as he'd said. The slow pulsations between her thighs grew and swelled until the pounding nearly drove her mad. She thrashed beneath him, her hips bowing up off of the sofa as she spent, a flood of moisture accompanying spasms that shook her to her core.

Amelia did not think she'd ever had such a powerful climax with nothing but a man's tongue to tease her. It must be the thrill of taking on a new pupil and seeing him excel.

At least, it had seemed he'd excelled. As she sat up and glanced down at him, she narrowed her eyes at the evidence of his disobedience. Michael's cock clenched in one large fist. She'd caught him mid-stroke, a look of sheer desperation and desire upon his face. He glanced down at the offending hand, then back at her. Seeming to realize his unwitting error, he cleared his throat, his neck flushing red.

"Forgive me, Mistress," he said. "I could not help myself."

Rising to her feet, she stared down at him with her arms folded over her chest. As much as she wanted to move to the next part—the part where she allowed him to fuck her—she could not let this transgression to go unchecked. Just as he must learn to obey, he must also learn that there would be consequences for failing to follow her directions.

"Oh, Mr. Darling," she scolded. "Now you've gone and done it. I'm afraid I have to punish you now."

# CHAPTER 8

$\mathcal{M}$ ichael felt as if his cock would explode at any moment. Yet, no matter how hard or fast he'd stroked himself, it seemed he couldn't bring himself to spend. It must be the damned cock ring, which functioned just the way Amelia had described. The organ throbbed in his palm, the head so sensitive that even the slight brush of his thumb over it proved enough to make his knees buckle.

He was a man, not some green lad who could not control himself. Yet, the taste of Amelia and her juices dripping down his chin, her moans echoing from the ceiling as she climaxed in his mouth—it had been an assault upon his senses too strong to combat. Before he'd known it, he'd found his hand upon his cock, the urge to frig himself overcoming all good sense.

Of course, he'd been caught, and now, he must endure punishment. If Amelia was anything like Lady Dane, he supposed he ought to be prepared for physical pain. That, he could tolerate. While he would not choose to endure being flogged or whipped, he felt certain it could do nothing to temper his desire. If what Amelia said proved true, it might even enhance it.

"I am sorry, Mistress," he apologized again, hoping that getting back in her good graces would mean he could have access to her cunt. "I will endeavor to exercise better control in the future."

Going back to the table where she had retrieved the cock ring, she lifted something from the surface. "I am certain you will, Mr. Darling."

He inclined his head at the sight of the wooden paddle held between her hands. "The instrument of my torture?"

She laughed, approaching him with the paddle. "I prefer the whip, but I left mine at home. This will do for tonight's lesson. Do you see that footstool in the corner?"

Following her gaze to said furniture, he nodded. "Yes, Mistress."

"Bring it here."

He obeyed, his cock steadily throbbing with every step as he crossed the room to retrieve the footstool. Perhaps this was meant to be the true torture—withholding his release this way. He felt ready to beg and plead to be inside of her, if only to ease his agony.

Placing the footstool on the floor in front of her, he knelt before it. What other use could it have other than to serve as a place for his punishment?

"Rest your body over the stool and hold still," she said imperiously.

"As you say, Mistress," he replied, laying his upper body across the footstool and allowing his head to fall forward toward the floor.

The position felt demeaning, which he supposed must be the point. He might never allow anyone else to have him in such a posture, but Amelia's promise that there would be no buggery put him at ease. She seemed to take this seriously and would not go back on her word. He trusted her to continue leading him as she had from the beginning.

He flinched when one of her hands caressed his thigh, stroking up toward his buttocks. The pleasure of her touch only made his erection even more unbearable.

"When I give an order, I expect you to obey, Mr. Darling," she reprimanded, bringing her palm against his buttocks in a light swat. "Is that understood?"

"Yes, Mistress."

Just as the last word had fallen from his lips, the paddle fell against him. She used a light hand, allowing the wood to glance off him just hard enough to make his skin grow warm. That warmth combined with the heat in his groin, the pain melting away as quickly as it had come. His eyes widened as he realized he'd liked it.

Each fall of the paddle—a bit harder than the last—sent more heat through his muscles, the sting becoming a pleasant tingle that seemed to resound all the way to the tip of his cock.

She struck him again with a great deal more strength, the paddle falling with a thud against his arse and forcing a grunt from him. He groaned as moisture dripped from his cock, the confused muddle of discomfort and desire proving far more delicious than he could have imagined.

"Please, Mistress," he begged before he realized the words were coming from his mouth. "I have learned my lesson. If you'll allow it, I'd still like to be allowed to fuck you."

The paddle fell to the ground beside him with a thud, and a moment later, Amelia's gentle hands caressed his buttocks. He hissed at her touch, far more arousing now that his skin had been set on fire by the paddle. She soothed him with soft strokes, moving up toward his back, then down toward his thighs.

"Will you be a good boy from now on, Mr. Darling?"

He chuckled. "Perhaps not always, but for as long as I am able, Mistress. I think we both know I have a propensity for mischief."

She laughed. "One of the many reasons I am fond of you, Mr. Darling. Rise."

He lurched to his feet, his throat constricting as he turned to face her and wait for her verdict. If she didn't give him what he needed, he might die on the spot.

Backing slowly toward the couch they'd occupied, she gave him a coy smirk. "Come and get me, Mr. Darling. Take me."

He lunged forward as the shackles of her limitations fell away, freeing him to fulfill his urges. A primal growl tore from him as he grasped her shoulders and threw her back onto the couch. Resting his knees against the cushions, he fell between her thighs, nudging them apart and poising his cock at her entrance. Using one arm to brace himself on the back of the sofa, he used the other to lift her hips off the cushion, angling her the way he wanted before driving home.

Wet heat enveloped him, and he groaned, burying his face in her neck, taking up a swift cadence inside of her. He did not have it in him to go slow, to think of her enjoyment. The roaring of his own blood in his ears drowned out all sound, and every sensation faded away save for the pleasure of her tight sheath wrapped around him.

He faintly registered her legs wrapped around him, the heels of her boots digging into his skin. But he couldn't stop, not with her cunt pulsating around him, her wetness drenching him, her lips and tongue teasing his earlobe as he pumped into her like a madman.

Yet, still, the urge to spend seemed to hang just out of his reach. And so he fucked her hard and fast, as relentlessly as he could—all while she cried out and quivered in his hold, climax after climax rippling through her body.

By the time she reached her third orgasm, his skin was covered in a sheen of sweat, thighs sore from the constant movement of his hips.

But then, as suddenly as a blow to the head, his own release came. He pulled out of her just in time, dropping her onto the cushions and trying to get a hold of his cock before spilling his seed all over her.

Yet, he could do nothing to stop it. He came with a roar, the streams of his mettle spurting up onto her chest, staining the neckline of her chemise. His knees now weakened and his strength sapped, he backed away from the couch and fell into the first chair he encountered.

The sense of euphoria he'd experienced before overwhelmed him, and despite knowing he should help Amelia clean herself up, he could do no more than sit there, floating in that languid place.

A moment later, he heard her moving, and opened his eyes to find her wiping herself clean with a handkerchief. He cringed at the evidence of his climax staining her chemise.

"I apologize for that," he murmured, his eyelids heavy, his voice thick and foreign.

She grinned and tossed the handkerchief aside before approaching him. "Never apologize, Mr. Darling. The things we do together might seem taboo to others, but there's nothing wrong with them. Besides, I'd rather you spill your seed anywhere but inside me."

He inwardly cringed, but reminded himself that he and Amelia approached their sudden and odd relationship in different ways. He already thought of her as his bride, which meant the need to impregnate her had already crossed his mind. Conversely, Amelia seemed content to remain a spinster—and of course, an unplanned pregnancy could not factor well into those plans.

"What is this feeling?" he mumbled, pushing aside thoughts of marriage and babies for the moment. "It's as if I'm floating."

Approaching his chair, she sank down onto his lap. Running a hand through his hair, she kissed him, softly and tenderly.

"It is difficult to explain, but it is why so many men and women enjoy submission," she replied. "The euphoria feels better than being in your cups, than riding your horse as fast as it will run … it is indescribable."

That was certainly true. He had never felt this way after his past sexual encounters. Only with Amelia … only by submitting.

If this was what bending to her will earned him, he did not think he would mind submitting to her for the rest of his life.


Three days passed between Lady Dane's soirée and Michael's next encounter with Amelia. He'd purposely taken that time to compose himself—to think over the events of that confusing—albeit arousing—evening. The power she'd exerted over him, and the way it had made him feel, had proven so intense that he could hardly close his eyes without remembering the things she'd done to him—the things he'd done to her once she'd pushed him past the boundaries of his control.

He had not yet decided if the discovery of her unorthodox nature would be a benefit to their marriage or a problem. One on hand, a man with a lusty wife would never go to bed unsatisfied. Nor would he have to worry about tutoring some young virgin on their wedding night, freeing him to enjoy the experience without restraint. In truth, he could think of no true drawback to such an arrangement, and decided to allow her to continue tutoring him even after they'd wed. If nothing else, her tutelage could make him a better lover—something no man should refuse if given half the chance.

Now that he'd gained her interest and attention, the time had come to snare her for good. He would much rather take his time and allow a few more weeks for them to get to know one another, but the state of Oakmoor would not permit it. He needed Amelia and her dowry *now*.

And so, on the fourth night following Lady Dane's dinner party, he let Oliver dress and groom him, then walked to the same gaming hell in which he'd first met Amelia. A grin spread across his face when he found her inside, seated at the same table she'd occupied when he'd first lain eyes on her.

This evening, she wore a gown instead of her usual breeches and boots, though its neckline revealed so much flesh, it proved far more scandalous than her masculine attire. With her hair piled on top of her head and a cameo choker gracing her slender neck, she looked like his every carnal fantasy brought to life as she glanced over the shoulder of her current opponent and smiled at him.

The only thing that might heighten the effect would be knowing she wore those scandalous boots beneath her dress.

A slow grin spread across his face at the thought. Dismissing her companion, she gestured for him to join her at the table, responding to his smile with one of her own. It was catlike, lending her the appearance of a predator ... and Michael felt very much like her prey as he sank into the chair across from her.

"Lady A," he murmured, folding his hands on the table. "How do you fare this evening?"

"Better now that you have arrived," she replied with an arch of one eyebrow.

He chuckled. "Are the tables that dry tonight, then?"

She shrugged one shoulder, calling attention to her daring décolletage.

His mouth watered from the need to snatch down the front of that gown and ravage her with his mouth.

"Not at all," she stated. "However, the company hasn't been nearly so … stimulating."

Taking up the Piquet deck between his hands, he shuffled the cards. "Shall we play?"

Waving her hands to indicate that he should deal, she then leaned back in her chair and took a sip from the sherry glass resting on the table before her. They remained silent while studying their cards and selecting which ones to purge.

Observing her over his hand, he found her composed, with no hint to what she might think about the cards she held.

No matter. He'd been holding back with her thus far, purposely throwing their first game and allowing her to think him weaker at Piquet than he actually was. And, despite having been practically born in the saddle, he'd also allowed her to win their horserace. With her confidence so bolstered, he should have no trouble trouncing her soundly, thus gaining his own ends.

"Shall we make another wager?" he asked, keeping his tone light as he fiddled with his cards. "I have so enjoyed losing to you the past few bets."

Her musical laughter taunted him, even while it heated his blood.

"As I have thoroughly enjoyed slaughtering you and claiming the spoils of my victory. Very well, what would you want if you win?"

He smirked. "I simply ask for the same terms as our first Piquet game. If I win, you must allow me to do whatever I wish to do to you."

Biting her lower lip, she lowered her gaze. "Certainly, you understand that as a Mistress, I am not accustomed to such demands."

"That only makes it all the sweeter," he replied. "Come, my lady … surely, you are not *afraid* to agree to such terms."

Her gaze snapped back up to meet his, heat flaring in the depths and turning the grey irises into pools of liquid silver.

And with those words, he effectively snared Lady Amelia Fitzwilliam into his carefully laid trap.

"Me, afraid?"

He inclined his head. "Perhaps. Unless you wish to prove otherwise by agreeing to the terms."

"There can be no agreement until I've named my own terms," she pointed out.

"Naturally," he agreed. "Name your requirements."

"If I win," she began, her gaze burning hotly into his. "You must allow me to bind you hand and foot to a St. Andrew's cross, and show you just how efficient with the whip I am. Lady Dane's demonstration was child's play compared to what I am capable of."

Equal parts excitement and trepidation sent a tremor through him at the thought of allowing her to whip him. Excitement because the paddle had aroused him in ways he couldn't understand, but had still enjoyed. Trepidation because the whip seemed far more nefarious— yet, great risk would yield a greater reward. While he did not intend to lose this game, he did wonder what such an encounter might be like. Perhaps after they had wed, he would allow it, if for no other reason than to slake his own curiosity.

"Done," he stated, reaching into the breast pocket of his coat.

She frowned as he retrieved a slip of paper and pencil, placing them on the table beside the pile of cards they would draw from.

"What's this?"

He shrugged and began scribbling out the terms on the paper in his haphazard scrawl. It would be readable, and that would be all that mattered should he find himself needing to use it.

"Just a bit of insurance for my sake," he murmured. "As you are not accustomed to submitting, I find it prudent to ensure your cooperation in writing … in case nerves cause you to think to cry off."

She scoffed, shaking her head. "So certain that you'll beat me, Mr. Darling?"

Signing his name beneath the terms, he then slid the paper across the table toward her, laying the pencil within her reach.

"I certainly intend to put forth a valiant effort," he retorted. "Perhaps with such terms on the line, so will you."

Giving him an assessing stare, she reached for the pencil.

He tensed, thinking for a moment that she meant to refuse. It would seem the idea of having to allow him such freedom with her person truly unnerved her—something he'd have to examine more closely some other time.

To his relief, she lifted the pencil and signed her name beside his.

She raised her eyebrows and slammed the instrument down on the table beside the signed paper. "Do your worst, Mr. Darling. I certainly intend to."

Thus the game proceeded, their easy humor and lighthearted banter dissipating in favor of silent concentration. Michael studied his opponent closely through each *partie*, hoping to anticipate all of her moves and acting accordingly. She won the first *partie*, with him claiming a victory in the second. Back and forth they went, until they reached the final round with a draw.

"We have reached a stalemate, it would seem," she remarked as she shuffled the deck to prepare for the last bout.

"Apparently," he replied, running a hand through his hair as she dealt. "Best of luck in the remaining *partie*, my lady."

As she lifted her cards to study them, he sensed her discomfiture. It proved odd, watching her brow furrow and her lush mouth pinch at the corners. The prospect of losing this game did not sit well with her.

The silence between them grew tense as they played through the last round, their gazes clashing over the cards as they sat locked in a battle of wills, seemingly controlled by chance. He had not anticipated such a close game, and was forced to concede that Amelia was at least as good a Piquet player as him, if not better.

Yet, one last turn of the cards saw him the victor in the end, narrowly besting her by the difference of a few points.

Laying her cards facedown upon the green baize, she drew in a deep breath and sighed, then glanced up to meet his stare.

"Congratulations, Mr. Darling," she murmured, her voice low and strained. "I underestimated you, for certain, but your victory was well-earned."

He rose to his feet, his every sense on alert as he realized that he now approached the moment of truth. There could be no going back now—not when he couldn't be certain when he might have her at his mercy again.

Extending a hand, he stared down at her … at the woman who would become Lady Amelia Darling.

"Come," he said, the command in his tone clear.

She stiffened, but placed her hand in his, allowing him to assist her to her feet. He tucked her hand into the crook of his arm and escorted her toward the entrance, pausing to retrieve his hat from a footman before stepping out into the night.

He began leading her toward the inn, wanting to get her alone in his rented room before informing her of his demands. She remained uncharacteristically silent during the short walk, her hand unmoving upon his arm. His heart thundered wildly as he realized she would not cooperate—not at first. He was going to have to coerce her. At least, after tonight, she would know where he stood. Pressuring her to the altar would not be easy. However, with the signed slip of paper resting against his chest, it proved possible.

Once alone in his inn room, he released her, grateful to find that Oliver had lit a few lamps to illuminate the space before retiring to his adjoining chamber.

Turning to face him, Amelia folded her hands before her and lowered her gaze. "We may begin at your leisure, Mr. Darling."

He couldn't help a smile at that; she commanded him even while in a position of submission … as if he would need her permission to begin, when she'd already agreed to allow him freedom to do what he wished.

"Please, sit, Amelia," he said, gesturing toward the bed. "We must talk."

Her gaze turned quizzical as she glanced up at him, but she lowered herself onto his neatly made bed without question.

"You may rest easy," he began, pacing for a moment before pausing before her, hands clenched behind his back. "What I want from you does not require you to act as my submissive for a night."

Her shoulders sagged a bit, though her frown deepened as she seemed to try to understand where this conversation was going.

"Then what is it that you want from me, Michael?" she asked, her voice low, her gaze probing his.

Clearing his throat, he approached her, reaching out to cup her chin. Running his thumb across her plump lips, he took a deep breath and plunged in before he could talk himself out of it.

"I want you to marry me."

# CHAPTER 9

*A*melia felt as if she had been punched squarely in the gut, the impact rippling through her entire body as Michael's words sank in. Her throat clenched, her lungs burning as she attempted to draw in air.

It wasn't as if she'd never received a marriage proposal before. To date, she had turned down over a dozen. However, unlike the others, this one had caught her completely off guard. Michael had been nothing more than a pleasant diversion—a new submissive for her to teach and torment. Things had been going so well, and he'd never given any indication that he might be considering *her* as a marriage prospect. After all, none of the other men she'd conducted affairs with had ever dared to declare themselves in this way.

Yet, Michael Darling proved himself to be a different sort of submissive. The sort to push her to her limits and challenge her boundaries. Just now, he stood on the edge of the strictest limit of all.

"I beg your pardon?" she managed once she'd found her voice.

His gaze never wavered from hers as he continued staring at her as if able to see through to her soul.

"You promised me that I could have whatever I wanted from you, did you not? Well, what I want from you happens to be marriage."

Her mouth fell open as the realization of what he'd just done sank in, sparking heat in her veins. She vaulted to her feet, forcing him to backpedal a bit as she advanced upon him, hands braced on her hips.

"I promised you freedom with my *body* for a *night*," she retorted, her face flaming hot with anger.

Raising an eyebrow in that infuriating way of his, he reached into his coat pocket and retrieved the slip of paper he'd coerced her into signing at the gaming hell. He read his own words with a smirk twisting his lips.

"It says here that you will do whatever I command," he informed her. "There is no mention here of your body or the timeframe. I won our game fairly, and I am entitled to name my prize as spelled out, quite clearly, in our signed agreement."

Panic flared in her middle, making her pulse race and flutter. Her palms began to sweat, her stomach roiling.

"You bastard," she hissed, using anger to chase away her other emotions—most distinct of which was betrayal. She had thought they got on nicely, enjoying their arrangement as it was. If she'd suspected for a moment that he planned a stunt like this, she'd have never allowed their affair to continue.

"Now, now, my dear," he teased. "Perhaps we could save the fighting and name-calling for after we are wed?"

"We are not going to *be* wed," she retorted, jabbing his chest with her index finger. "Not when you've conspired to trap me into marriage instead of simply asking as a real man would."

Crossing his arms over his chest, he appeared unruffled by her insult. "Would you have accepted my offer if I'd simply asked?"

She clenched her teeth, annoyed that he'd figured her out so easily in such a short time. Of course she would not have accepted.

"That does not give you the right—"

"To play this little game of ours as I see fit?" he challenged. "Isn't that what this is, Amelia? A battle of wills? A test of our resolve? You've beaten me twice now, and gotten what you wanted from me. I acquiesced without question when you claimed your rightful prize from me, not once, but twice. Now, the time has come for me to collect what is rightfully mine, and I have decided that I want you … permanently."

She trembled as his words penetrated her skin and sank as deep as her bones. No man had ever proposed marriage to her this way— shunning flowery speech in favor of the bald truth. He wanted her, badly enough to risk his proposal on a wager he could not have known he'd win.

"Why?" she blurted before she could think better of it.

He wrinkled his brow. "Why, what?"

"Why do you want to marry me?" she clarified. "You must have your reasons … reasons you ruminated over before this disaster of a proposal."

"Because, of all the chits in London, you are the only one to capture my interest," he answered, his gaze holding hers steadily. "While my methods may be unorthodox, my intentions are good, Amelia. I believe we would suit, and not only inside of the bedroom. If you allow yourself to think past your anger, you might come to see that I am right."

She squared her shoulders and raised her chin, his high-handedness bristling her spine. "You would force my hand with your ridiculous wagers and a contract written out in pencil?"

"If that is what it takes, though I would much rather win you over with facts," he stated. "I am in need of a wife, and you are searching for a husband."

"Correction," she interjected. "My *brother* is looking for a husband for me. I simply went along with the farce at his behest."

"That was before you met me," he argued. "Which leads me to my next fact … you actually *like* me. Do not deny it, Amelia."

Grudgingly, she remained silent, knowing she could not find the words to disagree with him. While she was certainly wroth with him at the moment, it was true that she did like him. He was witty, possessed a sharp sense of humor, and seemed perfect as her submissive. She could not have chosen a better man had she tried.

Except for the fact that she hardly knew him. And who was to say he hadn't gone along with playing at her submissive just to win her hand? Once they were wed, she would become his property, and the tables would turn. He would be her master, and per the law, could treat her any way he wished.

As if sensing the direction of her thoughts, he came closer, resting his hands upon her shoulders.

"Fact number three, Amelia … I would *never* harm you in any way. As your husband, I would endeavor to ensure you never want for anything. You would have my respect and admiration, as well as my protection. Is that not enough?"

A bitter taste crept into her mouth as a sudden realization left her feeling cold. "And while you are meeting all of my needs, will you be doing so with your own funds, or with my substantial dowry?"

His expression hardened, and his gaze darted away from hers, and she had her answer. Shrugging out of his hold, she sneered at him, disgust propelling her away from him.

"As I suspected," she snapped. "Yet another fortune hunter."

"My need of your dowry does not negate the things I just said," he countered. "Your dowry will go to your husband, regardless of who he is. Why not someone you actually like? Someone who you know will indulge your secret passions?"

That gave her pause. If she wed him, he would allow her to continue acting as a Mistress? *His* Mistress?

She shook her head and forced herself to think objectively and not with her cunt. A submissive could be found anywhere—London was filled to the rafters with men who would pluck out their own eyes for a chance to get beneath her skirts. Just because she'd enjoyed fucking him did not mean she must wed him.

"I do not wish to marry," she informed him, composing herself and schooling her face into a mask of indifference. "Not you ... not anyone. Now, I do believe our affair has just come to an abrupt end, as your motives have been revealed, and I find I want nothing to do with them."

She attempted to breeze past him, but he halted her with a firm grip on her arm, pulling her against him.

Fighting his hold, she swung out with one hand to slap him, her temper getting the best of her. His other hand shot out, lightning quick, and halted the blow, his fingers biting into her wrists as he pulled her closer. She gasped at the feel of his cock, hard and full, pressed against her belly. Her anger flamed his lust, even while he tried to keep his grip on the annoyance tensing his jaw.

"You will not do that again," he growled, lowering his head until their lips hovered mere inches apart. "Bed play is one matter ... you taking out your rage out on my face, quite another."

Glaring at him, she writhed in his hold. "Let me go."

He obeyed, releasing her and setting her away from him. "You will be mine, Amelia. Mark my words."

She walked swiftly past him to the door, stifling the tremor that threatened at his possessive words. Men had been trying to claim her from the moment she'd made her London debut, yet, none had ever done so with a threat in his voice. None had ever approached her with such self-assurance. It caused her to realize that Michael Darling was unlike any man she'd ever known in all the ways that counted.

He would not let her get away without a fight.

Steeling herself for the battle, she departed from the inn, hands balled into fists at her sides. With that announcement, he had just declared war. What he did not know was that she intended to give as good as she got. The man had no idea what he'd just gotten himself into.

The next morning, Michael woke to find Oliver quietly preparing his clothing in the corner of the room. Sitting up in bed, he groaned, rubbing his bleary eyes and trying to ignore the pounding in his head. His sleep had been fitful, thoughts of Amelia disturbing his rest. He ran both hands through his tousled hair, then turned to place his feet on the floor. Raking his fingernails through his itchy stubble, he yawned.

Despite his fatigue, he must gather his wits. Today, he would continue waging war against his betrothed … a woman who would not admit they were betrothed. Nonetheless, he already thought of her as his. The rest proved simple semantics.

"Good morning," Oliver said as he went about methodically sharpening a straight razor. "I assume you must prepare for a visit to His Lordship, the Marquis of Ashton this morning. You'd best move quickly—you need a haircut and a shave if you're to be in such high company."

Rising, he stretched, noting that Oliver had laid out his best clothing for the morning call.

"Oliver, I find you to be indispensable. When I'm wealthy again, remind me to increase your pay."

"It shall be the first thing I do, you can be sure," Oliver quipped dryly.

Michael lowered himself into the chair and submitted himself to the valet, who rang for a bath before going about the haircut and shave. By the time his hair had been trimmed and his jaw scraped with the razor until it was smooth, a steaming tub sat waiting for him in the corner of the room.

He lowered himself into the water with a happy sigh, allowing the heat to relax his tense muscles. While he had expected resistance from Amelia, he certainly hadn't expected her to be so ambivalently set on refusing him. He'd thought that by appealing to her carnal nature in the beginning, he could soften her toward him. A woman like her would grow bored married to a man who did not understand or enjoy her predilections. He'd hoped that by showing her that he could come to her bed with an open mind and willingness to try anything to please her, he could coerce her to the altar.

It would seem she proved far more complicated than he'd first supposed.

That would not deter him. If anything, it made him more determined to have her.

Leaving the bath, he toweled off and then suffered under Oliver's fussing, until at last, the valet declared his appearance to be above reproach. After a hasty breakfast in the downstairs taproom, he hailed a hansom cab and set off for Ashton House. His arrival in the early hours, as opposed to the later social calling time, would ensure the marquis knew he meant business. He would not leave until he had secured the man's blessing to wed his sister.

Alighting from his cab before the large, imposing Ashton House, Michael stared up at the elegant façade. It proved one of the largest townhomes in Mayfair, dwarfed only by the ridiculously opulent home of the Duke of Avonleah, situated on the opposite side of Grosvenor Square.

Pulling at the lapels of his coat to straighten it, he ascended the stairs and took hold of the polished door knocker.

An appropriately aloof butler answered the door and took his calling card before ushering him inside. The man sniffed, raising an eyebrow as he read it, discovering that he entertained a mere 'mister' as opposed to a member of the nobility. He held Michael's card as if it were filthy and disdainfully informed him that he would endeavor to find out if the marquis were 'at home.'

The treatment did not ruffle him. He remained aware of his place in the world, and it was not among these people. Thankfully, once he'd married Amelia, he could whisk her away to Oakmoor and the seclusion of the country. He smiled, realizing that he missed home. As well, he wondered how Amelia would make Oakmoor her own, as he intended to allow her free reign to remodel and redecorate to her heart's content. After all, a lady of her status and wealth was bound to have better taste than him, and his concern lay in Oakmoor's farmlands. He would have not the time nor the energy to expend upon choosing wallpaper and drapes.

"Right this way," the butler called out, appearing suddenly from a corridor to the right of the foyer.

Falling in step behind the servant, Michael quietly absorbed his surroundings, noting the luxurious floor runner beneath his feet, as well as the polished sconces and expensive wall art adorning the corridor. Soon, he found himself ushered into a cavernous study.

Shelves brimming with leather-bound tomes lined three of the four walls, and the understated décor spoke volumes about its occupant. Wealth and taste were on full display, but with a light hand that hinted at an austere personality. Straightforward, no frills, masculine.

Michael liked the man who would become his brother-in-law already.

He found said man standing behind a large mahogany desk, hands clasped behind his back. Lord Simon Fitzwilliam IV, Marquis of Ashton, stood slightly taller than Michael, his frame slender yet wiry. Like Amelia, he possessed a headful of thick, black hair, a lock of which tumbled over his forehead. His eyes might be considered grey, though Michael found them a bit unnerving in their pale hue—making them almost transparent.

There, the similarities ended. Where Amelia proved sunny and boisterous, the marquis appeared cloaked in darkness. The shadows of the room, due to the closed drapes and crackling fire, seemed to cling to him lovingly. Power exuded from him with very little effort, and Michael could now see why so many quaked in their boots at the mere mention of the man's name. A more formidable member of the peerage could not be found in all of England.

Pausing just before the desk, he bowed in deference. "My lord."

Inclining his head in response, Ashton motioned toward the two chairs facing the desk. "Mr. Darling, it is nice to make your acquaintance. Please, sit … and do inform me of the reason for your visit."

He sank into the high-backed chair, while Ashton resumed his place on the other side of the desk.

"My lord, it is my understanding that you are not a man who

entertains folly," he began. "So, I shall endeavor to cut right to the chase. It is my intention to wed your sister, Lady Amelia."

Ashton raised one dark eyebrow at him. "You don't say? And you have come to ask my permission … is that it?"

He cleared his throat, refusing to be intimidated here. Ashton might be Amelia's guardian and brother, but Michael would soon become her husband. He must establish himself from the beginning as a man who claimed and protected what was his, and did not back down—even when faced with a powerful marquis.

"Your permission … no. At her age, your permission is not necessary. What I have come for is your blessing."

This time, both of Ashton's eyebrows lifted as he studied Michael closely. "And why would you think I'd give you my blessing when I've never laid eyes upon you in my life? Amelia has not seriously courted anyone this Season, and—no offense meant—but the card presented by my butler leads me to believe you are not titled."

"True enough," he acquiesced. "And while I have not courted Lady Amelia publicly, I have come to know her in the time that we've been acquainted. I believe we suit each other well."

Folding his arms across his chest, Ashton leaned back a bit in his chair. "Does Amelia know that you are here?"

"No," Michael admitted. "But I have made my intentions known. I have asked her to wed me."

"And did she agree?" Ashton pressed.

Michael fought back a smirk. "Yes, and no."

Ashton frowned. "I do not understand."

Rising, he reached into the breast pocket of his coat, retrieving the hastily scribbled contract. He had ensured it was on his person before leaving the inn. Setting it before Ashton, he stood back and waited while the marquis read over the words.

He went still for a long moment, then glanced up at Michael, the corner of his mouth curving into a smirk. Michael relaxed a bit as he chuckled, the low, rumbling sound humanizing the man who had, up until now, seemed to possess all the warmth of an icicle.

"Am I to believe that you secured Amelia's promise to marry you through a *wager*?" he asked, shaking his head in disbelief.

Michael shrugged. "It seemed the best way to ensure she could not cry off."

With a dry laugh, Ashton rose, crossing the room to the sideboard holding several crystal decanters. "I believe this calls for a drink. Brandy?"

"Yes, please," he replied, allowing his tense shoulders to relax a bit. The man hadn't thrown him out yet, which he took to be a good sign.

The marquis poured two fingers of brandy into each tumbler, then approached to offer him one. The two clinked glasses and sipped, Michael's eyes widening at the first taste of the rich liquor.

"I say, this might be the finest brandy I've ever tasted," he declared.

"Being outnumbered by women makes it a requirement," Ashton quipped, though Michael could see he only jested. He spoke of his 'women' with affection.

"I'm certain you find comfort in the presence of your newly born heir," he replied. "Congratulations, by the way. You must be pleased— a son and a daughter at once."

"Quite," Ashton agreed. "Now, back to the matter of my sister. I take it she was not pleased when you pressed the issue of the wager."

"You know her well," Michael replied.

"I do. I also know that she has resisted marriage for a long time, for her own reasons. Reasons which I understand all too well. And while I have increased her dowry in hopes of attracting a mate for her, I do not intend to force her to wed anyone ... contract or no contract."

"I surmised as much," Michael said.

"If Amelia refuses you, there isn't much I can do to sway her," Ashton continued. "Nor do I intend to. My sister is no ordinary lady, and her ... eccentricities ... are not well understood."

Michael stiffened at the mention of Amelia's oddities. Of course, the marquis could simply refer to her penchant for wearing breeches and acting in a manner considered unseemly by the *ton*. Yet, something in the man's tone put him on edge. Could he possibly know about his sister's bedroom activities?

"I am well aware of Lady Amelia's ... tastes," he tested, watching the marquis closely. "And while I did not understand them at first, she coerced me to approach the situation with an open mind. When I allowed myself to do that, I found that I enjoyed her company no less. In fact, I discovered that I enjoyed it more."

Ashton stared at him pensively for a long moment, and Michael realized the man must understand what he was trying to say. Yes ... this man *was* aware of what his sister got up to when alone with her lovers. How could he not be?

"You are not the first man to entreat me for Amelia's hand," the marquis said, between sips of brandy. "You are also not the first to discover that he enjoys her ... peculiarity. However, she has never accepted a single proposal, never carried on with any man for longer than a few months. What makes you so different, Mr. Darling?"

Tightening his hand around the tumbler, he straightened a bit. "I like your sister, my lord, and not just because of the things she has taught me. Perhaps I am not special—not in any overt way. However, my position as a gentleman farmer means I have no reason to curtail her behaviors for fear of some sort of scandal. You'll find that it takes far worse conduct to create a scandal out in the country. In short, your sister need not change who she is to wed me, nor do I intend to make her. With me, she will be admired, respected, protected, and indulged. I am not a perfect man, my lord, but your sister will be well taken care of."

Silence passed between them, with each man taking the measure of the other.

Michael finished his brandy and awaited the marquis' verdict. He intended to pursue Amelia with or without the man's blessing, but could see the sense in having him as an ally.

"Mr. Darling, how's the fare at your inn?" Ashton asked suddenly.

Michael scowled. "Abysmal considering that I am used to the talents of my cook back home."

Ashton nodded. "I'd thought as much. Come … you and I have much more to discuss, and I would prefer to do it over a meal. Breakfast is being served in the dining room, and I'd like you to join me."

Sagging with relief, he acquiesced, setting his empty tumbler aside and following the marquis from the room.

# CHAPTER 10

$\mathcal{A}$melia reached up to massage her throbbing temples as she stumbled toward the staircase, the smells of food wafting from the dining room making her stomach tremble. She would prefer to have slept until afternoon, but due to the tumult in her gut after last night's encounter with Michael, she'd found herself unable to rest. Thoughts of him had tormented her, memories of their nights together mingling with the bitter sting of what had felt like betrayal.

They'd gotten along so well, hadn't they? At least, they had when she had thought they were both being honest about their desires and intentions. As it turned out, Michael had been after her dowry all along. Just like many other men of the *ton* who had pursued her.

As she reached the landing and turned toward the small, intimate family dining room, she vowed to put the man behind her. It did not matter that she'd lost their ridiculous wager—one designed to snare her into a trap. She would not be manipulated into marriage.

Pausing outside the dining room, she frowned, the sound of two male voices floating out into the hall. Her throat grew tight, and her arms prickled with gooseflesh at the sound of the familiar tones, not quite as deep as Simon's, the accent slightly less refined.

"Michael?" she blurted as she pushed the cracked door all the way open and stumbled into the room, her head spinning.

Her bare feet fell silent on the thick rug, the hem of her morning gown swirling around her ankles as she reached out toward the door-knob for support, her knees suddenly weak at the sight of him.

Slouching in a chair to Simon's left, he smirked at her, appearing all-too pleased with himself.

"Ah, my betrothed has arrived," he drawled, winking at her over the rim of his teacup before taking a sip.

Recovering quickly, she straightened and raised her chin, glaring at him as she folded her hands demurely before her. "I am *not* your betrothed."

Simon raised an eyebrow at her, absently buttering his last slice of toast. "Did you not sign a contract to that effect?"

Her mouth fell open as she glanced from her brother to Michael, and back again. "You must be joking. Surely, I am not to be expected to uphold the terms of such a contract ... one, I might add, that *he* tricked me into agreeing to."

"It is no less than many chits have gone through to snare unknowing men in the marriage trap," Michael quipped, exchanging conspiratorial glances with Simon.

Her face heated at the realization that the bastard had made an ally of Simon. How the devil was she going to get out of this, with her brother determined to marry her off to the man?

"Besides," Simon added. "Aren't you always prattling on about women being equal to men? Were you a man, Mr. Darling here would have the right to call you out for shirking the terms of a contract you willingly signed. Why, it's a wonder he does not."

"Not a terrible idea," Michael replied with a grin. "Are you any good with a sword, my lady?"

"Simon, if you please—"

"The only sword she needs to concern herself with is yours," Simon mumbled, ignoring her and giving Michael a wicked grin. "I do hope you're up to the task. I, as you know, managed to sow two seeds in one go … a feat that will be hard for you to beat."

"I shall certainly give it a most valiant effort," Michael quipped.

"Simon, you cannot change from a dueling metaphor to a farming one within the same sentence … it displays a lack of imagination," she snapped. "And in case I was not clear, no one is going to sow anything, or impale me, or whatever nonsense you think to compare to intercourse. Because I will not be marrying this man."

Suddenly serious, Simon rose, adjusting his waistcoat. "That matter is for you to discuss with Mr. Darling. Perhaps it means nothing to you, but I've given him my blessing should you decide to go forward with the marriage … something I highly advise given the contract you signed. Think of the scandal it could create should word of such a thing makes the rounds in London. I know you do not care for propriety, but you are aunt to two children—who now bear the burden of our family name and the respect it commands. I shall leave you to hash it out."

Without another glance in her direction, he quit the room, signaling for the footmen to follow him. The doors clicked closed behind them, effectively trapping her alone with Michael.

She clenched her jaw as she turned to face him, arms folded over her chest. "You may as well follow them … I've nothing left to say to you."

Rising from the table, he approached her, hands braced upon his hips. "But I have something to say to you. It will only take a moment, and then you may eject me from the premises."

She dared a glance up at him, finding his face fixed into an expression of earnest sincerity. Despite still being angry with him, curiosity over what he might have to say kept her from telling him to sod off.

Skirting him, she took a seat at one end of the table, gesturing for him to resume his place on the other end. He ignored her, sinking into the chair directly at her side. Her scowl deepened at his impertinence, and she imagined taking her whip to his flesh in retaliation. Just the thought of being allowed to punish him again—watching his skin blush red while the burly muscles beneath tensed and then released—caused her blood to warm and the tips of her breasts to tingle.

"Amelia, I know that you are angry with me for tricking you," he began, resting one hand on the table, close enough that its proximity to her own hand sent a palpable energy through the air between them. "While I cannot confess to being sorry that you now know my intentions, I will relent that my methods might not have been honorable."

"It was an abominable thing to do," she agreed. "There are no shortage of young debutantes in London with large dowries you could have chased … all of whom would be perfectly content to wed you."

At the thought of him wed to some milky-faced chit with fat, sausage-like curls and the features of a porcelain doll, Amelia became unspeakably enraged. She told herself it must be the dominant nature of a Mistress—a possessiveness she felt toward the man who had submitted to her so beautifully. Of course she did not wish to think of him with anyone else. That didn't mean she wanted to marry the man.

"That might be true," he relented. "However, I find myself unable to even consider pursuing any of them. You are the one I want, Amelia."

She snorted, shaking her head. "I'm certain the sixty thousand pounds you stand to gain have nothing to do with it."

Lowering his gaze to the table, he curled one hand into a fist. He rapped his knuckles steadily against the wood, as if thinking of what he would say before speaking. After a while, he glanced up to meet her gaze again.

"I will not lie to you. Oakmoor is in dire straits, and your money would be needed to set that right," he admitted. "However, during our conversation, your brother and I came to an agreement on the terms of our wedding contract … terms which I think would appeal to you, if you'd like to hear them."

Straightening in her chair, she inclined her head. "I do not relish being spoken about when I'm not in the room."

He chuckled. "My dear, you may as well grow used to it. You are the sort of woman who inspires conversation. Would you like to hear the terms or not?"

Gesturing for him to go on, she forced herself to relax against the back of her chair. Michael continued, stilling his hand and ceasing his drumming on the surface of the table.

"Twenty thousand pounds of the dowry will be yours to spend as you please," he began. "You have my word that I would never seek to take it from you, nor access it for my own needs. The money belongs to you, from now until the day you die … and anything that might be left of that at the end of your life may be bequeathed as you see fit."

Her eyebrows shot up at his unexpected generosity. Most men of the *ton* would pilfer a woman's dowry as well as her maidenhead, then cease to think of her again until she bore him a son.

"And the rest?" she prodded, unable to pretend that these terms did not, thus far, appeal to her.

"Will become ours as a family, of course," he replied. "While I will control the funds, I am willing to ensure that you are consulted on all purchases as it pertains to Oakmoor. I want you to come into this marriage secure in the knowledge that your dowry is being used as it should. As well, I would give you carte blanche to see to the renovation of the manor … do with it as you see fit."

Folding her hands and resting them on the table's surface, she thought over his words in silence. It was certainly better than any other offer she'd gotten. Aside from that, Michael proved to be the only man she could confess to liking—and not just because he pleased her in the bedchamber. The man was witty and charming, his lack of airs and pretense refreshing.

But could she envision a future with him—see him as the father of her children and the man she would spend the rest of her life with?

Trying to decide now only made her head pound harder, the incessant throbbing at her temples obliterating all rational thought.

"I appreciate your honesty," she said. "However, I find it difficult to give you an answer just yet."

He nodded. "I understand. Perhaps a day or two to think it over?"

"Yes, that might be best," she replied.

Rising to his feet, he executed a graceful bow. "As you wish, my lady. You know where to find me once you are ready to send word of your answer."

"Of course," she said, unable to look at him as he stared at her, his pensive perusal causing her to feel exposed and vulnerable.

He stood there for a long while, staring at her with his hands clasped behind his back. Amelia sat contemplating the paneled wall, fighting the urge to squirm under such close scrutiny.

Finally, he moved, his voice ringing out in the quiet room as he made his way toward the door.

"By the way … should you refuse me, I intend to return to Oakmoor alone. You're the bride I've chosen, and I cannot fathom settling for anyone else. We might not have made a love match, Amelia, but you cannot deny how well we suit each other. I think, in time, love would come … if that is something you might want."

With that, he was gone, silently closing the door behind him.

She released a heavy sigh, sagging in the chair once she sat alone. Closing her eyes, she rested her head against the cushioned back. He'd given her much to consider, a heavy task considering that she'd been adamantly opposed to marriage before now. Yes, she'd agreed to try to find a husband at Simon's behest, but she'd never expected to find a man like Michael—one she could consider marrying without the urge to cast up her accounts.

And perhaps that would prove the most dangerous aspect of it all. Michael would never allow her to hold him at a distance—something that her hidden secrets required. Even Simon was not privy to the deepest of them, and he was the man she loved above all others. The only man she had ever really felt any real affection toward.

Marriage to Michael meant that, eventually, there would exist someone in the world who knew everything there was to know about her.

Amelia could not yet decide if that would prove a beautiful gift or a bitter curse.

. . .

That evening, she went to her sister-in-law, hoping for some much-needed distraction. Truly, what she wanted was for someone to affirm her first decision—to tell her that she shouldn't marry Michael because they did not know each other, or because he'd turned out to be a fortune hunter. Yet, Amelia should have known not to expect Sophie to be rational. After all, she'd just given birth to her husband's twins, and practically glowed with the love radiating from her in tangible waves. It was truly sickening.

"Simon tells me he seems to be a good sort, and he is generally right about these things," Sophie said once Amelia had finished pleading her case.

The two shared an after-dinner pot of hot chocolate in Sophie's private sitting room, which connected to both the bedchamber she shared with Simon and the nursery where the twins slept peacefully.

"Of course you think so," Amelia scoffed.

Never mind the fact that Sophie was right, damn her. Simon had an uncanny way of seeing right down to the marrow of a person, which made sense considering the wife he'd chosen. If ever there had been a woman created to tame a man like her brother, Sophie must surely be it.

"Aside from that," Sophie added, pausing with her cup halfway to her lips. "There's the fact that you've been walking about in a state of giddiness from the moment you met the man."

Nearly choking on her own drink, she sputtered and set her cup aside, deciding that it would be wiser to avoid consuming anything during this conversation.

"I most certainly have not!"

"You have," Sophie insisted. "I can always tell when you've taken a new lover, but this one ... well, I could see he was different from the start, and I did not need to meet him to know that. And perhaps 'different' is just the thing for you, Amelia. After all, you are no ordinary woman."

No. She was a shrew and a hoyden, as well as a Mistress who could never take just any man into her bed—not if she meant to enjoy it.

"You are right about him," she murmured, sighing and leaning against the back of the chair she occupied and propping her feet up onto a stool. "He isn't anything like the others. Being with him is … oh, Sophie, it's so perfect. He knows how to submit without turning into a sniveling little cunt."

Sophie giggled, and Amelia grinned, amused at her sister-in-law's comfort with her frank speech. Just last year, the poor girl would have flushed beet red anytime she said something crass. It would seem marriage to Simon had cured her of all her maidenly sensibilities.

"If I were going to marry, I would choose him," she admitted, her voice low as she avoided eye contact.

Sophie's voice struck her with its softness and the empathy threading it when she replied. "Then what is wrong? What does it matter if he needs your money? The Fitzwilliam family has more than we could spend in three lifetimes."

Shaking her head, she waved a dismissive hand. "I do not care about the money. But the truth is … well, like my brother, I have my secrets. Things I never thought I'd have to let anyone see."

A short silence followed, during which she could feel Sophie's probing stare on the side of her face.

Leaning forward in her chair, Sophie pressed her hand against the one resting in Amelia's lap.

She turned to meet Sophie's gaze, finding her expression grim.

"So different from Simon, yet so similar," she whispered. "Was he very terrible to you, too, Amelia?"

Tears sprung to her eyes at the mention of the man who had made her and Simon's existence a living hell. Blinking them back, she raised her chin and forced the emotion back down. It was how she'd always survived, pasting a smile on her face and laughing when she did not want to be seen with tears in her eyes.

"What does it matter?" she said with a shrug. "The man is dead."

Sophie sighed, removing her hand and sitting back in her seat—

having enough experience to likely know Amelia would not allow herself to be pitied.

"Yes, but I think we both know what his legacy is," she replied, her tone still gentle and soothing. How the devil did she do that? "It will haunt you daily if you let it—even when you do not realize that it's happening. Your façade of happiness to mask the loneliness you really feel … the parts of yourself you won't let anyone see … your unwillingness to marry. Don't you realize what you've done? You've allowed him to keep you from happiness."

"I am happy!" she snapped, rising to her feet. "I do whatever I want, whenever I want, with whomever I want. I ride, and traipse about barefoot, and drink, gamble, and fuck. No one will control me ever again. Do you understand? Uncle Gregory does not win, Sophie … I do!"

Inclining her head, Sophie gave her a sad smile. "I am sad that you think that. Because, in truth, that you are too afraid to take a husband because you worry he will try to control you … well, that gives him the victory, does it not?"

"Damn you," Amelia rasped, swiping at her face and finding her fingertips wet with tears. "You know nothing."

"Perhaps I do not when it comes to you," Sophie relented. "But I know everything there is to know about Simon and what was done to him. I was there for every painful, beautiful moment that passed with him fighting to be free from the past. Now, he wants the same for you, and so do I.

"But you must be the one to make the first move, Amelia. You must try. Otherwise, you will ruin what might be your best chance at happiness. I do not know Michael, but I trust Simon's judgement in this. Should you decide to wed him, you have our most ardent blessing."

Rising to her feet, she approached Amelia, reaching out to grasp her shoulders. Amelia pressed her lips together to keep from sobbing, the pressure in her chest expanding so swiftly, she could hardly contain it. Kissing her cheek, Sophie released her. With one last pitying look, she left the room, going into the nursery and closing the door behind her.

Now alone, Amelia collapsed back into her chair, discharging her held breath on a sob. Burying her face in her hands, she released the torrent of emotion welling in her throat, surprised by the overwhelming surge. She'd never allowed herself to feel this way, because Uncle Gregory had abhorred tears. In truth, he'd hated females in general—her being just a child having no bearing on such feelings. Her tears made her weak, a sniveling, overemotional burden that her uncle had never wanted to carry. He'd never ceased reminding her that she was unwanted, unloved, and a waste of his time and effort.

She was not certain how long she sat there, sobbing into her palms, but eventually, her shoulders stilled, and her breathing became even. The stream of tears stopped, though the remnants still clung to her eyelashes as she sat back in the chair and stared absently into the fire.

She did not want to admit it, but Sophie had been right. Despite being known as the most daring female of the *ton*, she was terrified of the one challenge she'd avoided thus far in her life.

Marriage had always seemed like an institution designed to imprison the woman. The man owned his wife like chattel, while the law gave him the right to do with her as he pleased. While her sister-in-law and some of her friends had found bliss in loving unions, Amelia hadn't been willing to risk it. Marriage to the wrong man would leave her trapped in a nightmare—the likes of which she never wanted to find herself in again.

Yet, Michael's promises came to mind now, and she could not find it in her heart to condemn him as being the same sort of man as Uncle Gregory. Perhaps he had been dishonest with her, but he'd had his reasons. With the entire legacy of the Darling family resting upon his shoulders, he'd had no choice but to assess his options and act accordingly. No woman in London could boast as large a dowry as her. Could she blame him for hoping to find a wife and a fortune at the same time?

No, she could not.

Besides that, his promises had seemed sincere. When he'd looked her in the eyes and promised to protect and respect her, she'd believed him. What had she to lose?

Nothing.

Everything.

And yet, her brother had risked it all on Sophie, placing all his faith in a woman based solely on her smile. Closing her eyes, she imagined Michael, his devilish grin causing a low flutter in her belly.

Bets had been won based on far less.

Resolute, she rose to her feet, swiping away the last of her tears. Crossing to Sophie's escritoire, she found several sheets of stationary and a quill resting beside a half-full inkwell. She wrote out a quick note to Michael, hardly possessing the patience to wait for the ink to dry. Once it had, she shoved it into an envelope and left the drawing room. She took the stairs two at a time, grasping the first footman she encountered by the arm. Impressing upon him the importance of the note being delivered this evening, she sent him off, then went in search of Simon.

She found him in his study—likely attending to some pressing bit of business before turning in for the night. He glanced up at her from behind a cloud of smoke, the steady trail wafting up from the cigar resting in a crystal ashtray, giving the room an inviting aroma. Taking a sip of brandy, he leaned back in his chair, waving her in.

Approaching the desk, she met his gaze and felt the same resounding pangs of affection she always had. She might tease him about being cold and aloof, but she'd always loved Simon—always trusted him as the only man who had ever tried to protect her, to shelter her from the world. She would never allow him to know that he'd been successful almost every time ... almost, but not quite. It would kill him to know, and he'd become so happy, she was loath to ruin it.

No, her secrets were her own to keep, until she could find the courage to share them with Michael. Perhaps, in time, she would be ready.

"If you've come to castigate me for that performance with Mr. Darling this morning, it will have to wait until tomorrow," he murmured, humor dancing in his eyes as he put out his cigar. "I'm off to bed and my wife, if you do not mind."

Amelia shook her head. "No, I only … well, I thought you'd like to know that I sent a footman off with a note for Michael."

Standing, he studied her closely, as if trying to discern her decision just by looking into her eyes. "Well?"

She cleared her throat. "We are going to need a special license."

A wide grin stretched across Simon's face, the rare expression blinding in its intensity. Rounding the table, he took her into his arms and into a crushing embrace.

She returned the affection, closing her eyes and inhaling his familiar scent. It reminded her of the nights she would climb into his bed, looking for comfort when they were children. Now, the only person she would share a bed with would be Michael. Oddly, she felt a steady sense of calm in the pit of her gut at the thought. As if her body had made peace with something her mind had not yet arrived at; she'd made the right decision.

"I thought this day would never come," he said, setting her back from him with a chuckle.

She rolled her eyes. "Never fear, I will not be underfoot to aggravate you any longer."

His expression melted into a stern one as he grasped her shoulders. "Nonsense. You could have remained with me until you were an old, grey spinster, and you well know it."

Shaking her head, she absently fiddled with his crumpled cravat, destroyed by their tight embrace. "No, Simon. This home belongs to you and Sophie. Now, I must go make a home of my own."

He nodded. "He is a good man, Amelia. I can feel it. He seems to care a great deal about you."

She forced a smile, not certain Michael cared quite as much as her brother seemed to think. "Yes, he is a good sort. I will be happy, I think."

"He never would have wanted it for us," he replied, his gaze growing haunted. "But we showed him, did we not?"

"That, we did, Simon," she replied, even though she still felt more uncertain about her future than ever. "That, we did."

# CHAPTER 11

They were wed a sennight later, in an intimate ceremony at Ashton House. Their only guests consisted of Oliver, and his brother and sister-in-law. Michael experienced an overwhelming sense of relief when Amelia appeared in the drawing room, a small cluster of fresh flowers gathered from the garden and tied with ribbon clutched in her hands. A rose satin gown enlivened her complexion, and the matching crown of blossoms resting on top of her loose hair made her look like something out of a dream.

When her note had arrived at his inn, informing him of her decision to accept his suit, he had hardly been able to believe it. Standing here with her made it all real, and contentment swept through him as the recital of their vows began.

For a moment, he had feared his efforts might all come to naught. But with an exchange of words and rings, she became his—permanently. Sure, the wealth she brought with her would solve all of his problems back home. However, he now found that he would have mourned her loss, above all. With the morning light filtering through white lace curtains, and her cheeks and lips kissed by just a hint of rouge—causing her to appear deceptively innocent and charmingly alluring—he experienced a surge of pride at the knowledge that they belonged to each other.

Once news of their hasty wedding made its way through town, the gossip would spread like wildfire. Thankfully, they would not be here for the resulting fallout. Arrangements had been made for their return journey to Norfolk, and they would be on their way at the conclusion of the intimate wedding breakfast planned by the marchioness. Sophie, he must remember to think of her as Sophie—his sister-in-law now. Never would he have thought to be connected to such wealth and power, even through marriage. That aspect of his new union would take some growing used to.

Once vows had been exchanged, he slipped a beautiful sapphire ring onto her finger—a gift from Simon. It had once belonged to their mother, Lady Joanna. Sophie now wore one of similar design, hers sporting a red ruby. For him, a plain gold band sufficed.

The moment they'd been declared man and wife, he swept her into his arms and kissed her. She returned his ardor, gripping the lapels of his coat and coming up on tiptoe to meet his mouth with her own. Simon cleared his throat and shifted while Sophie giggled at the display of amorous affection.

"At this rate, they'll never make it to the wedding breakfast," the marquis grumbled.

"They had better, after all Cook and I went through to prepare," Sophie declared, pushing herself between them to take Amelia into a tight hug. "Oh, I am so happy for you. Congratulations, sister."

"Thank you," Amelia had replied.

Michael was next to be crushed by Sophie's surprisingly strong arms. Her excitement and sweet nature reminded him of his own sister, whom he hoped would get on well with Amelia. He shook hands with Simon, and together, they indulged in a champagne toast while waiting for the meal to be served.

The rest of the day passed him in a blur of food and conversation —most of which he would likely not remember in the years that would follow this day. Yet, Amelia's radiant beauty as she sat between him and Simon at the table, smiling and laughing unabashedly between sips of champagne, would remain with him always. It proved difficult not to feel so damnably smug when he was more certain than ever that he'd made the right choice by selecting Amelia as his bride. Now, he must work to ensure she never found cause to regret marrying him. After they'd returned to Oakmoor, he would set out to make it a home worthy of a lady of her caliber.

Once the meal had concluded, Amelia and her lady's maid joined him out front of Ashton House, where his coach awaited, loaded down with as many of her belongings as would fit. The rest would arrive by wagon later. Changed into a pair of breeches, boots, shirt, and waistcoat, Amelia bid her family farewell while he stood by, waiting patiently.

"Do write often," Sophie urged her as the two embraced. "I shall miss you terribly."

"We are fortunate that Oakmoor is not far outside of London," Amelia replied. "I will visit frequently."

Michael hated London, but would make an effort to abide it whenever she wished. She hadn't left the city since arriving for her come-out, after all, and would likely miss the bustle and fast pace of life here. It was his hope, however, that she would come to enjoy the peace of the country, where he'd remain for the rest of his days if he had anything to say about it.

"We hope to see you for the christening of the twins in a few weeks," Simon reminded them, taking his turn with Amelia.

"We would not miss it for the world," Michael assured him as Simon clung to Amelia with one hand while offering him the other.

The two men shook, and Simon gave him a firm nod, his level stare speaking volumes. He was about to hand his little sister over to Michael for good—no easy feat. As the brother of a beautiful young woman, Michael understood entirely.

"I will take care of her," he assured the marquis. "I made that promise to her, and now, I'm making it to you."

Simon nodded again, as if satisfied with that. Then, glancing down at his sister, he smiled, his affection for Amelia clear. "Will you be happy, Amelia … for me?"

Bussing his cheek, she returned his smile. "For you? No. For Sophie? Perhaps."

"Harridan," he teased, giving her a gentle push toward Michael. "Go on now … go to your new home."

"I love you," she said to her brother, though the sound of those words said in her voice did queer things to Michael's chest.

What would it feel like to one day hear her say that to him? He hadn't realized it until just then, but he wanted those three words from her.

Dear God, he had grown besotted with his wife.

He decided it was not a terrible state to be in—this utter absorption in another person. The desire to know her, to discover her secrets and understand her in ways no one else did … it made him eager to get her home so they could begin their life together.

Giving her a hand up into the carriage, he ensured that Kate, her maid, sat comfortably perched beside Oliver on the seat opposite. Then, with one last glance back at Ashton House, he climbed in and settled beside Amelia. Taking her hand in his, he clung to it tightly as the coach pulled away.

Glancing over at her, he found her staring back at him, her eyes wide as if in awe. If she felt anything similar to what he experienced right now, she was likely shocked that they'd actually gone through with it.

He wanted to pull her into his lap and kiss her soundly—to tear her breeches off and consummate their union right there in the coach. A wide grin curved his lips as he wondered how thoroughly she'd punish him if he bent her over the seat and fucked her from behind without waiting for her to direct him to take her. It would likely be worth it—both having her the way he wanted, and the following punishment. Yet, with his valet and her lady's maid sharing the carriage, he would be forced to behave himself.

"What on Earth has you grinning like the cat who ate the canary?" she teased, inclining her head as she took in his expression.

Taking her hand, he chuckled. If only he could tell her the true directions of his thoughts.

*Soon,* he reminded himself. By this time tomorrow, they'd be at Oakmoor—the massive estate boasting several places he could get her alone.

"Nothing, Lady Darling," he murmured, enjoying the way her new name rolled off his tongue. "Shall we go home?"

Her smile was softer, less boisterous than he had become accustomed to. Still, she nodded and tightened her fingers around his.

"Yes, Mr. Darling," she replied. "Let us go home."

Pounding his fist against the roof of the coach, he leaned back in the seat and tried to settle in for the trip. Outside, the sound of the cracking horsewhip preceded the clop of horse's hooves. And with that, the journey home began.

The following evening, Amelia sat staring through the parted curtains over the coach's window as the vehicle slowed to a stop in front of the ancestral home of Michael's family. Her family now, too, she recalled as she drank in the large manor.

It stretched wide, easily as large as Ashton Abbey—the country home she and Simon had been raised in—and rose up three stories. The longstanding lineage of the Darlings showed itself through the architecture of the home—a hodgepodge of old bones renovated over time with modern touches. Yet, an old world charm remained in the tower-like structures at the east and west corners, their pointed rooves reaching up toward the sky. Smooth white pillars flanked the wide steps leading up to the massive front doors—which had been made of beautiful oak wood and boasted a large, ornate door knocker.

From the outside, the manor itself appeared well-preserved, but closer inspection revealed the evidence of Michael's financial woes. The foliage and hedges surrounding the manor were overgrown, flowers tangling in a wild display. Apparently, gardeners proved an expense that Oakmoor could no longer afford. As the coach had entered Darling lands, she'd spotted other signs of neglect—fences that needed mending, and livestock that wandered where they shouldn't because of it, stables in need of a new roof, and areas of land where weeds and trees had overgrown into spaces previously cleared.

The inside of the manor would likely prove to be in a similar state. Michael had truly been desperate in coming to London in his search for a bride. If nothing else, she must applaud him for his ingenuity in snaring her for himself. While she had no love for her family home—a place where she and Simon had been abused and terrorized instead of sheltered and loved—she could understand what it would mean to Michael to see his restored to its former glory.

A footman opened the coach doors, and once the steps were in place, Oliver alighted first, offering a helping hand to Kate. Then, Michael jumped down and, instead of offering her a hand, reached into the carriage and took her by the waist. She gasped as he lifted her, his grip strong and sure as he set her on her feet. The sun shone into her eyes, sending bright rays through his hair and turning several of the strands to gold. His hands remained on her waist, and he nudged her closer, bending his head to kiss her. She faintly registered the sound of the front door flying open, but could not think past the tingle electrifying her lips as he fit his mouth over hers. He claimed her lips in an ardent kiss, his chest swelling against her breasts with a deep inhale—as if it weren't enough to taste her; he needed to pull her in through his other senses.

Her limbs turned to jelly, but he kept her on her feet with nothing more than the strength of his hands and nearness of his body—a pillar of might that never ceased to amaze her with its warmth and hardness in tandem.

By the time he pulled away, she'd grown breathless, her eyelids drooping heavily as her blood hummed swiftly through her veins, causing her entire body to prickle from the top of her head to the tips of her breasts, straight down to her toes.

"Christ, I don't think I can wait another moment to make you mine," he murmured, his voice a low vibration caressing her skin and causing her to tremble in his arms.

What the bloody hell was happening to her? Never had a man rendered her so weak with nothing more than a kiss.

Their night spent at the inn last night had led to nothing more than a good night's rest—the journey having exhausted them both. Tonight would mark the consummation of their marriage.

"It will have to wait," intruded a soft, imperious female voice. "At least until after you have introduced her to your Mama."

Amelia swiveled her wide eyes to the woman standing just at the foot of the front staircase, hands folded demurely before her.

Michael released her, clearing his throat, but doing nothing to put distance between them. Darting a glance back up at him, she found his face flushed with embarrassment, though he did drape his arm around her possessively. Amelia turned back to Mrs. Darling and straightened, squaring her shoulders and meeting the woman's gaze. She refused to be ashamed of being affectionate with the man who was now her husband. She refused to be ashamed of anything.

Instead of censure, she found kindness in the eyes of Michael's mother. The woman smiled, coming forward with her arms extended, the lines around her eyes crinkling, indicating a face that smiled often. Michael released her and went to the woman, drawing her into a tight embrace.

"Welcome home, Michael," she said as they pulled apart, him grasping her hand and pulling her closer to Amelia.

"Mama, may I introduce you to my bride … Lady Amelia Darling —formerly Lady Amelia Fitzwilliam," he said, pride in his voice, his smile wide. "Amelia, my mother, Mrs. Perdita Darling."

Releasing her son, Perdita turned to appraise her, her smile still warm and friendly. Michael had inherited his blue eyes from her, though her hair shined a brighter shade of blonde than his. Petite, her form was a bit plump, and her skin held the same golden tone as her son's—as if she spent a lot of time out of doors. Her clothing was at least four years out of fashion, but she carried herself with a quiet dignity Amelia could not help but admire.

"My lady," she said, executing a flawless curtsy. "I am pleased to meet you. Welcome to Oakmoor."

Amelia's mouth dropped open in horror. "Oh, please … don't do that! And call me Amelia, I insist."

With a nod, Perdita came closer and took both of Amelia's hands in hers. The gesture stunned her, and she blinked rapidly, trying to understand such affection when they'd only just met. Yet, Perdita gazed at her as if she were a long-lost child … as if she'd been waiting for Amelia for years.

"Amelia," she replied. "And you shall call me Perdie. Once you and Michael have settled in, I do hope you'll allow me the honor of familiarizing you with the manor. It is quite a walk from one floor to the next, so if you'd prefer to rest and conduct your tour in the morning, I am at your service."

"I would like that, thank you," Amelia managed, still overwhelmed by this woman's kindness toward her.

Was this how mothers behaved? Having never known Lady Joanna Fitzwilliam, she hadn't had an example of what one was like. She liked Perdita already.

"Where are the others?" Michael asked, taking Amelia back against his side, his arm an iron shackle around her waist.

She'd come to know him enough to recognize the tension in his muscles as a state of heightened arousal. He truly meant what he'd said about not being able to wait much longer to consummate their marriage. She'd have to relieve him of the tension, and soon. As footmen approached the coach to begin unloading their things, she smiled at the sight of her special trunk—the one containing her personal collection of implements for the bedroom. Perhaps she'd introduce him to a few of them tonight.

"Lydia is out for a ride with friends," Perdita replied. "Archie, Hesper, and the children have gone to visit the Smallshaw family and should return in time for dinner. Shall we go inside? Perhaps you'd like some refreshment before the evening meal? I could arrange for tea."

Amelia exchanged a glance with Michael, whose expression told her the last thing he wanted was tea.

"If you do not mind, Mama, I think we'd prefer to rest a bit before dinner," he replied. "Amelia is sure to be tired after the journey, and will need her wits about her if she's to endure dinner with you lot."

She gasped at the insult, but calmed once she realized that Perdita was laughing. So odd, this relationship between mother and son. Had Simon laughed this way with their mother before she'd died? He'd been a lad of six then, just old enough to know her, to be able to remember her fondly to this day. She'd always envied him that.

"Truer words have never been spoken," Perdita said with a hearty chuckle. "Very well, take your rest, and I shall see you both for dinner. Michael, I trust you haven't been away long enough to have forgotten the way."

"Of course not, Mother," he quipped. "Your other son is the nitwit, remember?"

Perdita laughed, the sound becoming thinner as she retreated back into the manor.

The moment she had disappeared through the front doors, Michael reached for her, sweeping one arm beneath her knees and the other at her back to lift her swiftly off her feet. She clung to his neck with a squeal, holding on tight as he started up the stairs with her.

"Michael, what the devil are you doing?" she managed between laughs.

"Carrying my bride across the threshold, of course," he replied. "We cannot begin a proper marriage without the tradition."

"And here I thought your prick penetrating my cunt was the required form of consummation," she whispered, burying her face against his neck.

A hearty chuckle made his chest tremble, and he kissed the top of her head. "Such a foul mouth you possess, wife. I wonder what other wicked things it is capable of."

She bit her lower lip and whimpered, the throbbing between her thighs growing stronger as she thought of sucking him off, of him quivering and groaning and at her mercy.

"Get me to a bed, and I will show you," she purred, taking his earlobe between her teeth.

He groaned and increased his pace, his long strides carrying them up a staircase, and then another, where he turned left on the third floor and carried her down a long corridor. Amelia only caught glimpses of her new home, but saw enough to recognize the good taste and charm of the family who had inhabited it for generations. Despite faded, worn carpets, and empty walls where precious pieces of art had likely hung before being sold, Oakmoor struck her as being both charming and beautiful. With a bit of polish, it could become an opulent home rivaling any other in Norfolk.

"Here we are," he declared, pausing before the fifth door on the right.

Setting her on her feet, he then took her hand in one of his and turned the knob, pulling her inside behind him.

She took in the large chamber—a cozy space decorated in masculine shades of navy and grey. A massive four-poster bed rested against the wall, its heavy curtains pulled back to reveal the turned-down counterpane. Rugs that had once been thick were now threadbare and worn, while the wallpaper had begun peeling away from the paneled wood underneath, curling and showing signs of age. Yet, the room appeared clean and smelled like Michael—rich, woodsy, and manly. It suited him.

Through an open door, she spotted the dressing room. Inside it, Oliver moved about quietly and efficiently, putting away Michael's things. Through another open door on the other side of Michael's dressing room, she spotted her own. Inside it, Kate worked to hang her gowns—the few she'd brought with her on the coach. The lady's maid would have her work cut out for her once the bulk of Amelia's things arrived from London.

Turning to her with a sheepish expression, Michael ran a hand through his hair. "It's in need of a woman's touch, I'm afraid. The entire manor is, truly. I know that it isn't as grand as what you're accustomed to, but Oakmoor is special to me. My siblings and I grew up in this house … and I've always intended to raise my family here. I hope you'll come to think of it as home, Amelia. I am excited to see what sort of changes you will bring about as lady of the manor."

Placing her hands upon his chest, she rose on tiptoe to kiss the tip of his nose, giving him a smile. "Michael, do stop apologizing. I was aware of the state of Oakmoor before I arrived, and having seen it now, I can assure you I do not intend to go running back to London. Truly, it isn't at all as bad as you led me to believe. In fact, I think it is quite charming."

He raised his eyebrows and took her back into the circle of his arms. "You do?"

She nodded. "I truly do. It has character, and is obviously loved by the people who live here. I'm proud to live here, too, and am not so high in the instep that I require lavish surroundings everywhere I go."

For a moment, he simply observed her in silence, his expression becoming serious, his irises darkening as he took her in. Then, he began backing her toward the bed.

"Leave us," he commanded without another glance at the dressing room.

Without preamble, Oliver closed the door of the dressing room, and a moment later, his and Kate's footsteps echoed across Amelia's adjoining room and out into the hall, eventually fading away altogether.

"Are you pleased, Mistress?" he whispered against her lips, pressing her against the side of the bed.

"For the nonce," she replied coyly, reaching up to snatch his cravat free. "Though, as you know, I am quite the demanding dominant. I shall require you to attend me constantly … to ensure that I remain happy."

Lifting her onto the bed, he shrugged out of his coat and dropped it haphazardly to the floor. "I do believe I am up to the task."

Reaching out to cup the erection displayed by his snug breeches, she grinned. "You most certainly are, Mr. Darling."

"We've only an hour before dinner," he declared, working quickly to open his breeches while she lifted her skirts and petticoats.

Falling back onto her elbows and spreading her legs, she licked her lips at the sight of his cock jutting out from his open fall.

"Then I suppose you'd better work hard and fast to please your Mistress," she declared, meeting his gaze. "Don't let me down, Mr. Darling."

Grasping her hips and driving himself into her with one rough thrust, he forced a cry from deep in her throat. Closing his eyes, he shuddered, resting inside her for a moment while he seemed to wrestle for composure.

"Never, Lady Darling," he moaned as he began pumping in and out of her, his grip on her hips tightening. "Never."

# CHAPTER 12

The moment they entered the drawing room where the family sat waiting for dinner to be served, Michael's little sister, Lydia attacked them—as he'd known she would. Jumping up from her place on a settee beside their mother, she squealed and bounded across the room. One moment, she'd been a demure, polite young lady, and the next, she became a bouncing force of nature—a body filled with infinite energy, draped in soft pink bows and ruffles.

"Oh, Michael, she's absolutely *darling!*" Lydia chirped, wrapping her arms around Amelia and jumping up and down with glee. "Archie declared you would never nab a bride who is both wealthy *and* beautiful. But, just look at her … she's as pretty as a doll and as stylish as a fashion plate!"

While Amelia leveled an amused smirk at him, he managed to pry his minx of a sister off her. Fixing Lydia with a stern look—which she effectively ignored—he smoothed a wayward strand of hair at the top of her head and beamed.

"Amelia, allow me to introduce my little sister before she makes even more a cake of herself," he teased. "This little shrew is named Lydia, and I'm of the opinion that she's fit for Bedlam."

Jabbing him in the ribs with her index finger, Lydia scoffed. "You're still as much a brute as you were when you left. It is a wonder you convinced such a lady to wed the likes of you."

"It is true, he is most unworthy," Amelia joked, giving him a sly glance. "But I have always had a most pitying heart."

Giggling, Lydia approached Amelia once again and took her arm. "Oh, I like you already, Amelia. May I call you Amelia? I suppose I should since we are family now, but Mama would insist I ask."

While most people quickly grew overwhelmed with Lydia, who could speak more words in the span of one minute than anyone else he knew, Amelia simply smiled at the girl and patted her hand.

"Please, do call me Amelia," she assured her. "We are sisters now, after all. I look forward to coming to know you better."

"And I you," Lydia declared. "Come, let me introduce you to my other brother, sister-in-law, and their brood."

Michael stood back and allowed Lydia to take over the introductions. His brother, Archibald, took Amelia's hand and kissed it politely —his demeanor more reserved than the others in the family. It would take him longer to warm up to Amelia, but Michael would not have to worry that he would treat her badly. The Darlings had always been close knit, and whether by marriage or birth, their motto had always been 'once a Darling, always a Darling.'

Archie's wife, Hesper, smiled and embraced Amelia, then proudly presented their children, Serena, Janet, and Bartholomew.

While the women chatted and fussed over the well-dressed and unusually clean children, Michael poured two fingers of brandy for himself, then filled another glass once he noticed his brother approaching. The two clinked their tumblers together in a toast and stood gazing upon their family.

"She's lovely, Michael," Archie declared in his low, quiet voice. "Well done. I do hope you at least like the lady ... considering the haste of your union and the urgent needs of the estate."

Taking a sip of his drink, he was hardly fazed by his brother's tactlessness. It was simply his way—speaking his mind without holding back, and the somber manner with which he carried himself. The two proved polar opposites in every way—Michael preferring the freedom of the outdoors, while Archie thrived at his desk, where he worked as a solicitor; Michael being a man of quick smiles and boisterous laughter, and Archie proving more reserved and restrained. Yet, they'd always gotten on well, perhaps because their opposite natures balanced each other.

"Would you like to know the truth?" he murmured, his voice muffled by the feminine laughter and chatter, mingling with the children fighting for the attentions of their new aunt. "I am besotted, Archie. I daresay I'm half in love with her already. It's the damnedest thing. I set out to solve all our problems and never imagined ... well, to answer your question, I do like her. Quite a lot."

Archie graced him with a rare smile. A man who had made a love match himself, his brother could understand his feelings more than anyone else. Michael had always envied his younger brother this sort of happiness, and now, it seemed to be within his grasp.

"Then, congratulations on a match well made," Archie replied. "I am happy for you, brother."

Michael clapped him on the shoulder and drained the last of his brandy before crossing the room to claim his wife once more. The moment her arm was back in his, the butler entered the drawing room to announce that dinner would be served.

Ignoring the rules of propriety that dictated decorum in London, the family moved to the dining room in no particular order, with the children joining the adults at the small, intimate table reserved for family meals. Taking his place at the head of the table, he put Amelia to his right, instead of at the other end where she would traditionally sit. He wanted her close. His mother took the seat that should have been Amelia's, while Lydia sat to his left across from her. Archie and his brood filled in the other chairs.

The Darlings—who had always possessed hearty appetites—all reached for dishes at once, conversation ceasing only long enough for them to fill their plates. There were no courses here at Oakmoor—

Cook simply sent out a variety of dishes and allowed them all to eat their fill, the way they all preferred.

Michael watched as Amelia tasted each of the available offerings, her eyes going wide with shock, then closing in rapture in reaction to the rich sauces and tender meats. While Oakmoor had fallen into disrepair, one thing it could always boast was one of the best cooks in all of Norfolk. Their neighbors never turned down party invitations, knowing that the food at a Darling affair would always be something to talk about over tea the following day.

"You're likely to gain a stone or two living here," Lydia chirped between bites of lamb. "Cook's food is the best in the entire region."

"I suppose you are right," Amelia agreed as she helped herself to another serving of French green beans à la crème. "Though, I suppose I'll simply have to increase my daily exercise to balance things out a bit."

Lydia's eyes widened at the notion that her new sister-in-law might prove an athletic woman like her, as opposed to one who preferred the pianoforte and crocheting like Hesper.

"Do you ride, Amelia?" she asked.

Amelia nodded. "Every morning. I also practice fencing, Pall Mall, and shooting—with a rifle, mostly, but I'm a fair hand with a pistol."

Michael pinched his lips together to hold in a laugh as every adult at the table fell silent, forks clattering to plates and eyes swiveling to Amelia. Lydia watched her as if discovering a priceless gem, while his mother, Archie, and Hesper portrayed varying degrees of shock and amusement.

"Well," his mother declared, the first to pick up her fork and knife and resume eating. "We've certainly gained an accomplished family member."

"I'll say," Lydia agreed. "Amelia, I'd be ever so grateful if you'd teach me to use a rifle. It seems like a dashed good time."

"Lydia," their mother said, her tone holding a heavy warning. "Your studies."

"Of course," his sister replied with a sigh. "I meant, *after* that."

Giving her youngest child an indulgent smile, his mother inclined her head. "Very well … but only if you practice the pianoforte for at least an hour before you go off shooting. I'll not debut into society a daughter who can shoot a rifle, but not play a proper composition."

Lydia grinned, bouncing on her bottom in the chair. "I'll practice for *two* hours if it means I can learn to shoot."

"One will do," their mother replied.

"It certainly will, given that the girl is tone deaf," Michael muttered between spoonfuls of peas.

Several of the green vegetables struck the side of his face, and he glanced up to find Lydia holding up her spoon, which she'd just used as a catapult. Narrowing his eyes at her, he scooped up another spoonful of his own peas, prepared to volley them at her.

"Children," their mother chided without raising her gaze from her plate. "Behave, or Amelia will regret marrying into this family."

Glancing over at Amelia, he found her silent but observant, soaking in the spectacle with obvious curiosity.

"Oh, I do not mind," she said. "I take great pleasure in tormenting my elder brother, Simon, so I understand. Do go on."

Giving Lydia a smug look, he let the peas fly, chuckling when they struck her square in the face, one of them falling into her bodice.

His sister glared at him, a look that promised retribution. He could likely count on finding horse manure in one of his shoes tomorrow morning, or his bedsheet shortened, or some other childish prank. He and Lydia spent most of their spare time attempting to repay the other for some lark or other.

"Tell us more about your family, Amelia," his mother urged.

Amelia paused, her wineglass halfway to her mouth.

For a moment, Michael thought he registered panic in her expression at the question, but it quickly disappeared. As he covered her free hand with his own and gave it a squeeze, she smiled. He could see that it was forced.

"There is only my brother, Simon, and myself," she replied. "Oh, but he is recently wed to Sophie, and they've welcomed twins just a few weeks past."

"Oh, that is marvelous!" Hesper spoke up. "How happy you all must be."

"We are," Amelia replied graciously.

"What of your parents?" Archie pried.

Michael shot him a scowl and shook his head, far too late to warn him off. He did not know much about Amelia's family, but his investigation into her had turned up two parents who had died when she'd been only a babe.

"Both deceased, I'm afraid," she replied, her tone remaining light, as if it was of no consequence. "My brother and I were raised by my Uncle Gregory, who died some time ago."

"Your brother, he is the Marquis of Ashton, yes?" Archie continued, seeming to have heeded Michael's warning and now sought to change course.

"He is," Amelia confirmed.

"What luck," Lydia said. "Not only does my new sister know how to shoot a rifle, she's one of the most connected women in all of England."

"Lydia, really," their mother chided.

Amelia simply laughed. "She's quite right, though it's really all a bunch of bollocks if you ask me—titles and bloodlines and all that."

Archie raised an eyebrow and met Michael's gaze. "Ah, now I begin to understand how such a lady would lower herself to marry you."

Michael laughed, reaching for his wineglass and taking a healthy sip. Archie so rarely joked, which proved eagerness on his part to steer the conversation back toward the pleasant ease they'd begun with as opposed to the uncomfortable strain caused by bringing up Amelia's family.

"It's all hogwash," Amelia insisted. "Though, I suppose the name and connections come in handy from time to time. For instance … if Lydia would like me to sponsor her debut in London, I am certain it can be arranged. In fact, an entire Season could be planned for her, if she's amenable."

Lydia leapt to her feet and squealed, her eyes bright with excitement. "Oh, she's more than amenable. She's downright giddy!"

"What a generous offer," his mother said, clasping her hands against her chest. "I hardly know what to say."

"Say yes, for a start," Lydia urged.

Squeezing Amelia's hand, Michael drew her gaze to his and smiled. "Thank you."

He hoped she heard how grateful he was in those two words. Lydia had always wanted a London Season, but they'd lacked the connections to ensure a proper sponsor. With Amelia's assistance, his sister could become one of the most sought-after debutantes in all of London. It surpassed both his sister's and mother's wildest dreams.

Nodding in response, she squeezed his hand in return and turned back to Lydia, who had turned the conversation to gowns and party themes.

Michael leaned back in his chair and surveyed the people seated at the table—which now seemed complete with Amelia seated beside him. Yes, Oakmoor had needed money, but it had also needed *her*. Barely here half a day, and she'd already breathed new life into the place. If for no other reason than for this, she had earned his devotion. He did not know her as well as he wanted, but that didn't matter. This need to know her, to discover what lay beneath the layers he'd already peeled back—it struck him as the strongest desire he'd ever had. It was more than he'd hoped for when first setting out to find a wife. It was everything.

Amelia stared absently at her reflection in the mirror of the vanity as Kate brushed her hair to ready her for bed. While her body was relaxed after an evening of good food, wine, and pleasant company, her mind seemed to rush at a pace too quick for her to keep up.

So much had changed in the span of a few days, she could hardly fathom it all. She had gone from being The Incomparable Lady A, the most sought after eligible lady in London, to Lady Darling, wife of a gentry farmer and a member of a large family who seemed to like her with no notion of the person she truly was.

"That will be all, Kate," she said, dismissing the maid.

Rising to her feet, she snatched the belt of her dressing gown free, allowing it to slide down her shoulders to the floor. She'd covered herself to keep from shocking Kate, but now that she had been left alone, could be free.

"You are still Incomparable," she said aloud to her reflection, holding her head high and smirking at herself in the mirror. "You are still a Mistress ... *his* Mistress."

Instead of a traditional wedding night negligee, she wore an oversized white shirt—one of Michael's which she'd had Oliver pilfer from his closet. Beneath it, she wore nothing, but over it, she'd cinched a black leather corset adorned with red ribbon. His shirt stopped just at the backs of her thighs, and from there, the black riding boots he'd seemed to like molded to her legs like a second skin.

Bracing her hands upon her hips, she grinned. Her life had changed, and she had promised herself she would try to find happiness here, with Michael. Part of that included further exploring their connection as Mistress and submissive. She'd never thought of how liberating it would be to marry one's submissive. However, having him constantly within arm's reach had its benefits. Add to that the fact that she actually enjoyed his company out of bed, and she could find no reason to lament the institution of marriage—at least not where she and Michael were concerned.

Pausing to retrieve a few of the implements she planned to use with him tonight from her trunk, she sauntered through their connected dressing rooms. The steady baritone of Oliver's voice had faded away ten minutes ago, so she knew Michael would be alone.

Alone, and waiting for her.

She found him slouched in a chair near the fire, barefoot, stripped to the waist and nursing a glass of brandy. Since he hadn't noticed her presence in the room yet, she took a moment to simply observe her husband.

He was truly remarkable to look upon—handsome in a rugged sort of fashion, large and strong in a way that might have frightened other women, but only titillated her. That she could command every inch of that hard, male body, make him crawl and beg for her … by God, what had she done to become so fortunate?

Locks of disheveled hair kissed the back of his neck and fell over his forehead, shadowing his eyes, while his large chest rose and fell with every breath. After draining what was left of his drink, he set the empty tumbler on a nearby end table and ran a hand through his hair. A soft sigh, a sound of contentment, rushed between his lips, making her smile.

She must have made some answering sound, or he'd simply sensed her presence, because he glanced up suddenly and met her gaze. His jaw tightened, and his eyes glittered with a primal light that sent a shiver down her spine. He did not have to say with words that he appreciated her getup.

Slouching further in his chair, he reached down and adjusted the front of his breeches, causing her mouth to grow dry as she noticed the heavy bulge pressed against the fabric. A single glance at her, and he was already hard as stone.

Still holding her gaze, he inclined his head, as if summoning her to him. The Mistress in her wanted to remind him who was in charge … to retrieve her whip and crack it through the air, demanding submission. The wife in her propelled her to him, drawn forward by the raw hunger in his gaze. For the first time, her need to be close to someone, to be understood and wanted, needed, superseded all else.

Once she stood near enough that her legs came up against his, she paused, setting her tools on the table beside his empty glass. Standing over him silently, she waited for the one thing every dominant needed before taking control of an encounter.

She waited for him to submit.

Sitting up straight, he reached for her, grasping her hips in his large hands. He pulled her between his spread legs, still staring silently up at her. She stood still, keeping her hands at her sides, even though all she wanted to do was touch him.

He slipped his hands beneath her shirt, cupping her buttocks and kneading them. Then, he came out from beneath the garment, skimming his hands up her waist, his fingers caressing the leather of her corset.

For once, she wished she stood naked before him, nothing separating his hands from her flesh. Yet, just the thought caused nausea to well up in her throat. Closing her eyes, she swallowed past the taste of bile and took a deep breath. She might not be ready now, but for Michael, she would try to be … soon, someday.

Opening her eyes, she found him still watching her, his gaze seeming to bore straight through her. Giving her a gentle push, he set her away from him, enough to give him space to ease out of the chair. But, instead of standing, he sank to his knees before her. Then, winding his arms around her thighs, he pulled her against him, turning his head to rest his cheek against her, just below where her corset ended. Warmth spread through her middle, his breath seeping through her shirt.

She released a sigh of relief at his acquiescence, raising a hand to rest upon his head in acceptance of his capitulation. Then, running her fingers through his hair, she gently pulled until he raised his head to look at her. Giving him a soft smile, she smoothed a hand over his brow, then cupped his cheek.

"Remind me of your safe word, Mr. Darling," she commanded, keeping her voice soft but firm.

"Dimple," he replied, then added, "Mistress."

Running her thumb over his lips, she nodded. "Very good. Stand."

She backed away enough to allow him to follow her directive. He kept his hands at his sides, though she could see it pained him to do so. His muscles tensed, the plump veins beneath his skin seeming to pulsate from the control he exercised in waiting for her to allow him the liberty to touch her.

"Finish undressing for me," she demanded.

Without hesitation, he opened his breeches and pushed them down to his ankles, stepping out of them. He wore no smallclothes, so his cock bounced free, standing proud and tall.

She closed the distance between them, standing just close enough that their bodies touched.

Rising on tiptoe until their lips brushed, she wrapped her arms around his neck. "Kiss me."

He obeyed before the last word had finished coming out of her mouth, muffling it between their lips. Even while keeping his hands balled up at his sides, he devoured her mouth, overwhelming her with the force of his desire. His tongue invaded her mouth, seeking hers and engaging in a sultry dance of flesh.

"The chair," she managed between kisses.

She gasped against his lips as he abruptly lifted her and began backing toward the chair. Holding on tight, she drank from his mouth as he sank into the chair with her in his lap, spreading her legs so they dangled over the sides.

Finding the decanter he'd been drinking from resting on the table beside his empty tumbler and her tools, she took it up and refilled the glass. Raising it to her lips, she took a sip, humming at the pleasant taste of the liquor on her tongue. Then, she dipped her first finger into the glass and offered it to him dripping with the amber liquid. He opened his mouth, taking in her finger and swirling his tongue around the digit. The hot caress caused her nipples to harden, the desire to feel that tongue in other places overwhelming. But, he had put himself in her hands, likely because he wanted to know what else she might be capable of. She would not let him down.

She went back into the glass with her finger, this time trailing the liquid along the side of his neck. Then, she lowered her head and lapped at the brandy with her tongue, following the glistening trail up to where his pulse thrummed just beneath his jaw. He drew in a sharp breath as she closed her lips around his skin, flavored by the brandy, sucking hungrily and sinking her teeth into his flesh. He groaned, his hips surging against hers and brushing his cock against her mons.

The feel of him, so close to her entrance, hard and thick, caused her to grow wet, the glide of his flesh against hers sending ripples of pleasure throughout her body.

Lifting the glass, she swallowed what remained—all but a few drops, which she promptly poured over his naked chest. He gasped as the liquid sluiced over his skin, while she set the glass aside and applied her tongue to licking him clean.

She moaned at the taste of him—heady and wild, masculine and complimented by the flavor of brandy. He went rigid beneath her, his fingers digging into her thighs as she lapped at him, tasting both him and the brandy, teasing him with little kisses and nips of her teeth.

"Hmm, brandy tastes better paired with you, Mr. Darling," she murmured against his skin before flicking her tongue out at one of his nipples.

He gasped, then groaned as she closed her lips around it and sucked. His cock surged, growing harder when she nipped at his nipple with her teeth; softly at first, and then with increasing pressure. He hissed from the pain, then sighed when she soothed it away with her tongue. She moved to the other, teasing his flat nipple until it hardened against her tongue, then nibbling on it with her teeth.

"Ah, Mistress," he groaned as she rocked against him, teasing him with the wet flesh of her quim without allowing him inside. "More … give me more."

Raising her head, she met his gaze and found he truly did crave more of the pain—more of the challenge she could offer by testing his limits. His eyes had begun to glaze over, and desire radiated from him in tangible waves. He fairly trembled from anticipating what she might do next.

"As you wish, Mr. Darling," she replied, reaching toward one of the items she'd brought from her trunk. "Do you know what this is for?"

She held up the implement—a silver ring attached to a slender, silver chain, which forked into two strands bearing metal clamps.

"I recognize the cock ring," he said, studying the device. "But this one is different from the one we used previously. What are the clamps for?"

With a grin, she reached out to pinch one of his nipples, pulling another shudder from him. "These go here ... and here."

He writhed beneath her as she teased first one nipple, then the other. "It looks positively Medieval."

Pursing her lips, she pinched one of the clamps to open it, then allowed it to close with a snap. "Does it frighten you?"

With a lopsided grin, he leaned back in the chair and slouched a bit, giving her full access to his body. "I cannot wait to wear it for you, Mistress. I think I shall look quite fetching."

Unable to help a chuckle—even though she tended to prefer to remain serious when acting as a Mistress—she took the silver ring and slid it over his engorged member.

"So you shall," she agreed, stroking him a few times.

He drew in a deep breath and released it slowly, seeming to brace himself for what would come next. While his cock grew and swelled for her, filling with his blood, she would affix the clamps to his nipples.

But first, she lowered her head and suckled at the left one to prepare it. She wanted him ready so the pain would not be more than needed. The moment he relaxed beneath her, the tension melting from his limbs, she pulled her lips away from his nipple and affixed the clamp with a speed she had mastered with years of practice.

He flinched, grunting as the first bite of pain registered, then closed his eyes and furrowed his brow as the deep throb settled in.

Stroking his jaw, she kissed his lips, then his cheek.

"Breathe, Michael," she whispered. "You will find the throbbing subsides after a moment."

Opening his eyes, he met her gaze, pain warring with desire in his eyes. She went back to rocking against him, prompting a sharp cry.

The cock ring had done its job, and now, he had become so sensitive that the slightest touch would heighten his pleasure.

Closing his eyes, he moved his hips in time with hers, moaning as she soaked him in her juices. While he remained distracted, she bent down and pleasured his free nipple, taking her time and ensuring he was practically in a frenzy by the time she affixed the second clamp. He roared, the sound a mingling of pleasure and pain, resting his head against her breasts and fighting for breath.

Stroking his hair, she held him close, continuing to rub herself against him, drawing his attention to the heat simmering between them.

"Do not forget your safe word if you need it," she reminded him, kissing his brow.

"No," he growled, grasping her buttocks and grinding her harder against his cock. "Don't stop … for the love of God, don't stop now."

His eagerness brought a smile to her face, while the steady friction of his cock against her inner folds and clit steadily pushed her toward the edge. But, she was not ready to spend yet … she did not want to do that until he was buried deep inside her.

Lifting just out of his reach, she straightened her legs and stood, straddling him. He growled at her, clenching his teeth, his eyes flashing with annoyance and anguish at the loss of his pleasure.

Grasping the chain running between the clamps and his cock ring, she gave it a sharp tug. He groaned, the muscles in his chest and abdomen clenching and bulging, his hands balling into fists.

"You want me, don't you, Michael?" she taunted, giving him a sly smile. "So badly you can taste it."

"Yes," he ground out through gritted teeth, his gaze upon her downright murderous.

She half wondered if he wanted to kill her or fuck her. The danger of finding out only made her want to push him further.

"That's why you resorted to tricks to win me," she teased. "Because you could never have had me otherwise. You and your calloused hands and big body ... hardened by *labor*, of all things! To think you would dare to covet me ... a true lady."

He grinned in response to her taunting, the gesturing menacing yet arousing in the way it transformed his face from that of a man to one of a lion biding its time until it could tackle its prey and rip it to shreds.

"That is correct, Mistress," he murmured, his voice a low, sensual caress stroking down her spine. "I wanted you ... I wanted to get my filthy, work-roughened hands on you. Hands that have done manual labor with wood, and tools, digging in the dirt. But that is why *you* want *me*, isn't it? You want me because I'm dirty and low and beneath you ... but I'll fuck you like none of those pampered lords can."

She gave the chain another jerk, and he grit his teeth, his head falling back as he muffled a growl, his entire body jerking beneath her. Repeating the motion with more force, she simultaneously sank back into his lap, taking his cock to the hilt. He bucked beneath her, his bellow loud enough to shake the rafters. Trembling and shuddering beneath her, he panted as she began to ride him, resting her hands upon his shoulders and giving him everything she had.

"Permission ... to touch you ... Mistress," he managed between strokes, the words panted out each time her thighs met his.

"Granted," she moaned, holding on tight as he penetrated her deepest places.

Thrusting his hips upward in time with her downward move-ments, he reached up and tore her shirt open, sending the top buttons flying across the room. Her breasts bounced free above the corset, and he promptly latched on to one.

Amelia threw her head back and moaned, shuddering as he suckled and nipped at her breasts, treating her to some of the pleasure and pain she'd subjected him to. She hissed at the bite of his teeth and then sighed with bliss at the soothing of his tongue. He held on to her hips, his fingers digging into the flesh of her arse as he urged her on, harder, faster.

His cock nudged against a sensitive place deep within her, and she angled herself to achieve more of the earth-shattering pleasure it caused. She moaned, resting her head against his shoulder and giving herself over to him, no longer able to maintain control as her insides began to shudder and clench around him.

He gasped at the feel of her sheath gripping him tightly, holding her tight against him and rocking her so that her clitoris fell against his pelvis with every stroke. A scream tore from her as her climax seemed to crescendo, the waves of it growing more powerful by the second. She collapsed against him, not caring that the nipple clamps now bit into her skin as well as his, riding the ebb and flow of the most powerful finish she'd ever experienced.

They went still for a moment, Amelia struggling to catch her breath, Michael holding her tight against him. Before she could regain control of the situation, he was on his feet, still holding her tight, still buried deep within.

"Permission to take you to bed and fuck you into oblivion, Mistress?" he asked, even as he began walking her to the bed.

"Granted," she replied, clinging tight to his neck as they approached the bed.

Tearing the curtains aside, he threw her onto the counterpane, his cock slipping out of her momentarily. She hardly had time to bemoan its loss before he swiftly turned her over and pulled her roughly to the edge of the bed until her legs hung over and her feet touched the floor. He kicked her feet apart and grasped her hips, then impaled her with one powerful thrust.

Amelia gripped the counterpane and held on for dear life as he pounded into her, the sound of his pelvis smacking against her arse resounding through the room, mingling with his hoarse groans. She gasped, the exhales forced from her with each brutal thrust, the feel of his cock slamming into her seeming to echo to the far reaches of her body.

Never had she allowed a man to take her like this—to have her in a position of submission. Yet, as a pleasure she'd never known swept through her, bringing her climax back to life, she could not find the will to resist. Instead, she closed her eyes and groaned as her core began to spasm around him forcefully, this orgasm far more powerful than the last.

"Oh, God, Michael!" she cried, her vision growing hazy as the climax swelled to its pinnacle, lifting her swiftly before throwing her over the edge.

He grunted in response, fucking her even faster as he grasped the edge of her corset and held on for leverage, using it to propel her harder against him. He would come any moment—she could feel it in the tension coiling through his body, the thrusts which grew less precise with each passing second, the sound of his breath becoming harsher and uneven.

With the last bit of strength she possessed, she lifted her head and reached back with one arm, blindly fumbling over Michael's body to find the chain connecting his clamps to the cock ring.

"Come for me," she moaned, finding the chain and wrapping her finger around it. "Now, Michael!"

Yanking on the chain, she heard the telltale snap of the clamps pulling free of his nipples, swiftly muffled by his hoarse moan as he slammed into her one last time before spending with a shudder that shook him from head to toe.

"Fuck!" he bellowed, stroking in her a few more times as his climax seemed to go on and on, his seed spilling into her with a volume that would have alarmed her if not for what she'd done to achieve it for him. He'd likely never had a climax so powerful.

Pulling out of her, he collapsed onto the bed beside her, rolling onto his back as his breath sawed in and out of his lungs. Now that he'd raptured, the euphoria would set in, and she would need to care for him. While this had not been a task she'd relished with her previous submissives, she found herself eager to do it for Michael.

Standing as soon as her legs would allow, she crossed to his washstand and cleaned between her legs. Then going into her room, she quickly changed out of her seductive getup and into a clean nightgown.

When she returned, he remained where she'd left him, watching her intently. In his gaze, she perceived the affection he felt for her, but there was also something else. Something that would frighten her if she allowed herself to dwell on it.

She admired and respected Michael; she liked him a great deal.

She could not fathom anything beyond that just yet.

Climbing up onto the bed beside him, she pressed a damp, cool cloth against his forehead. She smiled as he sighed and closed his eyes.

"Let me take care of you now, Michael," she whispered, keeping her voice low so as not to disturb his tranquil state.

Nestling closer to her, he nodded in acceptance of her ministrations. "Thank you, Mistress."

# CHAPTER 13

$\mathcal{M}$ ichael leaned back against his headboard, Amelia held tight against his side. The heady exhilaration that always followed her domination had begun to dissipate, leaving in its wake fatigue and contentment. After removing the tortuous cock ring and clamps, then bathing the sweat from his skin, she had applied a healing salve to his nipples. The substance had soothed the soreness left by the clamps almost instantly.

He reveled in her attentiveness—the way she stilled her own restlessness in order to let him hold her, the way she pressed little soft kisses against his skin, the way she asked him how he felt and what he might be thinking. She'd told him that this was the duty of the dominant—caring for their submissive after each encounter. Yet, a part of him hoped she treated him different than her past lovers because he was her husband. Perhaps even, because she was coming to care for him.

Stroking one hand down her arm, he smiled when she trembled, gooseflesh breaking out in the wake of his touch.

"I apologize if my family made you uncomfortable," he murmured, nuzzling the crown of her hair and inhaling her scent. "They have waited a long time for me to take a wife, and might have been a bit … overzealous."

Lifting her head to gaze up at him, she smirked. "I thought they were all delightful. Particularly Lydia. Why would you think I might be uncomfortable?"

He shrugged one shoulder. "Their questions about your family. The Darlings have always been close knit. It would never occur to them that asking someone about their family might bring up unpleasant memories. I do not know much about your family, but I am aware that your parents died when you were only a babe."

Her smirk fled, but her gaze remained shuttered when she replied, keeping her tone light. "It is hardly their fault … they did not know. Besides, it is difficult to mourn something I never knew. I am aware that I once had a mother and a father, but I never knew them. Now, Simon … I pity him, having known and lost them both so close together."

His eyebrows drew together as thoughts of his own father caused pangs of longing deep in his gut. The loss of Phillip Darling had been a crippling blow to the entire family. As a father and husband, he'd been beyond compare—loving, attentive, generous. Michael and Archie had been equal in the man's eyes, and he'd doted on Lydia.

It had always been his ambition to become just like Phillip; a hardworking landowner who took care of his tenants, a devoted husband, a good father. While his beginning with Amelia had been unconventional, he still held out hope that they could achieve the same sort of happiness his parents had shared.

"When did he die?" Amelia asked. "Your father?"

Snapping out of his reverie, he sank down onto the mattress, taking her with him. Turning onto his side to face her, he kept his arm around her.

"It's been six years," he replied. "His absence is felt every day. As large as Oakmoor is, it seems a bit hollow without him."

"I'm sorry," she whispered, reaching up to smoothing a lock of hair back from his forehead. "What was he like?"

He grinned. "Just like me. I was born with Mother's eyes, but the rest of me was inherited from him. He was a large man, tall and broad. He loved the outdoors and working with his hands. While most of our neighbors would never stoop to working in the fields alongside their tenants, Papa believed that a man had a responsibility to his family to work his own land. Now, Oakmoor is over twelve thousand acres, so it seems impossible, but he knew every inch. When I was old enough, he would take me out riding with him every morning, teaching me what it meant to own land, to work it and earn your living from it. I've spent most of my life striving to become just like him ... the sort of man people could admire."

She smiled, her wide grin making his chest tighten with its genuine beauty. "He sounds wonderful."

"He was," he agreed. "As a father, there was none other like him. When he wasn't tending his duties, he was chasing us through this house—all four of us, him, me, Archie, and Lydia, putting up such a racket."

Amelia's smile faded, her eyes growing haunted. "I cannot imagine what that must be like. My uncle did not tolerate noise. In fact, he seemed to prefer for us to stay out of sight altogether. At least, that was how he preferred things when it came to me. Simon, at least, served a purpose as the heir to the marquisate. He needed training, educating. I, however, proved no more than a nuisance until I would come of an age to marry."

Thinking of Lydia, who had been his father's pride and joy, Michael experienced a twinge of pity for Amelia. A young girl should have a doting papa to love and spoil her so completely that no man would ever be good enough to wed her. At least, this was how he'd always imagined being the father of a daughter should be.

Taking one of her hands in his, he raised it to his lips.

"Your uncle sounds like a tyrant," he said.

She scoffed. "You have no idea. I was never happier than on the day he died."

Studying her expression, he saw she truly meant it. "Was there no one there for you? No one to love you or protect you?"

"Simon," she replied. "He was all I had in the world. He protected me … and even though Uncle Gregory tried to smother all the joy and love out of him, he loved me."

Kissing her knuckles, he tightened his grip on her hand. She lowered her eyes, as if the confession had shamed her somehow. Here he lay, telling her about his perfect father after having introduced her to his perfect family, when she had no notion of what it felt like to possess either of those things. More than pity, he experienced the overwhelming urge to give her everything she'd never had. Protection, love, a family.

Releasing her hand, he reached out to gently raise her chin so she was looking at him again. "He tried to crush your spirit, but he could never have counted upon you growing up to become The Incomparable Lady A."

Her grin was back, transforming her face and revealing the adorable dimple in her left cheek.

"You are damned right, he could not."

He returned her smile, caressing her cheek with his knuckles, then leaning closer, resting his forehead against hers. "I've grown quite fond of you, you know."

"Is that so?" she teased.

"Quite so," he replied. "And I want you to know that you can be who you are with me. A harridan. A Mistress. I will never try to change or manage you. You have my word, Amelia."

"And our children?" she prodded, her tone growing serious as she seemed to search his gaze for something.

Thinking of spending inside of her this afternoon, and again just a short while ago, heat suffused his veins at the thought of her, even now, being pregnant with his child.

"They are free to be whatever they wish to be, as well," he replied. "I might not ever be the perfect father, Amelia, but our children will know love. They will know affection and joy and freedom."

Closing the distance between them, she wrapped an arm tight around his waist, burying her face against his chest.

For a moment, he could only lie there, taken aback by the sudden gesture of affection. In the time they'd been together, her touches had been mostly sexual, dominating … serving a purpose. Yet, she seemed to draw something from him just now, resting against him in a way that put him in a sheltering position.

Tightening his hold on her, he cradled her close, kissing her forehead and stroking her hair. Whatever it was she sought from him, he could only hope he had it to give. As it was, he had already begun to fall rapidly under her spell. The hope that she would come to return his affections had seemed farfetched.

But, just now, with her cheek pressed against his heart and her arm holding him tight as if she did not wish to let go, it seemed far more inevitable.

"Michael?" she said, her breath tickling his bare chest.

"Yes?"

"I've grown quite fond of you, too."

The first fortnight of Amelia's new life at Oakmoor rushed past her at a dizzying pace. With Perdita as a guide, she spent the first few days familiarizing herself with the manor and staff. The large country house boasted dozens of rooms, a massive ballroom, more drawing rooms than she could count, three music rooms, sunrooms at each corner of each floor, and two long galleries—one for family portraits and one for a fine art collection. There was also the library, Michael's study, and the adjoining office of his steward, and another study where Archie worked when not at his solicitor's office in town.

Many of the rooms had remained closed before her arrival, the furniture covered to ward off dust. The musty smells in the shuttered chambers told her that they hadn't been cleaned in some time. With a limited staff working to keep the estate running, this did not surprise her.

After taking inventory of all that needed to be done, she had set to work taking over as the lady of Oakmoor. It was, after all, what she'd been bred for. Just because she had shunned marriage did not mean she did not possess what it took to efficiently run her own household.

Finding an unused study, she had ordered it cleaned for her use and claimed it as her own. There, she reviewed the household books and ensured that all their accounts were settled and debts had been set right. Then, she charged the housekeeper with hiring new chambermaids and footmen, and leaving the replenishing of the outdoor staff to Michael's steward.

Within days, Oakmoor's windows stood open to air out the unused rooms, while an army of chambermaids scrubbed and dusted every surface, polishing furniture and beating rugs. The hedges outdoors were tamed, overgrown wildflowers trimmed and brought in to decorate the drawing rooms in fresh bouquets.

Then, with Perdita, Hesper, and Lydia at her side, she swept through the entire house, taking inventory of repairs and renovations to be made. Orders were placed for new rugs, wallpaper, chandeliers, and drapes. Once that had been done, a modiste and tailor had descended upon the house with more assistants than she could count, their mission to update the family's outmoded wardrobe.

Aside from those duties came those of entertaining visitors. As word spread that Michael Darling had wed Lady Amelia Fitzwilliam, sister of a marquis, their neighbors began to arrive to assuage their curiosity. She entertained them all, offering tea and refreshments and engaging in idle small talk whenever she was not engaged in the renovation of Oakmoor.

She hardly saw her husband during the day—something to be expected when he had so much work to do. While she saw to the house, Michael occupied himself with riding the lands with his steward, making note of the improvements to be made. She was kept abreast of their progress, as the steward arrived promptly in her study each afternoon at three o'clock to present her with a list of materials to be ordered. She approved them all, trusting Michael to spend her money wisely and finding nothing frivolous or unnecessary in his lists. Materials for mending fences, repairing the grain mill, patching the stable roof, and improving their tenants' homes ... all of it would be put to good use.

They met each night for dinner with the family before retiring to Michael's bedchamber for the evening. Though she had her own suite of rooms, they preferred to sleep together in his bed. Some nights, they fell under the counterpane together and drifted right to sleep, too exhausted from all their hard work to do more than trade a perfunctory kiss. Other nights, they fumbled in the dark, finding enough energy for a quick bout of lovemaking. She reveled in those stolen moments, but missed their longer encounters—the times when he had submitted to her so perfectly. And while she had been taught that the time spent caring for one's submissive afterward was for their benefit, she had come to enjoy it, as well.

With her previous lovers, once the initial satisfaction that followed a bedding dissipated, she had not been able to get away from them fast enough. Yet, she felt none of this urgency with Michael. Quite the opposite, really. She enjoyed his company and actually missed him when he left her to tend to duties all day. Her first night at Oakmoor, she had revealed things to him she'd never said to anyone—things about her uncle and her brother. And while it certainly counted as progress, there remained other things she simply was not ready for. As fond as she was of her husband, just the thought of being completely undressed with him caused her to feel nauseous. Once he saw what she hid, she would be forced to tell him all of it—every foul, disgusting thing her uncle had subjected her and Simon to.

Someday, she told herself, she would be ready. She would trust her husband with her deepest and darkest secrets. Until then, she would strive to find happiness here at Oakmoor. With the manor on its way to reaching its former glory, she must now find other ways to occupy her time. In London, an active social calendar had filled her days and nights. Here in the country, life moved at a slower pace, her surroundings far quieter than she was used to.

Perhaps a day out of doors would be just the thing, she decided on the first morning she awoke without a gargantuan list of tasks to attend to. She'd risen to find the bed beside her empty—something she'd grown accustomed to. Michael rose before the sun, and surely possessed the most silent feet ever created, as she never heard him leave.

She dressed herself, not needing Kate to pull on breeches and boots. Donning a worn waistcoat over a white shirt, she attached one of her many cameo pins in the cravat she'd tied herself and set out from the room. Her hair arranged into a braid and draped over one shoulder, she forwent a hat, wanting to feel the sun on her face, uninhibited.

Finding the dining room occupied by Lydia and Perdita, she joined them for breakfast. The enticing aroma of the various foods sitting on the sideboard caused her stomach to grumble. It had been so long since she'd lived in the country, she'd forgotten how much heartier breakfasts were than in the city. Along with the customary tea and toast with various spreads, the sideboard sat laden with coddled and boiled eggs, ham, and venison. Her mouth watered as she piled her plate high, then joined the other women at the table.

"I must say," Perdita commented as Amelia waited for a footman to pour her tea. "I've never known a woman to wear breeches, but you cut quite a figure in them, Amelia."

She beamed at her mother-in-law, who seemed to readily accept all of her eccentricities. Apparently, she could do no wrong in the woman's eyes.

"Thank you, Perdie," she said between bites of egg. "You should try them for riding and lounging about the house. They're quite the most comfortable thing you'll ever wear."

Perdita chuckled. "Oh, dear, I'm afraid age and giving birth to three children have made that quite impossible. I haven't the pert backside I once possessed, unfortunately."

Lydia giggled. "My backside is still pert. Might I start wearing breeches?"

"I have several pair," Amelia offered. "I'm happy to give you a few … that is, if your mother does not object."

Shaking her head at her daughter's hopeful glance, Perdita sighed. "I supposed it could not hurt. But only when you're riding on our lands, or about the house. I would not like to hear the tongues wagging should you go about calling on people in them, or wearing them to town."

Amelia took a bite of toast with a secretive smile, wondering what Perdita would think of the evening knee-breeches and tailored waist-coats she owned. When paired with a long cutaway coat, they proved some of her favorite items to wear for an evening out. Though, she typically spent her evenings in London at the theater or gaming hells … as opposed to the country balls and dinner parties Lydia would likely be attending.

"Yes, Mama," Lydia replied before turning her wide grin on Amelia. The girl seemed positively giddy at the prospect of being allowed to wear breeches. "I vow, Amelia, you've made Oakmoor ever so much more exciting since you arrived, and it's only been a fortnight."

"Speaking of which," Perdita spoke up, leaning back in her chair and stirring milk into a fresh cup of tea. "I had thought to suggest an event of some sort … a ball or dinner party to celebrate your marriage to Michael. Your wedding was swift and private, which will set the gossips to wagging their tongues if we continue hiding you away here."

While Amelia had entertained several neighbors since her arrival, she understood well how society worked—even on this rung just a bit lower than the one she usually inhabited. A hasty marriage could mean any number of things, and a public appearance could set any rumors about the state of her marriage to rest. Besides, with Oakmoor being whipped back into shape, now would be the perfect time to invite their friends and acquaintances to celebrate with them. If anyone knew about the diminished state of the Oakmoor lands and coffers, there would be no doubt that things were on the mend once they saw for themselves the improvements that had been made.

"A fine idea," she said, cutting into a slice of ham. "Perhaps a house party? A short one … no more than a sennight long, I think. It could serve a dual purpose—introducing me to your neighbors, and my official first event as Lady Darling, as well as practice for Lydia. Since she isn't officially out yet, this would be the perfect opportunity for her to mingle and make acquaintances before her London debut. And with my connections, the invitations would garner acceptance from families of influence … families with eligible sons for Lydia to consider."

Her sister-in-law's eyes lit up. "Oh, Mama, can we? We haven't had a house party in ages! Not since I've become old enough to be considered for marriage. Oh, and if people of title and rank come, I could end up engaged to a baron … no, a viscount! Could you imagine, Mama … me, a viscountess?"

Perdita chuckled. "Calm down, Lydia. It is only a house party, and there will be no engagements before your official coming out next Season. But, Amelia is right; this would prove a good opportunity for you to dip your toes into the proverbial pond. It is a wonderful idea, Amelia."

"I'll discuss it with Michael this evening," she replied.

And, perhaps coax him into a bit of play. There were still many items in the trunk hidden in her dressing room that she wanted to show him. Things that would whip him into a frenzy and earn her another explosive encounter like the one they'd shared their first night at Oakmoor.

While Lydia and Perdita chattered on about the various possibilities for activities during the house party, Amelia quickly finished her breakfast. Bidding them good morning, she left the dining room, and then the house altogether. A nice, long ride across the estate would clear her head and allow her to get some exercise.

When she approached the stable, a groom began readying her mare, Aries. She had arrived from London, along with the rest of her belongings, a few days prior. Once the horse was ready for her, she thanked the groom and mounted, turning in the direction of the well-beaten path leading away from the manor. The dirt lane split off into others as she progressed, each new path leading to some other place. She selected one leading into the line of trees marking the edge of the house grounds—which were perfectly manicured now that a full gardening staff had been hired. She slowed Aries once the trees had swallowed her, enjoying the scenery of the woods passing on either side of her—the massive oaks from which the manor had taken its name shading her from the morning sun.

As time passed, the woods began to thin and gave way to acres upon acres of prime farmland. Tall stalks of wheat bent in the soft breeze, rippling like golden waves for as far as her eye could see. Michael had mentioned the grain harvest being upon them, one of the reasons the tools and parts for repair of the broken mill had been so imperative. Without it, this year's profits would have suffered.

She rode along the field's perimeter, finding other crops she could not identify growing in other areas alongside the wheat. More stretches of land beyond lay empty—the practice of crop rotation ensuring that the soil there could rest. New crops would be planted there after the other fields had been cleared.

Beyond it all, the homes of Oakmoor's tenants sprawled, taking up small parcels of land. She could not see them from here, but could recall spotting a few of them upon their arrival a few weeks back.

Men inclined their heads politely and murmured greetings as she rode past, before returning to their work. The mending of the fences had begun, she noticed, a task which would take quite a bit of time considering the number of acres they owned.

She'd been riding for a while, the manor now completely out of sight, when she happened upon Michael and Abbot, his steward. The two men rode on horseback at a sedate pace, coming toward her on a path stretching between two fenced-off pastures. One of those paddocks held what must be hundreds of sheep. The white, fluffy animals milled about inside the enclosure, grazing on the grass and fobs growing inside.

Michael grinned and spurred his mount toward her, approaching at a trot as she came to a stop, staring open-mouthed at the creatures.

"Good morning," he said as he reined up his mount beside hers. "What brings you from the manor so early this morning?"

With a grin, she gestured toward the pasture. "We own sheep?"

He chuckled, following her gaze to a smaller enclosure within the paddock where the baby lambs grazed separately from the adults. "So it would seem."

"Oakmoor is full of surprises," she replied, patting the side of Aries' neck to calm her. The horse snorted and stomped, seeming anxious to continue their ride.

"Had you not come along, we would have been forced to sell at least half of them this year," he informed her, his tone grave. "We could hardly afford to keep them fed. Now, the income from wool and milk can be put back into the estate. Not to mention mutton and lamb meat."

Amelia enjoyed mutton and lamb as much as anyone, but faced with the creatures the meat came from, she experienced a twinge of guilt.

"They are so darling," she murmured. "It's been years since I saw a lamb up close."

Michael swung down from his mount, tying its reins to one of the fence posts. Then, approaching Aries, he took her reins, leading her to the fence and tethering her beside his mount. Turning to her, he reached up and grasped her waist, plucking her from the saddle as if she weighed no more than a doll.

By now, his steward had caught up to them. A slender, silent man, he reminded her of Archie with his plain clothing and reserved demeanor.

"You may return without me, Abbot," Michael said without sparing the man a glance. He seemed to have eyes only for her. "I will meet you after lunch."

"Of course," Abbot replied, inclining his head to Michael, then tipping his hat to Amelia. "My lady."

Amelia nodded in reply, and the steward left them, spurring his horse on down the path. Taking her hand and leading her toward the fence, Michael gave her another of his belly-trembling smiles.

"Shall we?"

Bracing one foot on the bottom rung of the fence, she swung the opposite one over the top, keeping a steady hold on Michael's hand as she stepped over and hopped down to the grass inside the paddock containing the little lambs. He climbed in after her, coming to stand by her side as they became surrounded by the baby animals. She practically squealed with glee as the lambs pranced through the grass around them, their soft bleating widening her smile.

Reaching down, he slid a hand beneath one's belly, lifting it as easily as he had her. The lamb squirmed in his hold, but calmed once he wrapped his other arm around it, cradling it against his chest.

"This one's my favorite," he declared, as she approached to pet it. "Her name is Daisy."

"How do you tell her from the others?" she asked as she stroked the soft, newly grown wool coiling along Daisy's body.

Pointing to the smudges of some sort of dye on one of her flanks, he adjusted the lamb in his arms so she could get a better look.

"The fencing helps keep our animals on our land," he told her. "But we still follow the practice of marking them in case they get loose and wander. All Oakmoor sheep are marked on their flanks with a yellow dye. Lydia was present for Daisy's lambing, and helped with the marking. She drew a little flower, see?"

Amelia smiled, running a hand over the dye mark. Unlike the other lambs, whose marks appeared like haphazard splotches, Daisy's marking was distinct—a yellow flower.

"She's lovely," she murmured, taking the lamb's face in one hand and stroking its head with the other. "Where were you and Abbot returning from?"

"We've been visiting tenants," he replied, kneeling to place Daisy back upon the ground. "We've maintained their homes the best we could, but with our coffers bled dry, some of the houses fell into disrepair. We are taking note of the needs of each tenant, and Abbot will see to it that those needs are met."

Following him back toward the fence, she propped her arms on the top rung and leaned against it, turning to gaze at him as he joined her, mimicking her posture.

"I think that is admirable," she said. "Most of the landowners I know leave such duties to their stewards. Most would not know one of their tenants if they stood just before them."

Like Simon. Though, she had to admit it would be hard for her brother to cultivate a relationship of any sort with the people who lived on and worked his lands. After all, he owned several estates, each of them as big, or bigger, than this one, but spent most of his time in London. Michael, however, lived and breathed Oakmoor.

"My father always said a man who owns as much land as we do has a responsibility to the people who help cultivate it," he replied. "From the time I was a boy, I've been visiting the tenants—getting to know them. Many of their children are of an age with me. It is they who work the land with me. And because they know me, they care about Oakmoor as much as they would if it belonged to them."

Envy roiled in her gut at the mention of his father yet again. Michael did not know how fortunate he had been to have had such a man to admire and love.

"I should like to accompany you next time," she declared. "Oakmoor is my home now, too, and I want to come to know the tenants, as well."

"You do?" he asked, his stare incredulous.

"Of course I do," she replied. "Besides, it would serve to give me a reason to leave the manor. I vow, the past few weeks spent cloistered indoors have been quite taxing."

Climbing up and over the fence, he assisted her back to the other side. The moment her feet touched the grass, he swept her into his arms and up against his body. She gasped against his lips as he took her mouth in a kiss, ravaging her lips hungrily.

"Michael," she panted between kisses. "What has gotten into you?"

He chuckled against her neck, kissing his way up toward her ear. "It has been a long few weeks, Amelia. I've missed you."

Closing her eyes, she allowed her head to fall back as he went on kissing her, flicking his tongue over her thrumming pulse. He smelled of leather, horse, sandalwood shaving soap, and the outdoors—a combination that struck her as distinctly male … distinctly Michael.

"We've had dinner together every night," she argued. "We've shared a bed and even made love."

"It hasn't been the same," he argued. "We've been too tired for anything more than a few hasty tumbles. I've *missed* you."

His meaning was made clearer as he began running his hands over her body, squeezing her breasts and skimming her waist before palming her buttocks and pulling her tighter against him.

"We've plenty of time just now," she whispered, raising her head to kiss him again, growing dizzy from the heady feeling of being held by him, his kisses turning her limbs to jelly.

Releasing her, he took her hand and swiftly led her down the path he and Abbot had just taken. With a laugh, she trotted to keep up with his long, determined strides. After a while, he seemed to notice he was practically dragging her down the lane and paused to sweep her up into his arms. She held on to him, kissing his face, his jaw, his neck, his ear, as he carried her past the fenced-off pastures and toward a large tree shading a soft patch of grass in the clearing. Setting her down beneath it, he began undressing her, his fingers moving with swift, deft movements.

Desperation struck her, and she reciprocated, snatching his cravat from his throat and attacking the buttons of his shirt and waistcoat. They disrobed swiftly, boots and stockings tossed aside, waistcoats left lying on top of Michael's shirt.

Then, she stood before him wearing only her shirt, the hem of it falling just past her bottom. Michael paused with his hands on her shoulders, his breath coming harsh and swift as he looked her over from the top of her disheveled head to the tips of her toes buried in the grass.

His gaze dropped to the neckline of her shirt, his breath slowing as he gingerly pried one of the buttons at her chest free. Her lungs swelled, and she held her breath while he finished off the others, his knuckles caressing the bare skin left by the opening. Slipping one hand beneath the fabric, he slid it aside to reveal one breast. He sighed, stroking her nipple lightly.

"My beautiful wife," he whispered. "Let me undress you."

Her throat burned, and her vision became unfocused as she looked away, unable to hold his gaze when he was looking at her with such naked hunger and longing. They were married, yet he had never seen her completely undressed.

Taking her back in his arms, he lifted her, urging her legs around his waist. One hand strong at her back, he nuzzled the opening of her shirt, pressing soft kisses against her breastbone.

"I want every inch of you, Amelia," he murmured, his breath fanning over her nipple, his lips caressing it lightly, his tongue flicking out to taste it. "All your secrets, all your desires … all of your pain."

She whimpered when he moved to her other breast, treating it the same as the other. Yet, even while he kissed her revealed skin, he left her shirt on her back, placing the decision in her hands. A deep, resounding pang in her chest echoed throughout her body, and she longed to bare herself to him, to finally allow him to see her, the parts of her she'd been hiding.

And yet …

"I'm not ready," she choked out.

Raising his head to look at her, he sighed, hurt flickering momentarily in his eyes. It was gone as quickly as it came, and he raised his lips to hers for a kiss. She obliged him, twining her fingers in his hair and trying to tell him with a kiss what she could not say with words. She was not ready yet … but she wanted to be.

Silently accepting her rejection, he sank to his knees in the grass, taking her onto his lap. Then lying back on the ground, he lifted her off him enough to reach the fall of his breeches. Once free of his clothing, he pressed his cock to her entrance, slipping his hands just beneath her shirt to grasp her hips and angle her toward him.

"I am content to wait," he said, staring intently at her, his gaze disarming in its fervency. "When you are ready, I will be here."

Overwhelmed by the gift he had given her—what he was giving up by allowing her to keep her secrets—Amelia closed her eyes to blink back tears. He could not see her this way. If she cried, he would want to know why, and perhaps he wouldn't be content with her brushing him off as she had before. Perhaps he would demand to know the truth, and then she would have to tell him. She would have to unearth the things she'd buried and had hoped to never revisit.

Instead, she sank onto his member, taking him deep inside with a guttural sigh. Michael grunted and relaxed beneath her, lying back in the grass. He maintained his hold on her hips, urging her at the rhythm he wanted while bucking beneath her, rising to meet her.

She had never been with a man without directing him, commanding him, demanding her own satisfaction. Yet, she felt no desire to do that with Michael this time.

This time, she allowed her gaze to connect with his, her hands resting on his chest, her breath matching time with his as they moved together.

It proved the single most erotic moment of her life, making love with Michael beneath the sky and sun, grass tickling her legs, his big body beneath her—hers for the taking, hers to worship.

As she shuddered in climax atop him, she realized just how doomed she was now. Michael was stealing her heart, making her want to give him every part of herself.

But, what would happen when the only parts she had left to give turned out to be tattered and torn? Would he want them? Would she survive if it turned out that he didn't?

As he closed his eyes and gritted his teeth, following her to his rapture, she swiftly wiped away her tears so he would not see them. He could never know.

# CHAPTER 14

$\mathcal{M}$ ichael left his study for the day, bidding Abbot a good evening before setting off for his bedroom to dress for dinner. Tomorrow would be Sunday, and thank goodness for that. The past few weeks had exhausted him, and he wanted nothing more than to rest and spend the day with Amelia … after church, of course. It did not matter that he was a man grown and had inherited Oakmoor—his mother would box his ears for missing church.

He chuckled at the thought, but the sound died away as he thought of his wife. Their blissful time in the pasture had been on his mind most of the afternoon. Mostly, because it had been the first time in a fortnight they hadn't had to rush through making love. But also, because a part of him was still disappointed that she had, once again, opted to remain partially dressed during intercourse. It had seemed like an interesting quirk at first—something she might employ as a Mistress to keep him guessing, making him yearn for her. Yet, now, it became clear that she used that shirt as a shield—against what, he could not be certain.

Passing the open door of a drawing room, he spotted his mother inside, a pair of spectacles resting upon the bridge of her nose as she worked at her needlepoint frame. Lingering in the doorway, he observed her—lovely even in her advanced age, quiet and poised.

For a moment, he tried to envision Amelia at this age, but then could not. She had likely never had the patience to learn needlepoint, and he could never imagine her admitting to needing glasses or that her vision had begun to diminish with time. The thought of his wife, still wearing breeches and vexing him to no end fifty years from now, made him chuckle, which drew Perdita's attention.

Pushing the frame aside, she gestured for him to come in. "You haven't lingered in that doorway to watch me work since you were a boy."

With a short laugh, he sank onto the settee beside her, resting his hand on top of hers. "I must admit, I was mostly lingering in hopes that you'd have peppermint sticks in your pocket."

Turning to him with a soft smile, she reached into the pocket of her day gown and produced a bag of the striped candy sticks. "I am a Grandmama now. I can never be caught without them."

Accepting one from her, he leaned against the back of the settee and placed the sweet between his lips, sighing as the taste returned him to his childhood—off roaming the halls of Oakmoor with one of the candy sticks clutched in one fist. His governess would chide him for leaving sticky fingerprints on various surfaces, but his mother would simply smile and ruffle his hair, then use her apron to wipe him clean.

"Did Amelia address the house party with you today?" she asked.

Opening one eye, he peered at her. Amelia had broached the subject of the house party as they'd dressed after making love.

"She did," he mumbled around the peppermint stick. "I think it is a marvelous idea. The two of you should begin planning it at your earliest convenience."

Folding her hands in her lap, she nodded. "Splendid. It will be good to have guests again. It's been so long."

Indeed, it had. It had seemed like ages since Oakmoor had been filled with such life and vitality. He had Amelia to thank for that ...

yet, his concern over her reticence in other areas left him concerned.

"Mama," he said suddenly. "Might I ask you something … about women?"

Removing her spectacles, she allowed them to hang from their chain around her neck. "Of course, Michael."

Taking a bite of the peppermint stick, he crunched it between his teeth before continuing. He avoided her gaze, twirling the sweet between his fingers, hypnotized by the swirl of its red stripes.

"What reason would a wife have for keeping … certain things … from her husband?" he asked.

From the corner of his eye, he noticed her eyebrows rising.

"What sorts of things?"

Hunching in the chair, he rested his elbows on his knees, taking another bite of the candy. "Secrets, I suppose. Certain types of affection. Details about her past."

With a sigh, she reached out to him, taking his chin in one strong hand and forcing him to turn his head to look at her. A motherly smile curved her lips as she fussed over his hair as she had when he'd been a lad, arranging it to her liking.

"Are you certain it isn't just a matter of how little you know one another?" she asked. "You were only in London a few weeks before you returned with her, and you've barely been married a fortnight. Knowing someone takes time, Michael."

He shook his head, dislodging her hold. "It is more than that. There is something … I do not know what it is, but she's frightened to let me know her, to let me know things about her that she'd rather not speak of."

She nodded in understanding. "Patience, my son. Give her time, and give her your love. I assume you ask me these things because you do love her?"

Having polished off the peppermint stick, he retrieved a handkerchief and used it to clean his fingers. He then ran a hand through his hair and sighed.

"I do, Mama … I love her more than I would have thought possible given our short time together."

"Then love her," she replied. "And simply allow your presence to make her comfortable enough to reveal what she's hiding. The security of your affection and your steadfastness … it will show her that you will not be put off by a few secrets or a less than stellar past. Do you understand?"

He supposed he did, but that did not make it any easier to go on the way he had been thus far—dancing to her tune in hopes that she would give him back even a fraction of what he gave her.

"I understand," he answered. "Thank you."

Patting his knee, she rose. "It is what mothers are for. Shall I see you for dinner?"

A sudden idea came to him, and he rose slowly, shaking his head with a smile. "No. I think Amelia and I will dine alone tonight."

She pressed a hand to her heart and sighed. "How romantic. Amelia is sure to be pleased. Shall I arrange for the meal to be sent to you … say, in two hours' time?"

He nodded. "That would be good, Mama. Thank you."

After kissing his cheek, she left, heading in the direction of the kitchen.

Michael departed the room and went the opposite way, bounding up the stairs and to his chambers. Even after their time together this afternoon, he was loath to share her with anyone. Perhaps an evening alone could cause them to grow closer. With two hours left until dinner arrived, he would have time to bathe and make himself presentable for her.

He entered his room to find Oliver waiting, the sharpened straight razor in his hand and prepared for shaving. His evening clothes lay neatly on the bed.

"Have you seen Amelia, by any chance, Oliver?" he asked, stripping off his coat and pulling off his cravat before sinking into the chair beside the washstand and giving himself over to the valet.

"She is in her chambers dressing for dinner," he replied while laying a warm towel over the lower half of Michael's face. "Her lady's maid sent word that she wishes an audience with you before the two of you join your family."

Perfect. That would give him the opportunity to inform her that they would be dining alone tonight. Perhaps afterward, he could carry her to bed and indulge in a bit more of what they'd shared beneath the tree that afternoon. As much as he enjoyed her domination and mastery, she had never simply been with him before—taking him into her body and surrendering to the feelings of the moment instead of exercising control.

He sat through the shave, then hastily bathed and allowed the valet to fuss over his clothing. Then, dismissing Oliver, he crossed through his dressing room, then hers. Finding the door to her room closed, he knocked, not wanting to intrude if she wished to be left alone.

"Enter," she called out from the other side.

He pushed the door open and found her standing in the center of the room, freshly bathed and devoid of her riding attire. His mouth fell open as he realized she had not dressed for dinner, but for an evening of play in the bedchamber.

As always, the black leather boots clung to her legs to the knee, revealing the black lace edging a pair of stockings. She had donned a clean shirt, but had buttoned it to the throat and placed a cameo brooch there. A red satin corset cinched in her waist over the shirt, its edges adorned with more black lace. She had piled her hair on top of her head, a few stray strands kissing her cheeks and the back of her neck.

But it was the instrument she held in her hand that caught and held his attention. The black coil made him shiver, the sound it made as she unwound it and allowed it to slither to the floor causing his pulse to race.

"Come, Mr. Darling," she commanded, her tone terse and demanding. "I haven't got all night."

Raising his eyebrows at her, he sauntered into the room, closing the door behind him. "Had I known you wished to play, I might not have come dressed for dinner. Hell, I would not have bothered to dress at all."

She gave the whip a flick, letting it crack through the air before falling back to her feet. "I want to watch you undress. Then, you will kneel for me."

At the hungry way she raked her gaze over his body, he wanted to fall to the floor then and there. She never ceased to get his heart racing and his mouth watering for a taste of her. Thankfully, dinner would be sent to his room, not Amelia's. Hell, it could wait. His plans for romance fell to the wayside as he found himself wanting to know exactly what she planned to do to him with that whip.

He hastily undid all of Oliver' hard work, leaving his clothing in a pile on the floor before coming to stand just before her. Holding her gaze, he sank to his knees, hands clasped tight behind his back.

Coming forward, she ran her fingers through his hair, then circled him, out of his line of sight. Her fingernails tickled his back, sending a shiver down his spine. Anticipation hummed through him, excitement and arousal already filling his cock with blood.

"Remember your safety word, Mr. Darling?" she asked.

He chuckled. "It is Dimple, Mistress ... though I have never had cause to use it."

Her voice came at him, harsh and biting as the sound of the whip whirling through the air warned him what would come next.

"Tonight, you just might, Mr. Darling," she replied just before the whip landed.

The first blow stung, the annoyance making him grit his teeth. Another came, a bit harder than the first, the echoing tingle from the first strike mingling with this one. Each crack of the whip fell against him with increasing force, with Amelia barely pausing between them to allow him to draw breath.

Closing his eyes and sinking into a place where his mind disconnected from the pain his body experienced, he couldn't help but wonder if she punished him for getting too close—for daring to attempt penetrating the barrier she had erected between them.

When she ceased whipping him and changed the encounter from one of pain to one of ecstasy, he decided that it was worth it. Any torment she delivered would be worth it if perhaps, he could show her that no lengths were too great for him to reach. If it would prove that she could trust him, he would gladly do it.

"Amelia, have you heard a word I said?"

Turning to glance at her husband—who rode at her side down the lane cutting through Oakmoor's pastures—she frowned. She had been walking about in a daze since their emotional encounter in this very same pasture. Her thoughts twisted about her mind in a muddle, the turmoil settled in her gut like a stone weight growing heavier by the day. She was being distant, and remained acutely aware of her behavior and how it hurt Michael. For the past week, he'd been trying to reach her with kindness and the sort of witty jokes that typically made her smile. Yet, she'd remained closed off, unable to move past a single thought.

The only time she found clarity and peace was when, in the dark of night and the privacy of their bedchamber, he would kneel upon the floor to submit to her. It was as if Michael knew it was the only way to reach her—the only way to be as close to her as he seemed to want to be. Yet another aspect of her personality he might not ever understand.

During the day, she remained aloof and quiet, but in the evening wielded her whip and other implements with cold skill, pushing him to the limits of his control before allowing him to unleash every ounce of his passion and desire onto her.

She would never be able to tell him the truth.

To show him the things she kept hidden, to tell him her darkest secrets … a part of her would not allow it. After all, how could he ever fathom it? Perfect Michael, who even when tricking her into marriage had had the noblest intentions—the salvation of his family and their lands and the tenants depending upon them. Perfect Michael with the lovely family who all treated each other with affection and respect. How could he ever understand what had been done to her ... the things she'd witnessed being done to her brother?

And once he knew, he would pity her, perhaps even think of her as damaged. And while she often thought of herself that way, as well, she just could not bear for him to. Yet, the truth remained that she could not avoid it forever. Thus her sullen mood. She'd painted herself into a corner, and now had no notion of how to get out. She and Michael were bonded for life, the inevitable revelation of her secrets no longer a matter of 'if,' but 'when.'

"Of course I did," she replied, turning away from his probing stare and fixing it upon the road stretching ahead of them.

He had approached her this morning about joining him on a ride to visit a few of their tenants. Since she had previously expressed an interest in doing so, she could hardly have turned him down. So, they rode side by side in strained silence, only the sounds of chirping birds and bleating sheep breaking through the quiet of the countryside.

Michael raised his eyebrows. "And? What do you think?"

Heaving a sigh, she shrugged one shoulder. "Whatever you want, Michael."

"Ah," he replied, his tone light and teasing. "Then it is settled. Tonight, I'll tie you to our bed facedown and fuck that beautiful arse of yours."

Her eyes widened, and her head whipped toward him. Their gazes met, and she found his full of mirth, his lips twitching as if he bit back a laugh.

She scowled. "That was not very funny."

"It isn't well done of you to pretend you were listening to me when you clearly were not," he chided. "In case you are interested to know, I asked how you would feel about bringing Lydia with us to London. She has never been, and expressed interest in visiting at least once before she begins her Season."

Furrowing her brow, she glanced at him from the corner of her eye. "We've only just arrived at Oakmoor a few weeks ago. Why would we take Lydia to London?"

His expression of amusement faded to one of concern. "The christening of your niece and nephew is next week. Don't you remember?"

Amelia closed her eyes and released her breath on a pained sigh. She had completely forgotten about Phineas and Joanna's christening—they had promised not to miss it.

"Of course," she said, forcing a light tone.

As the neat rows of cottages housing their tenants came into view, Michael reached out and snatched the reins of her horse from her grasp. Pulling both their mounts to a stop, he leaned toward her—so close, she could smell him over the clean air of the outdoors. It made an even greater mess of her senses, the urge to lean into his strong chest and weep gripping her swiftly and tightly.

"Amelia, I wish you would tell me what the matter is," he urged, his expression of concern so genuine that it made her chest ache. "If it is something I have done, then simply tell me so I might set it right."

Squaring her shoulders and lifting her chin, she schooled her face into a mask of indifference. "Nothing is the matter. Don't be silly."

His jaw hardened, his grip tightening upon her reins. The vein in his neck stood out as the tension seemed to overtake his entire body. The hurt she'd been witnessing all week flickered in his gaze, stabbing her like a knife to the gut.

*You could never understand, Michael. I care more for you than I ever thought I could ... and that frightens me most of all.*

Nostrils flaring as he composed himself and released a noisy breath, he dropped her reins and nodded decisively.

"Very well," he said, his tone now clipped and brusque. "As always, I am waiting ... if ever you decide you are ready to trust me with whatever it is you are hiding."

Spurring his mount onward, he left her behind, heading toward the cottages at a steady trot.

She stared after him a moment, her heart sinking into her stomach. Perhaps she need not worry about him uncovering her secrets. Her treatment of him would be enough to push him away before long.

Despite her trepidation, that notion struck fear deep within her and brought the stinging of tears to her eyes. Either way things went, she would lose him. It did not matter that they were wed—eventually, Michael would tire of her avoidance and decide she might not be worth the effort.

Gently nudging her mare along after him, she resigned herself to her fate.

Michael pressed a hand to his ribs, the slight soreness there mingling with the sweet bliss of the memories that accompanied it. The stir of desire began in his loins as he remembered kneeling before Amelia, unable to take his eyes off her as she'd circled him with her bullwhip. The crack of the thong through the air had sent a surge of energy through him, making his pulse race as he'd wondered when the braided end would make contact with his skin.

If someone had told him before he'd met Amelia that he would enjoy being struck with a bullwhip, he would have called them daft. Yet, as she'd let the leather strike him with blows that began as slight annoyances and advanced to sharp stings, he'd found himself sinking into the moment and losing himself to the beautiful madness Amelia created with an expertise that left him in awe. She'd taught him how to breathe between strikes, to flex and relax his muscles when the whip fell, tracing red lines between each of his ribs. Then, she'd teased his flaming skin with a feather, the delicate caresses at odds with the pain she'd created using the whip. He'd bowed his head and taken it all —everything she placed upon him, every bit of the pleasure and pain. And even as he sank into the place of perfect submission and comple-tion, he realized that she needed it as much as he did.

Something was wrong with his wife, and she would not tell him. She would not let him in or allow him even a glimpse of what she might be thinking or feeling. Yet, when she stood over him while he knelt, waiting for her to push or pull him in some direction, he tapped into a hidden part of her. A part of her no one else but him knew. He did not have to ask to know that she'd never had such a visceral connection with any of her former submissives. Perhaps with those other men, her role as a dominant had been about control and pleasure ... a bit of sporting fun. Yet, with him, it was more.

They sat now in one of his tenants' cottages—their last visit of the day. The sun had begun to set, and they'd been invited to stay and take tea with the Whittle family. His own cup sat in the saucer he balanced on his knee, practically untouched, as he gazed over at his wife, who sat beside him, listening to Mrs. Whittle carry on about what a talented seamstress her daughter was. The single braid hanging over her shoulder had become a bit disheveled from their long day of riding, leaving a few loose tendrils framing her face. The longing to stroke those strands, to grip that braid and jerk her head back, forcing her to submit to his kiss, slammed into him with all the force of a fist to the gut. The urge to shake her and demand to be let into her heart, her soul, proved even stronger.

Yet, his mother had urged him to be patient with her. So patient, he would be.

"I would love to see some of Miss Mary's creations," Amelia said in response to Mrs. Whittle.

Michael supposed the woman had offered to show off some of her daughter's work, though he'd gotten so lost in thought, he hadn't actually heard the offer. Yet, Amelia rose and set her cup on the side table to her right, while Mary materialized from the kitchen, her eyes bright at the prospect of being able to show off her hand-sewn gowns to a noble lady. Mrs. Whittle beamed proudly as she led them down the hall and toward the back of the cottage—presumably to Mary's room where said gowns were kept.

"Congratulations are in order," said Mr. Whittle from where he sat in an armchair across from the loveseat Michael had been sharing with Amelia. "Your bride is a fine catch ... a beauty and a charmer.

He inclined his head. "Yes, she is. Thank you."

Oh, she had been all smiles and charm in front of each family today, as if she'd wanted them to approve of his new wife. Meanwhile, she'd barely looked at him all day.

Glancing down into his tea, he found himself wishing for something a bit stronger. Becoming foxed seemed a better prospect by the second.

"Word of the house party has been spreading," the man added with a grin. "Mary has not stopped speaking of it since she heard the news from her friend, Alice Stanley. Good of you to invite your tenants, as well, if you don't mind my saying so."

Michael forced a smile. "A tradition of my father's that I intend to uphold. Oakmoor is your home as well as the Darlings' … we want everyone to celebrate our new addition to the family. As well, the opportunity for eligible young ladies such as Miss Mary is one that my mother is most excited about."

Mr. Whittle laughed. "The schemes of a matchmaking mama are always in play."

"So they are," he agreed with a chuckle.

Just then, a small figure in a white nightdress appeared from the back of the house, one finger hanging out of his mouth. John, the youngest of the Whittle brood, had tears in his eyes as he made a dash for his papa.

"What's this?" Mr. Whittle crooned, reaching down to pull the young boy up onto his knee.

"Mama says I must go to bed now," John whined, much to Michael's amusement.

He could remember being that age and trying to escape the dreaded bedtime—which had seemed unfairly early when he'd been this young.

"I see," Mr. Whittle said, keeping his face serious while seeming to fight back a smirk. "Is there anything I can do?"

Wrapping his arms around his father, John nodded. "Make her let me stay up … just a bit longer, Papa. Please?"

Mr. Whittle chuckled. "And have your mother cross with me? I think not. But … how about a bedtime story?"

John nodded emphatically, his blond, cherubic curls bobbing around his face.

Rising and taking the boy under one arm, Mr. Whittle gave him an apologetic glance.

"I'll only be a moment," he promised.

Michael shook his head, his grin genuine this time. "Take your time, I insist."

His tenant returned the smile and turned away, bouncing the boy beneath his arm and tickling his ribs as the two retreated to the back of the house.

Now alone with his thoughts, they turned from brooding ones to happy ones. Watching Mr. Whittle with his son had reminded him of being with his own father. He wondered if, even now, Amelia carried his child. The thought of a young boy with her eyes made him smile. Perhaps that would mend things between him and his wife … new life to turn their collective focus upon something other than the nature of whatever secrets Amelia seemed determined to keep from him.

However, he frowned as he wondered if she would be as distant from their child as she had come to be from him.

"And, we arrive back at brooding," he muttered to himself.

He'd just made up his mind to try to finish off his tea, so as not to be rude, when a commotion from the back of the cottage caught his attention. He straightened, turning his head to glance down the darkened corridor in search of the source.

As he set his tea aside, Mary appeared, her hands clenched over her chest. Her eyes had grown wide, and she seemed to struggle to speak as she met his gaze.

Frowning, he stood. "Is something amiss?"

Mary gaped for a few more moments before finally finding her voice. "Please come … it is Lady Darling … she … well, you must come!"

He crossed the room in a few quick strides, Mary's slender form already halfway down the hall, leading him to an open door through which soft lamplight glowed.

Stumbling to a stop in the doorway, he found Mr. and Mrs. Whittle standing at the foot of their son's small bed—across the room from a larger one that must belong to his elder brother Henry. Mary lingered near the door, hands clapped over her mouth, eyes still wide saucers of disbelief.

On the bed sat John, whimpering with tears in his eyes … and Amelia's arms wrapped tight around him. His wife appeared half crazed, her chest heaving beneath her waistcoat, her eyes wide and wild as they darted about the room. The way she held the child gave Michael pause, and he understood it would be unwise to approach her in such a state. Whatever had happened, Amelia would likely maul anyone who advanced toward the bed, like a lioness protecting a cub.

"Amelia?" he said, keeping his voice low and soothing so as not to worry the family standing around and looking on in openmouthed horror. "My dear, what is the matter?"

Mr. Whittle took a step toward the bed, but a withering glare and a finger pointed accusingly from Amelia stopped him in his tracks.

"Do not come any closer!" she commanded, her face reddening as she kept her finger pointed at the boy's father. "I will not allow you to hurt this child again. Do you hear? I'll see you executed for your crimes, you … you *bastard!*"

Michael's frown deepened as he turned a confused glance to the man. "Whittle, what is the meaning of this?"

He shook his head in disbelief. "I swear to you, I know not what she means. I was simply—"

"I saw you!" Amelia accused, her raised voice causing John to begin sobbing—which only prompted her to hold him tighter. "I saw you climbing into his bed when you thought no one was looking!"

Mr. Whittle's eyes widened in horror, his face reddening in equal parts embarrassment and anger. "Mr. Darling, I can assure you, the lady did not see what she assumes. I did not … I would never … he is my *son*, for the love of God! He's only a boy!"

Michael's gut clenched as he realized what Amelia had assumed. He cast an apologetic glance at the couple and held one arm out, urging them to stay back and allow him to handle this.

Taking a step toward the bed, he moved slowly so as not to startle Amelia—who still watched Mr. Whittle as if she would castrate him if she held a knife.

"Amelia, dear, look at me," he murmured, pausing just beside the bed.

She swiveled her gaze to his, and the fear he found there broke his heart. He had never seen a person so terrified, like an animal cornered by a pack of hunters.

Shaking her head, she choked back a sob. "We can save him, Michael … we can help him. Don't let them hurt him anymore."

He nodded slowly, bracing a hand against the smooth wooden footboard before lowering himself onto the mattress. There remained enough space between them for her to feel safe, but he was close enough to make a grab for the boy if need be.

"No one is going to harm John," he assured her. "You have my word. You trust me … don't you?"

Biting her lower lip, she seemed to struggle with herself for a moment before nodding in agreement.

"Good," he crooned. "Just give him to me, and everything will be all right, I promise. Give me the boy, Amelia."

Her arm tightened around John, and he whimpered, but then fell silent, glancing longingly at his mother.

"Promise me," she whispered, a lone tear falling down one cheek. "Promise me he will be all right."

He forced a smile and nodded. "No harm will come to him … I promise."

She shivered as if cold, holding on to the boy for a moment longer before handing him over. The room remained deathly still as Michael stood, balancing the child on his hip, holding him with one hand while extending the other to Amelia.

"Now you," he urged. "I've got you, too. Come with me."

Keeping her gaze on him, she gave him her hand and allowed him to pull her to her feet. Leading her toward the door, he ensured she had crossed the threshold before turning to deposit the boy into his mother's arms.

Amelia lurched toward the door as if to prevent the exchange, but Michael swept her off her feet, gently putting her over his shoulder and getting a hold of her legs so she could not kick him. He strode for the front door, swiftly taking her outside and setting her on her feet near the post where their horses stood tethered beside the one owned by the Whittles.

"No!" she screamed, flailing as he sat her on her feet, maintaining a tight hold to keep her from running off. "Michael, we must go back! You promised me ... we cannot leave him in there!"

Giving her a little shake, he searched for her eyes in the darkness of the night and the tumble of hair falling into her face.

"Amelia, listen to me!" he bellowed.

"You lied to me," she accused, going limp in his arms and collapsing against him, sobs tearing through her slender body. "You said you would help me protect him."

A lump rose in his throat at the sight of her in distress, and he prayed for the right words—the right actions—to help smooth things over. She had become downright hysterical, and he had no notion of how to handle her this way.

"That man ... he is—"

"A father putting his son to bed," he said firmly, taking her face in his hands and giving her another little shake. "That is all, Amelia. You saw a father tucking his son in for the night."

She shook her head, more tears streaming down her cheeks. "No ... I know what I saw. There was no reason for him to be in that boy's bed."

He frowned, disbelief rippling through him in waves as he realized she honestly believed Mr. Whittle had planned to harm his son.

"Amelia, my father did it every night," he argued. "The man had a book in his hand, just as my father would have. He offered to read the boy a story ... of course he had a reason for being in the bed with him."

She fell silent for a moment, her gaze darting from him to the ground as she seemed to try to reconcile what he was saying with what she had seen. Squeezing her eyes closed, she released a pained sigh and shook her head.

"Oh, God," she whispered hoarsely. "What have I done? I've made a terrible mistake."

His shoulders sagged in relief. She seemed to be coming back to her senses.

"It is all right," he assured her. "You thought that boy was being harmed, and you tried to help him. It was damned brave of you."

Shaking her head, she backed away from him, her jaw clenching as she swiped her tears away. She raised her chin in that stubborn way of hers and sniffed.

"Please convey my apologies to the Whittle family for the misunderstanding," she said, her voice cold and clipped.

Without waiting for him to respond, she whirled and ran to her horse, pulling it free of its post and leaping onto its back.

"Amelia!" he called out as she wheeled the beast around and dug her heels into its side, prompting it into a swift gallop. "Amelia, wait!"

But, she was gone, swallowed by the trees, only her silhouette visible along the moonlit path.

Running both hands through his hair, he stared after her, at a loss as to what to do. One thing he felt certain of was the nature of Amelia's secret.

Someone had done something terrible to her when she'd been a child, and she, obviously, had never recovered from it. His heart ached for the woman he loved as he stood there wracking his brain for a way to help her, to heal her.

But, even if he could think of a way, the question remained: would she let him?

# CHAPTER 15

$\mathcal{A}$melia paced her chambers and sucked in deep breaths, trying to force herself to calm down. She'd been shaken to her core by what had occurred at the Whittles' house, and now her every nerve stood on alert, the palms of her hands tingling with the agitation plaguing her entire body.

She'd thought she had seen it all so clearly—little John in his bed with the imposing figure of his father looming over him. The covers being turned back, the man bracing one knee on the mattress as if to climb over the boy.

Closing her eyes now to blot out the memory, she whimpered, sweat breaking out over her brow from the effort it took not to scream.

She'd thought she had seen it all so clearly, but what she'd actually witnessed was, apparently, normal behavior for a father.

But, how could she have known when no one had ever tucked her into bed? Simon would allow her to sleep with him when she grew afraid of the dark or did not want to be alone. But no one had ever pulled the covers up to her chin or kissed her brow. No one had ever read her a bedtime story.

How could she have known that it was perfectly natural and normal for a man to share a bed with his son? How could she have known that the man hadn't meant his son any harm?

Her throat constricted as she thought of her brother, who had been abused almost nightly for years, with her helpless to do anything to stop it. She had watched her Uncle Gregory approach his bed, pull the covers back, and brace one knee upon the mattress … just as she'd seen Mr. Whittle do … and each time, she'd been paralyzed with fear. Not that there had been anything she could have done. She had only been a girl. But tonight, she'd been a woman grown—a lady with the power to save a poor boy from the same fate.

A boy who—as it turned out—hadn't needed her interference.

The family must think she was mad. And Michael … her heart sank as she wondered what her husband must think of her. If she hadn't driven him away with her distance and silence, then surely, she had done so with her erratic behavior.

The door of her dressing room swung open, and Michael appeared in the doorway, his face haggard and drawn. A day's worth of stubble had begun growing upon his jaw, and his eyes held a weariness she had caused. He approached her slowly, as if she were a skittish doe he was afraid to chase off.

"Amelia—"

"I do hope the Whittle family was not too put off by my behavior," she interrupted, turning to face him with her hands clenched behind her back. She needed to get a hold of herself … She *would* pull herself together.

"I explained that it was a simple misunderstanding," he replied, crossing his arms over his chest. "They were a bit confused, but understood once I smoothed things over. Mrs. Whittle was concerned about you, but I assured her you would be all right."

She shrugged. "And so I am."

He frowned, the exhaustion in his expression giving way to anger. "No, Amelia, you are not. I think we both know that. Additionally, I've grown tired of pretending I don't see that you are *not* all right."

Turning her back to him, she faced the hearth. "Nonsense. I haven't the slightest idea what you refer to."

His strong hands gripped her shoulders, and he spun her to face him, shaking her just as he had outside the Whittles' cottage.

"Enough! Enough avoidance, and enough of your games. I am your husband, and I am not asking here. You will tell me what on Earth led you to believe that Mr. Whittle intended to …"

He trailed off, proving to her that he was too naïve and pure to even say the words. A man wise in the ways of the world, perhaps, but one from such a perfect family, he could never imagine even saying it, let alone witnessing it.

"I do not have to explain anything to you," she snapped, shrugging out of his hold and moving swiftly around him to put some distance between them. "You do not make demands of me … *I* am Mistress here, and don't you ever forget it. I make the demands, Michael, not you."

Her skin suddenly felt too tight, his nearness causing her to become far too aware of how close she stood on a precipice. Once she fell over it, she might not survive what awaited her at the bottom—the truth, the realization that Michael was pure while she was sullied, dirty, broken. Not good enough for the likes of him. The irony of it was not lost on her—that she, the noble lady could be unworthy of a farmer with calloused hands and dirt beneath his fingernails. And yet, it proved truer than anything else she had ever known.

Turning to face him again, she hardened herself, clenching her jaw as she clasped her hands behind her back and squared her shoulders.

"On your knees," she ordered.

He blinked, starting as if taken aback. "What?"

Approaching him, she allowed the mantle of the Mistress to slip over her shoulders. Her emotions were too sharp, their edges pricking her and making her bleed from the inside. She needed to dull her senses and lose herself in the familiar.

She needed him to give himself to her.

"Kneel," she said, refusing to break his gaze. "Now."

For a long moment, he did not respond. He did not move, and seemed to even hold his breath as their eyes clashed.

Amelia could not breathe, her very soul vibrating inside her body as she waited for him to succumb—to submit and let her lose herself in him. It was all she had—this ability to turn the pain she'd been dealt into pleasure ... for them both.

Finally, he spoke, uttering the last word she would have expected to hear.

"No."

She advanced on him, hands clenching into fists. "That word means nothing to me."

Before she could get her hands on him, he rose one eyebrow and uttered another word she'd never have expected.

"Dimple."

She faltered, the word bringing her up short like a palm to the face. Her mouth fell open as the sting of his rejection radiated over her skin.

"Why?" she demanded.

Shaking his head, he sighed. "Because I will not allow you to go on using me to soothe your pain this way ... not until you tell me why. Not until you tell me who hurt you and how."

Panic flared swiftly at the thought of having to bare everything to him—tell him not only Simon's secrets, but her own.

"No," she declared.

Snorting derisively, he turned away as if to leave the room, and she felt as if he had snatched her heart from her chest and taken it with him. In their short time together, she'd done many things to him, treated him to her swiftly changing moods and odd behavior. Never once had he turned his back on her. Never once had he walked away.

Many men had taken their leave of her—she'd sent just as many packing when she'd finished with them.

But not once had she wanted to chase after one, do anything it took to keep one.

Until her husband.

"Michael, please," she called out, halting him at the door.

She had never begged anyone for anything—her pride had not allowed it. But for Michael, she would toss her pride aside. Couldn't he see she could not give him what he asked for? Not without tearing herself apart ... and then, what would be left of her for him?

With one hand braced on the doorknob, he turned back to look at her. The urge to stay and the need to leave warred in his eyes. She could not blame him for not knowing where he stood with her. She hardly knew herself.

"One night," he said, his voice low. "Submit to me for one night, and I will let the matter drop."

The panic she'd experienced earlier was now full-fledged terror. Give herself to him, fully, relinquishing all control? She could not do it.

"I cannot," she choked.

He shook his head. "You can ... you simply *will* not."

"You don't understand," she countered.

"No, I do not," he agreed. "And that is your fault, Amelia. You will tell me nothing, and I cannot see into your mind—as much as I might wish to. I've done all I know to do to prove that I would never hurt you ... that I care for you. Yet, you spurn me at every turn. As of this moment, I am done. I cannot do this any longer."

The knob turned, and the sound of the door creaking open brought tears to her eyes. Something told her that once he crossed that threshold, he would not be back. They would live separate lives unless she could give him what he wanted. She would lose him forever.

"Wait," she called out before he could leave. "Don't go."

Wiping her damp palms on her breeches, she swallowed through her tightly clenched throat. What she was about to do, she'd never done for any other man. None of them had meant as much to her as Michael. What could it hurt to give him this one night? If she did, perhaps he would stay true to his word not to continue prying into her past. Perhaps, they could both simply forget about it and move on.

The prospect of allowing him the freedom to do what he wanted with her terrified her to no end. But losing him forever frightened her more.

Clenching her shaking hands, she slowly sank to her knees on the floor. She clasped her hands behind her back and lifted her eyes to meet his gaze. The hunger and affection swirling in the blue depths captivated her, even while it sent a tremor of trepidation down her spine.

Forcing her tongue to move, she spoke her words of surrender.

"My safe word is darling."


Michael could hardly believe what was happening. As he began undressing his wife, slowly unfastening the row of buttons running down the front of her waistcoat, he wondered what had prompted her sudden change of heart. Perhaps she had been afraid she would chase him away forever if she did not give in. Or, she was more terrified of revealing her secrets than he'd first supposed—so terrified, she'd rather reverse their roles for a night than tell him the truth.

A part of him still wanted to walk through that door, to leave her behind and free himself from the frustrating mess she made of his senses. But like a fly trapped in a spider's web, he had become ensnared. The beautiful torture of loving her was one he willingly endured.

Tonight, however, he would take what she offered, if for no other reason than to show her without words what was in his heart. His domination would be of a different sort than she probably imagined … he would not punish her; he had no need to teach her. Instead, he would do everything she'd never allowed him, love her in all the ways she'd previously spurned.

Starting with undressing her.

She'd always come to him adorned in her boots, corset, and shirt. He had wanted the privilege of removing each layer of her clothing, and now, would let him—because unless she uttered her safe word, he was not going to stop.

He'd urged her to her feet and began by unwinding her long, black braid, combing his fingers through the strands. Next, he tossed her waistcoat aside, taking the time to run his hands over her arms, gripping her palms and intertwining their fingers. He kissed her knuckles, took each finger of her left hand into his mouth, caressing the digits with his tongue, then flicking it at the thin skin of one wrist. She gasped and squirmed against him, her eyes wide and naked in their dread as she watched his every move.

"Do not be afraid," he murmured, backing her toward the bed.

"I am not," she assured him as she sat upon the mattress and let him pull one of her boots off.

*Oh, my dear, but you are,* he thought as he freed her from the second boot and tossed it aside.

She was frightened witless, but he would not injure her pride by pointing it out. When they were finished, it was his hope that she would trust him as she never had before—understand that he loved her.

He made quick work of her breeches, leaving them in a pile along with her other clothing before reaching for the cravat still tied neatly around her throat. Loosening it, he freed it from her shirt and pulled it between his hands, folding it over until it resembled a blindfold.

She watched his hands, biting her lip again as she waited for him to take away her sight. Her limbs stiffened when the cloth fell over her eyes, but she remained silent as he tied it around her head in a quick, efficient knot. Her breath hitched, quickening into short pants, but he soothed her forehead with a reassuring kiss. If she could not see him, she could not anticipate his every move and steel herself for them. He wanted her defenses lowered, her body open and vulnerable to him in a way it had never been.

He left her perched on the edge of the bed as he quickly relieved himself of his own clothing, his cock already hard at the sight of the offering she presented, undressed except for her shirt, and his for the taking.

Lifting her effortlessly, he moved her so that she lay back against the pillows, then busied himself with the tasseled cords tying the curtains to the bedposts. He untied two of them, then climbed onto the bed and used them to bind her wrists. He stretched her arms out wide, lashing each to opposite posts, rendering her helpless. She sank into the pillows with a sigh, her even breathing telling him that she was fighting for control—of her own fears, of the anxiety that allowing herself to be helpless with him caused.

Straddling her hips, he stared down at her, his priceless offering. Cupping her face with one hand, he ran his thumb over her lips.

"God, that mouth of yours has been tempting me since the moment I first saw you," he murmured, applying pressure to her bottom lip to part it from the upper. "Such beautiful lips … and that smile of yours … you could drive a man to madness with just this mouth."

The smirk she used to tease him appeared, and she arched her back. "Would you like to fuck my mouth, Master?"

A heady tide of desire and primal sense of ownership washed over him at the sound of that title falling from her lips. His prick throbbed with the need to take her up on her offer, to shove his cock into her mouth and fuck those pretty lips.

He kissed her instead, gripping her chin and holding her at the angle he wanted and plundering her with his tongue. He kissed her until her chest heaved from heavy breath, until she grew limp beneath him, her mouth hungrily meeting his, her tongue engaging his in the familiar, sultry dance.

"Did I mention how much I love that dirty tongue?" he said once he'd pulled his mouth away from hers. "Maybe later, thank you. For now, I've something else in mind."

Moving down her body, he knelt at her feet. Then, taking one ankle in his hand, he raised her leg and lowered his lips to the top of her foot.

She shuddered when he kissed her there, then traced a path higher, over her shin and toward the inside of the leg. He flicked his tongue at her skin, then laved it up toward her knee and higher, to her inner thigh.

She cried out, her hips surging up off the bed as he neared her pelvis. But instead of giving her what she wanted, he pulled back, reaching for her other leg. She heaved a sigh and pouted, her lower lip jutting out and making him chuckle. He treated the second leg as he had the first, kissing his way toward her center, but coming just short of the one place she wanted him.

She grunted in frustration, pulling at her bonds, but finding them too tight for her to escape. Bracing his palms against her thighs, he pushed them open swiftly, spreading her and lying down on his belly right between them. He released her only long enough to push the bottom of her shirt up to expose her mons and the smooth patch of her lower belly above it. She whimpered, a panicked sound in response to the lifting of her shirt.

"Shh," he crooned, pushing at her thighs again and holding fast to keep her spread for him. "Just let me, Amelia. Let me …"

He nuzzled her lower belly, inhaling her scent and kissing his way downward. She shuddered beneath him, her skin breaking out in gooseflesh as he trailed kisses toward the dark curls shielding her core. She sucked in a sharp breath and held it, waiting, anticipating.

Using his thumbs to open her, he laid his tongue against her inner flesh and closed his lips around her, groaning at the taste of her, feminine and sweet. She cried out, hips bucking as he tasted and teased her, swirling his tongue against her clit and suckling with gentle but steady pressure.

His erection became painful as her taste and the musical sounds of her moans combined to drive him nearly mad. He wanted inside of her, but he hadn't finished yet. He had hardly even begun.

Still suckling at her clit with steady pulls of his tongue and lips, he released one of her thighs to ease his middle finger into her channel. The evidence of her pleasure soaked him, easing the way inside of her.

She shuddered, her back arching and drawing tight as a bowstring as he urged her closer and closer to completion.

"Michael," she whispered, her voice heavy and thick with desire. "God … Michael."

He gave her another finger, reaching deeper into her, using his combined digits to make love to her slowly, achingly, mimicking what he would soon do to her with his cock. Her hips bucked more forcefully, and her entire body quivered with the oncoming climax, so he gave her more. He quickened his fingers, reaching so deep that her juices soaked his third knuckles, and didn't stop—not even when she began convulsing around him, her satiny inner walls clenching his fingers as she screamed and trembled beneath him. He kept lapping at her, tasting her completion while she fell apart, her legs becoming limp as she sank into the mattress and gave herself over to her culmination.

Only when she'd gone completely still, her moans dissipating into soft sighs, did he cease, reluctantly pulling his fingers free of her sheath. Licking his fingers clean for one last taste of her, he crawled up over her body, settling his hips in the cradle between hers. He gritted his teeth at the feel of her cunt, hot and wet and pressed against his cock. Resisting the urge to impale her, he rocked his hips against hers, his eyes sliding closed as he took a moment to indulge, to revel in the pleasure of being pressed so tightly up against her.

She trembled against him, her arms jerking at the ropes, her hips undulating to meet each of his movements as if she searched for another rapturous ending.

"That's it, Amelia," he urged when she started moaning again, the friction between them creating the perfect pressure as he fit his cock between her lower lips and up against her clit. "Spend for me again, love … again and again."

She splintered with a cry, burying her face against his shoulder. He registered dampness against his chest—tears, he realized, wetting the cravat covering her eyes. Yet, she came forcefully, her body jerking beneath him as she moaned her pleasure while he went on rocking against her, drawing it out until the last possible second.

She became limp beneath him once more, her breath coming in rough spurts. As if she fought to contain whatever she was feeling, as if he was making her lose control of it all.

He began kissing her again, taking her mouth, then her chin, then her throat. She sobbed, arching her back as he tasted her pulse point, then her collarbone.

"Michael, please …"

Pausing just over her breastbone and the heart beating beneath it, he gazed up at her. "I know, love … I know. Just give in. Let me love you."

She tipped her head back as if in surrender, and he went on kissing her, unbuttoning her shirt as he went. He kissed the skin he bared inch by inch, slowly parting the open sides to reveal her breasts. Cupping them, he squeezed and kneaded, tweaked her nipples with this thumbs and forefingers, taking first one and then the other into his mouth. Her nipples tickled his tongue, hardening in response to his teasing licks and nips.

"Take me," she begged, arching her back as if to invite him in. "I can't take anymore … please, just fuck me."

Pausing, he glanced down at her face. Her cheeks had become flushed, her lips parted as she gasped for air. He could feel her heart pounding between them, in tandem with his. She was soaking wet, the tantalizing temptation of her channel just inches away from his cock and his for the taking.

"Is that what you want?" he murmured, nuzzling the side of her neck and gently biting her earlobe.

Surging her pelvis against his, she sent a shiver through him. "Yes … yes, Michael."

He would give in … but on his terms, in the way he wanted. Disengaging from her body, he came up on his knees and leaned over her to loosen her wrists. Once she had been freed, he rolled her over onto her belly. She stiffened and lifted her head, turning as if to search for him despite being blind.

"Michael?"

"Shh," he admonished. "I am doing what you asked … this is how I want to take you."

He re-tied one of her wrists to the bed, then straddled her hips while he leaned over to do the other. She squirmed beneath him, but he pressed his knees together, rendering her motionless between them as he finished his work. Now splayed belly-down, her arms stretched out and bound, she was more vulnerable to him than she'd ever been.

Head still raised, she released a panicked, strangled sound from deep in her throat. "Michael …"

He pressed a gentle hand to her head and eased it back down, caressing her hair and then moving it aside to bare her neck.

"No more running, Amelia," he said as he lowered himself on top of her and fit his cock against the cleft between her thighs. "You are mine now … say it."

She gasped as he entered her, resting his pelvis against her arse and pausing there, nestled deep inside. He grasped a handful of her hair and gave it a little tug, biting down gently on the delicate tendons of her neck.

She cried out, her channel squeezing around him and soaking him in another flood of moisture. "I am yours."

His chest swelled as he began to move inside of her. He released his next breath on a hoarse groan as her sheath stroked him, tight as a fist, and so, so wet. She raised her hips as much as his body atop hers would allow, taking him in deeper. He thrust at her, increasing speed with each surge of his hips, unable to stop the instinct of his body to drive as hard and deep inside of her as he could.

Her cries hit a crescendo as she reached her peak yet again, her hands wrapping around the ropes keeping her captive as she held on and surrendered to another release.

"Again, Amelia," he urged her, coming up on his knees over her and palming her buttocks without ceasing his movements inside of her. "Say it again."

"I am yours," she managed between moans, before her head dropped, her body going still beneath him.

She sighed softly as he continued fucking her, his fingers digging into the flesh of her taut buttocks as he strained toward his own release, needing to claim her with the marking of his seed, to fill her with his essence.

His gaze then fell to the accursed shirt still on her back—still separating parts of her from him, still hiding what she did not want him to see. Could she truly be his while she continued to don her armor while in their bed?

No, he decided. No, she could not.

Taking hold of the shirt's collar with both hands, he paused mid-thrust and seated himself inside of her. There could be no more barriers—nothing else between them. Not this night.

"Michael, don't," she said suddenly, the panic in her voice clear.

He paused for a moment, his arms clenching and rippling with the strength it would take to do what needed to be done. She'd begun thrashing beneath him again, twisting her body as if to angle her back away from him, but unable to with her arms spread out and tied to the posts.

"Please," she begged. "Please, don't do this."

Swallowing past the pity that her cries and tears had caused, he reminded himself that she had submitted to him. She was his tonight, unless she called out the one word that could put a stop to it. He'd been listening carefully for the word, vowing to stop the moment she uttered it.

Yet, she had not.

If she wished for him to leave her secrets intact, she would call out her safe word. In the absence of any such barriers, he did what he'd wanted to do the moment she first came to bed with him wearing a shirt just like this one.

He ripped it straight down the middle.

# CHAPTER 16

$\mathcal{A}$melia went still beneath Michael, grief stabbing her like the sharpest of daggers as the one part of her she'd always wanted to keep hidden from him was revealed. Deep down, she'd always known he would discover it, but she'd hoped to reveal it all on her own terms. Yet, he had not given her a choice, demanding her surrender and then tearing away the last piece of armor she possessed to protect herself.

A sob lodged in her throat, and she choked it down as she waited for him to pull away from her, to display disgust at the sight of what she could no longer hide.

Scars. So many of them, even the mirror could not help her keep count. They covered her back, white and puckered and hideous. His gaze upon them burned as much as the initial injury had, and she began to tremble from the force of her shame.

"My God, Amelia," he said, his voice so vehemently angry that a fresh flow of tears began.

Now he was furious that she'd hidden this from him ... that she had never told him he'd married a scarred woman. A broken woman.

She sobbed, turning her head to bury it in the pillows. At least she had been robbed of her sight so that she did not have to look him in the eye and witness his disgust.

But then, his hand was on her, his fingers tracing the scars with tenderness and reverence. She frowned, wondering what he could be about.

"He did this to you, didn't he?" he ground out, his voice strained as if he spoke from between clenched teeth. "Your uncle."

Unable to find her voice, she simply nodded as he went on touching her, smoothing his hands over her tortured back. The wounds had long ago healed, yet the phantom pain the memories brought had never been fresher.

Michael's hands left her to be replaced by his lips, and he kissed her so tenderly, she thought she might die from the way each touch of his mouth made her heart swell in her chest.

"My beautiful Amelia," he whispered against her skin. "I'm so sorry … I didn't know … I couldn't have imagined."

Her body unwound beneath his in acceptance of this—the affection she'd craved her entire life and had never been given. He was moving inside of her again now, ever so slowly, worshipping her with his cock while his lips paid her supplication, gliding over her scars like the most soothing of balms.

"You are safe with me, and so are your secrets," he told her as he covered his body with hers, as if to illustrate his own words. "I will never hurt you. Do you understand? I love you, Amelia. I love you so much."

She sobbed, the sound coming off on a tortured moan as he reached some place inside her that caused her toes to curl. The pleasure mingled with her tumultuous emotions proved too much. She wanted to beg him to stop. Yet, she never wanted it to end.

She must have uttered something to that effect aloud, because he replied as if she had.

"I will never stop," he said, his pelvis grinding against her arse as he dug deep into her, as if trying to touch her heart. "No matter what you reveal to me about yourself … no matter how ugly your past … I will never stop loving you."

She spent with a shudder and another sob, unable to still her convulsions or quiet the sounds he forced from her as he kept thrusting, stroking inside of her a few more times before following her, coming on a low groan.

The hot gush of his seed flooded her, bathing her insides in his possession. His arms came around her, and he clung to her for a long while, still lodged inside her as his harsh breaths tickled her ear.

After a moment, he finally moved from on top of her, quickly releasing her wrists from their bonds and pulling away the tattered remnants of her shirt. She sagged onto the bed, too exhausted and wrung dry to move, to try to escape him or cover herself. What was the use? He'd already seen her.

Yet, she was relieved when he turned her onto her back. She could feel him settling against her side, wrapping his arms around her and holding her close, then covering them both with the bedclothes.

Then, the cravat fell away from her face, and she stared into his eyes, warm and kind and filled with sadness on her behalf.

She forced a swallow, trying to get her voice to work so she could explain, so she could tell him that she'd had her reasons for keeping it a secret.

He pressed his lips to hers before she could speak, cupping her face and wiping away the last of her tears. When he pulled away, he shook his head as if to silence her.

"There will be time enough for talk later," he whispered, stroking the line of her jaw. "For now, just let me hold you."

She acquiesced, nestling her face against his chest and finding a moment of peace in his embrace. For now, she must give him what he asked—after all, she'd agreed to submit for a night that had not yet ended.

Yet, even as she surrendered to his comforting hold, Amelia knew this could not last. She could not allow him to undress her night after night, his touch upon her back forever reminding her of those scars and the man who had created them. By keeping them hidden, she'd been able to pretend they did not exist. That her Uncle Gregory had not irreparably destroyed her, leaving behind a reminder of who he was and what he'd done long after he had died.

She simply did not think she could survive it.

Michael came awake the next morning to find Amelia gone from their bed. Frowning as he blinked against the light streaming through the windows, he laid a hand in the place she'd occupied through the night. The sheets no longer held her warmth, so she must have risen early.

It should not have surprised him. Since becoming the lady of Oakmoor, she'd approached her duties with an eagerness that had consumed most of her free time. His mother had informed him that she rose early, in keeping with country hours, and he had it on good authority that she often worked and entertained up until it came time to dress for dinner.

However, after such an emotional night, he would have wanted her to rest. As well, he had hoped they could talk—about the scars on her back and their cause, about what had happened at the Whittles' home.

About the fact that he'd confessed his love for her.

Surprisingly, having said the words to her aloud had been freeing. As if he could now accept his feelings more easily because he'd voiced them aloud.

He loved Amelia.

It seemed like a simple fact, one among many others that made up the man that Michael Darling had become. He possessed blond hair and blue eyes. There was a scar on one of his legs caused by a fall when he'd been a lad. He liked his tea with lemon and nothing else. Unlike most of his peers, his left hand was his dominant one.

And, he loved Lady Amelia Darling.

With that revelation came peace of mind. Everything would be all right. Perhaps she would be angry with him for forcing her hand last night. She might even close herself off to him again for a time.

But, he had faith that loving her would be sufficient. Perhaps, it would even prove enough to earn her love in return. He'd grown up watching his father love his mother with all of his heart, every hour of every day. He had watched them navigate life together with the sort of joy and strength that inspired him. And he refused to settle for anything different when it came to his wife. It might be harder to come by, but that would only make it all the sweeter in the end.

Stretching with a groan, he left the bed, deciding to shirk work for the day in favor of finding her and hashing things out. Perhaps a ride across the estate would be in order. With so much open space around them and the privacy it would afford, they could say everything that needed to be said without worrying about others in the house listening in.

That decided, he dressed without ringing for Oliver. There was no time, and he did not have the patience to sit still while the valet shaved him. Raking a hand through the haphazard strands of hair falling into his eyes, he took the stairs two at a time and trotted toward the dining room, hoping he would catch her at breakfast.

He found his mother and sister seated alone, their near-empty plates resting on the table before them. Pausing near the door, he ignored his rumbling stomach and the tantalizing aroma of food.

"Have either of you seen Amelia?" he asked.

His mother stared at him in solemn silence, appearing as if the question required an answer she'd rather not give. His skin prickled with a premonition that only grew stronger when Lydia rose from her chair and approached him with hands balled into fists. His eyes darted about the room and through the parted curtains out the window—searching for Amelia in the corners of the room, then out on the estate grounds. Any glimpse of her to dispel the unease causing his heart to sink into his stomach.

"What did you do to her?" Lydia accused, her jaw hard as she glared up at him.

He flinched as if she'd struck him. "Nothing. I … she was just with me last night."

Lydia glanced away, her maidenly sensibilities coloring her cheeks at what his words implied. Though outspoken and brash, she was, after all, still only a girl, and a maiden.

"Whatever you've done, you must fix it," she said, crossing her arms over her chest. "Fix it, and bring my new sister home."

"Lydia, enough," their mother reprimanded, rising slowly from her chair at the table. "Whatever has happened between Michael and Amelia does not concern us. It is not our affair."

Michael gripped the doorframe, his entire body trembling as his mother's words seemed to come at him through a pane of glass. He could not think past Lydia's accusing words, of what they meant.

*Bring my new sister home.*

Did that mean Amelia had left him?

He shook his head and returned to the moment just as their mother cut Lydia's protests short and banished her from the room, sending her off to practice the pianoforte. His little sister cast him a glare on her way out, a promise of the tongue lashing to come—when their mother was not around to silence her.

Ignoring her, he turned to his mother, who folded her hands and met his gaze. In her eyes lingered pity and motherly concern.

"Michael …"

He drew a deep breath and attempted to compose himself. Once she told him what he already knew to be true, he could not be certain how he might react.

"Mother," he ground out, clenching his teeth to keep from releasing a tortured roar. "Where is my wife?"

With a heavy sigh, she reached into the pocket of her morning gown and retrieved a sealed envelope. She approached him and laid the letter in his hand. Glancing up at him, she creased her brow, the lines around her mouth becoming deeper and more pronounced.

"She asked me to give this to you before she left," she said while he tore open the envelope to retrieve the slip of parchment inside. "I tried to convince her to wait until you awakened so the two of you could speak, but she would hear nothing of it. She wanted to attempt to travel by hired post-chaise, but I convinced her to take one of our carriages. Oh, Michael, I tried to stop her, but once I realized she could not be swayed, I wanted her to be protected on the road."

He nodded absently as he tuned his mother out and read Amelia's brief missive. In short, clipped sentences, she informed him that she had returned to London for the christening of her niece and nephew. After that, she tersely explained that she thought it best to make the trip alone due to the events of the previous evening. Perhaps, she said, a time of separation would do them both some good. She would send for Lydia before the start of the next Season to begin preparing her for the big coming out.

She signed it simply '*Regards, Amelia.*'

Crumpling the paper in one hand and the envelope in the other, he closed his eyes and fought to get a handle on his temper. As it was, the impersonal note made him want to put his fist through the oak-paneled wall. Which would only upset his mother, and likely result in a broken hand. Neither appealed to him.

After a few deep, slow breaths, he opened his eyes to find her watching him closely, as if prepared for him to act on the rage causing his vision to grow hazy.

"You did the right thing," he managed around the lump in his throat, the grief threatening to choke him.

She nodded, releasing a breath as if relieved. "I meant what I said to Lydia, so I will not ask you what has happened. But ... what will you do?"

Tightening his fists around the offending letter and envelope, he whirled toward the door, his boots thudding over the carpet.

"She is my wife," he threw over his shoulder before exiting the dining room. "I am going after her."

He could have sworn he heard his mother mutter 'Thank God,' but he did not respond. Bounding up the stairs, he bellowed for Oliver.

Throwing open the door of his chambers, he screamed for the valet again, who appeared with wide, curious eyes.

"Prepare for a journey to London," he snapped, tossing the crumbled note into the hearth. "We will be joining Lady Darling for the christening of my niece and nephew."

Oliver inclined his head in acknowledgement and then disappeared into his dressing room. While the valet packed, he approached the hearth, deciding to channel his rage into burning the parchment and envelope. If he could no longer see them, he did not have to feel the pain of knowing she could toss him aside so callously.

Did he mean nothing to her, after he'd bared his soul to her, confessed his love, and attempted to show her that he cared nothing about her scars or the burdens of her past? Was this what being patient and willing to submit every time she asked had earned him?

Glaring into the flames, he vowed to extract the answers from her. She could not run from him … he would not allow it.

Once the paper had been burned away to ash, he sank into an armchair and stared into the hearth, his anger melting into despair.

Dash it all, he loved her. Was that not enough? Perhaps not, if his wife did not feel the same way he did. Part of him wanted to believe she loved him in return—or, at least, was coming to love him. He wanted to believe he'd seen it in her gaze, felt it in her kiss and her touch.

Yet, another part of him feared what he would find when he arrived in London. That he would come to see that it had all truly been one-sided … that he loved a woman who would prove incapable of loving him back.

Despite that fear, nothing would stop him from going after her, from taking her into his arms and demanding answers. For better or worse, he would know where he stood with her.

And, like it or not, he would accept whatever he was given and return to Oakmoor where he belonged when all had been said and done.

# CHAPTER 17

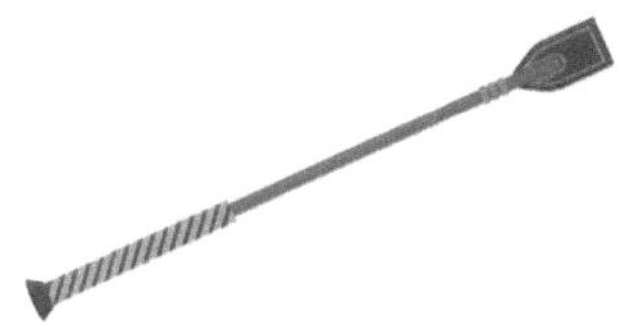

Amelia took another sip of her champagne, giggling as the bubbles tickled her nose. This would be her fifth—no, sixth —glass this evening, and she was not the least bit ashamed of that fact. Truly, the more she imbibed, the better she felt—the cares of her abandoned life at Oakmoor slipping away. She had hardly thought of Michael at all since arriving in London, taking up residence at Ashton House, and falling back in with her old friends.

No, she absolutely had not thought of him while lying alone in her bed, her body aching for the touch of strong hands. No, she most certainly did *not* think the gold waistcoat of the man who'd hosted last night's ball could be compared to Michael's blond hair. No, she had not cringed when putting her hand in the grasp of a male acquaintance for a waltz and finding it to be soft and free of callouses.

No, she most certainly did not miss her husband.

Keeping a tight hold on her champagne glass, she took up the dice and rattled them in her hand for a moment while those crowded around the Hazard table cheered for her. She'd lost heavily since arriving a few hours prior, but a few more rolls of the dice could change her luck. And even if they did not, she was exceedingly wealthy, more so than most of the people in this room. Besides, she had inebriated herself to the point of no longer caring how much money she'd lost. None of it mattered, anyway. Her husband possessed more than half her dowry, much of which had been put back into Oakmoor. The rest was hers to do with what she wished.

Rolling the dice, she closed her eyes and swayed upon her feet as the room began to spin. The cries of delight and hands pounding her shoulders in congratulations told her she had come out triumphant for this turn. Shaking her head, she opened her eyes and found herself confronted with another glass of champagne. A friend slipped it into her hand with a grin, taking her empty one.

Sir Arthur Reeves, a mutual acquaintance of the Widow Dane—who, she felt certain, had always wanted to fuck her. With her return to London so soon after being married, he must think her tired of her husband already and in search of a new lover.

Waving a dismissive hand, she accepted the champagne and turned away from him. He stood a snowball's chance in Hell with her, but she would never turn down a glass of champagne. Especially when it was making her feel so bloody good.

Somewhere inside the gaming hell, someone had begun playing a violin while another man sang in a pleasant enough voice. Hands grabbed her waist, someone spinning her playfully away from the Hazard table and toward a large opening in the middle of the room. The stranger swayed with her in a playful waltz, his frame too slender and not nearly as strong as Michael's. She huffed in disappointment, but did not try to pull away, allowing him to spin her about like a rag doll while she greedily consumed half the champagne in one gulp. She hiccupped and then giggled again, the giddiness that washed over her melting away the pain.

The pain of knowing she could never be good enough for her husband—a man as pure and as good as they came. The pain of remembering what had been done to her, what she'd witnessed being done to Simon … all of it a reminder that she was tainted … spoiled … damaged goods.

Another hiccup, then a burp, which she muffled with one hand. She tittered, and her dancing partner chuckled. He wanted to fuck her, too, she realized, the evidence of his lust pressing against her belly as they danced. It sickened her. All men ever wanted was her cunt. Why did none of them want her smiles, or her laughs, or her mind? Why did none of them know how to please her, or what she liked?

Why could none of them be as perfect as her husband?

Her partner suddenly stopped, slamming her into a wall. Scowling at him, she lamented the loss of her champagne—the rest of which had sloshed out of the flute when she'd collided with the wall.

Releasing her, the man backed away, his eyes growing wide as if he'd seen a ghost. With a shrug, she lifted her glass.

"It's only a bit of spilled champagne, silly," she slurred, swaying a bit as the spinning in her head grew faster. So fast, she felt as if she might be sick.

Shaking his head, the man continued staring at the wall behind her. Then, the wall shifted, and warm air stirred the back of her neck. She stiffened as she recognized the scent enveloping her, the hard plane pressed against her proving to be a man's wide, rigid chest.

Hands gripped her shoulders before she could blink, and she found herself spun around, her gaze lifting to clash with a pair of eyes that struck both fear and desire into the pit of her gut. Her knees went weak, but his hands tightened on her arms, dragging her against the sinful body encased in a bottle-green coat and buff breeches. He tore his gaze from her and glared at her dance partner, who quickly disappeared into the crowd to escape his wrath.

A low sound of surrender emitted from her as his eyes returned to hers—angry and relieved all at once. And yet, her body rebelled, stiffening in his hold, the familiar fear sinking in as he bent to lift her up over one of his shoulders.

Her breath was forced from her when her stomach bounced against his shoulder, and she grew even dizzier as he began walking, keeping a tight hold on her legs. The gaming hell became a blur around her, and then they were out in the alley, disappearing through a side door.

"Is she all right?" asked the familiar voice of Oliver, the valet.

"She is," Michael answered tersely before putting her back on her feet. "But I cannot promise that she will still be by the end of the night."

A shudder wracked her at the anger she heard in his tone, at the same time her head began spinning again from being set so suddenly back upright. Oliver disappeared onto the perch of the carriage along with the driver while Michael opened the door of the coach. His jaw and chin jutted out stubbornly as he pointed at the interior.

"Get in," he growled. "Now."

She hesitated for a moment, which seemed to be all he needed to take charge once more, because before she knew it, he'd practically thrown her onto the carriage seat before climbing in after her and slamming the door. Pounding on the roof of the vehicle with his fist, he alerted the driver, and they were off.

Swallowing past her suddenly thickened tongue, she pressed herself back against the carriage seat, seeking even an inch of distance between them. He seemed so large in this space, his bulky frame over-whelming her in its proximity.

"What are you doing here?" she managed, tearing her gaze away from him and staring off into the darkness.

The hour was late, and his attire had looked a bit rumpled in the moonlight streaming through the open curtains, as if he'd been trav-eling all day. Likely, he hadn't even bothered to stop at Ashton House before coming to seek her out. How had he known where she would be? Did he know her so well already after such a short time together?

He scoffed as if she'd insulted him. "When a man's wife runs off to London with nary a good-bye, he goes after her."

Folding her arms across her chest, she went on avoiding her gaze. "I did not run off. I came for the christening."

His fist slammed against the carriage wall, and she nearly leapt from the seat, startled by the sudden movement.

"You *left* me!" he roared, his thunderous voice nearly shaking the carriage. "All I have ever done since we married was try to get to know my wife. I have given you everything you've asked me for—submission, respect, the distance you needed to keep your secrets until you were ready to share them—"

"But I wasn't ready, was I?" she bellowed, cutting him off mid-sentence. "Perhaps, in time, I would have been, but you could not be content with that!"

"You left me with no choice," he countered.

"You *took* my choice!" she accused, not caring that she now yelled loud enough to be heard by their driver and Oliver. "You took that away from me when you tied me to that bed and tore the shirt from my back. What you revealed was *my* secret, *my* shame. It was not yours to uncover, Michael!"

She fell silent, swiping the tears that had begun streaming down her face. Damn him, he'd ruined the giddy feeling of the champagne. Instead of feeling light and free, she felt disoriented and disarmed. She could hardly raise her defenses against him in such a state. As it was, she felt like crawling into his lap, curling up against his chest, and seeking comfort in the shelter of his arms.

Would it be so bad if she gave in?

"It was not my intention to hurt you," he replied, his voice low and strained. "I truly thought that you would utter your safe word if you wished me to stop, and I … Amelia, I am tired of settling for parts of you. The parts you adorn yourself with to present a façade to the man who loves you."

She gasped, covering her mouth with her hand. To hear him say it again—not while making love and in the heat of the moment—struck her to her core. No man had ever confessed to loving her, except Simon, and his love was not the same kind as this.

"Yes," Michael confirmed. "I love you, Amelia. I said it, and I meant it. But I cannot love you if you do not let me."

"You do not understand," she croaked, choking back a sob. "You could never understand."

"Goddamn it, I want to!" he thundered. "But how can I when you will not give me a chance?"

Closing her eyes, she contained the well of emotions threatening to spill out of her. She had maintained control this long; surely, she could continue to. It was better for them both if she upheld a certain distance. Better for him not to have to bear the burden of her pain.

Turning her head, she went back to avoiding his gaze, sniffling as another tear rolled down her cheek. Even in the dark, she could feel his eyes on her, tracing the lines of her silhouette. After a moment of silence, he moved, so swiftly she could never have hoped to stop him.

"Not again, damn you," he growled, grasping her waist and hauling her across the carriage onto his lap. "Don't do that … don't shut me out."

Taking her face in his hands, he claimed her mouth in a bruising kiss. He didn't bother to be gentle about it, gripping her chin in one hand and plundering her mouth with this tongue, while using the other hand to grasp her hip and press her down on his rampant erection.

She groaned against his lips, the champagne lowering her inhibitions and making it impossible for her to refuse him. Their lips and tongues dueled, his rapid breaths colliding with her short, breathy pants. He ground his hips up and against hers, and she cursed her thin chemise and gown. At least wearing breeches would have made it harder for him to gain access to her body.

It took only seconds for him to snatch up her skirts and tear open the fall of his breeches, and then he was inside, breaking through her defenses and her body at the same time. She cried out as he filled her, grasping his shoulders and holding on tight as they undulated together, their connection a primal one. Visceral impulse, animalistic mating driven by pure instinct … possess and be possessed.

Michael buried his face against her breasts, each breath coming out on a low groan as he held tight to her hips, controlling her pace and angle. She surrendered to him, to the pleasure rippling out from her core with each stroke of his cock inside her.

In mere minutes, she shattered, gritting her teeth to keep from screaming in pleasure as her sheath clenched around his cock, the resounding spasms of her climax sending tremors through her body from scalp to toes. He followed closely, muffling his hoarse moan of completion against her shoulder as he jerked beneath her, flooding her insides with his seed.

Collapsing against him, she closed her eyes, breathing in the heady scent of sex and slowing her rapid breath. For a moment, he allowed it, but then he moved, lifting her off him and placing her back on her own seat. She watched him quickly clean himself with a handkerchief, then close his breeches.

Moments later, the carriage rolled to a stop before Ashton House.

Amelia quickly adjusted her skirts and ensured she appeared at least partially decent before the door swung open. Michael descended first, then gave her a hand down. As they stood at the bottom of the front steps, she noticed that the carriage remained in place, Oliver and the coachman both seeming to wait for someone to return to the vehicle.

"Are you going somewhere?" she asked.

Moonlight revealed his drawn features, the sadness in his eyes, and the tension around his mouth. It made her heart ache to see him this way and realize she had been the cause.

"A hotel," he informed her. "I cannot reside beneath the same roof with you under these circumstances ... not when I can hardly keep my hands off you for five minutes, it would seem."

Shaking her head, she held her hands out to her sides. "I do not understand what else you want from me, Michael. I've given you everything I have."

He lowered his head and sighed. "That is the thing, Amelia. You haven't, and we both know it. Simon can apprise you of my location should you decide you are ready to be honest with me about everything—what you want, your past, all of it. I cannot do things this way any longer. Do you understand? It is too painful."

Her chest ached as he met her gaze again, revealing the depth of the turmoil she had brought on.

Reaching out to cup his face, she stroked his jaw, bristled with days' worth of stubble.

"The last thing I wanted was to hurt you," she whispered. "Surely, you must know that."

Placing a hand over hers, he gave it a little squeeze, then pulled it away from his face, returning it to her side.

"I know," he murmured. "That does not stop loving you from being the absolute hardest thing I have ever done. And it's the damnedest thing, Amelia … even when it hurts, I cannot stop."

With that, he turned and re-entered the carriage, closing the door behind him without a look back.

Her knees grew weak, and she wanted to sink to the ground and surrender to the grief tearing her apart. Yet, she found the strength to turn and walk up the front steps. The carriage remained on the street until she had gone inside, then the sound of horses' hooves alerted her to Michael's departure.

Leaning against the front door and ignoring the inquisitive stare of the butler, she felt as if her heart had been ripped in two, half of it running after Michael. She had gone and done it. She'd lost him, likely forever if she could not give him what he wanted.

Peeling herself away from the door, she trudged up the stairs and sought her bed, not even bothering to change out of her gown. Her lady's maid had been instructed not to wait up for her, so there was no one there to help her prepare for bed. As she fell onto the sheets and pulled the coverlet over her head, there was no one there at all.

She woke the next morning with a pounding headache, her mouth as dry as sandpaper. Cursing herself for over-imbibing, she forced herself from the bed and allowed Kate to groom and dress her. After the night she'd had, she wanted nothing more than to cower beneath the covers and sleep the day away.

However, dreams of Michael plagued her when she closed her eyes —his lips on hers, his hands mastering her body, his cock filling her, his words of love warming her from the inside out. But lying awake brought her no relief, for her every thought became dominated by him—by memories of last night's confrontation and the way it had caused her to feel.

He had told her that loving her was painful, having no notion that she felt the exact same way. She had come to love him, to crave him as she did water and air. Yet, loving him hurt, because in her heart, she knew she could never be worthy of him. The way she'd treated him last night was proof enough of that.

Loving him not only hurt, it was confusing. As an emotion she did not entirely understand, it crippled her, leaving her vulnerable and exposed. How much more would it hurt once he realized that she was tainted and broken, unable to be fixed?

Now dressed, she supposed it could not hurt to attempt to take tea and toast for breakfast. Her stomach had itself in knots, and she was not certain whether it was due to the champagne or her clash with Michael.

Entering the dining room, she found Simon seated at the head of the table, an ironed copy of the *Morning Post* laid beside his toast and tea. He ate alone, dressed as if he planned to go out soon.

Watching her silently as she sat and waited for her tea to be poured, he held a heavy measure of censure in his gaze.

Wonderful. Now her brother was cross with her, too.

A few bites of dry toast and a sip of tea helped calm her stomach, allowing her to relax a bit in her chair. Closing her eyes, she sighed and pressed her fingers to her temples. Perhaps she should attempt a nap after breakfast to chase away the pounding behind her eyes.

When she opened them to find Simon still staring at her, his paper untouched before him, she huffed in annoyance and speared him with a glare.

"Out with it," she snapped. "You are dying to say something, I just know it."

"Actually, I have a question to ask you," he replied, fussing with his paper until it sat perfectly straight on the table and arranging his teacup so its handle rested at the perfect angle.

His propensity for perfectionism was often endearing, but just now, it annoyed her to no end.

"Oh, do finish rearranging the entire table," she grumbled. "I've got all day."

"It would seem you do," he countered, raising an eyebrow at her. "Since you are here instead of at Oakmoor where you belong."

"Simon—"

"Michael sent me a message with an address and his promise to attend the twins' christening," he interjected. "Why the devil is he staying in an inn? And as for my original question … what the bloody hell are you doing here?"

Rising, she threw her napkin aside, embarrassment heating her face. "If you do not want me here, then I can find an inn to occupy, as well."

"Sit down, Amelia," he commanded, his voice remaining low and steady.

While she usually enjoyed defying Simon, she obeyed, too tired to argue, too lonely to leave and go to a hotel. At least here, she had her family to distract her from how much she missed Michael.

"Now, when you arrived a few days ago, I promised Sophie I would stay out of it," he continued. "However, I cannot sit idly by and watch you suffer like this … not when I might be able to help you through it."

Scoffing, she rolled her eyes. "My husband loves me, and I am incapable of loving him back the way he deserves. How on Earth could you possibly help me with something like that?"

He issued a sarcastic snort. "It is almost as if you do not know me."

Meeting his gaze, she relented with a smirk. "Simon, you and I are not the same. I will admit, the things you endured could be considered much worse than the ones I did."

"Bloody hell, Amelia, it isn't a contest," he snapped, rolling his eyes.

"We were raised with no notion of what affection and love should look like. It only stands to reason we would, both of us, struggle with these concepts as adults. But, it is clear to me that you care for Michael very much."

Nodding, she folded her hands in her lap, toying absently with her wedding ring. "I love him, Simon. I did not think myself capable, but … it caught me quite by surprise."

"I know the feeling well," he replied. "I also know how hard it can be to allow yourself to feel as if you should accept the love of your spouse. Is that it, Amelia? You are struggling with allowing him to love you?"

She nodded again, her eyes stinging as if she would cry again. Fighting the tears back, she resolved not to cry … not this time, and not in front of her brother, who became uncomfortable when women began weeping in his presence.

"He hardly knows me," she managed once she could trust her voice not to wobble. "If he truly did … if I tell him the horrors we endured as children and … and the fears I have …"

"He will still love you," Simon said when she fell silent. "How could you think any different?"

"Perhaps he will," she argued, turning away from his probing gaze. Her brother was far too perceptive. "And perhaps he will see that I am broken. That there is nothing left for him after all of the pieces of me Uncle Gregory chipped away."

Reaching out, he took her chin in his hand and swiveled her head so she looked at him again. "Is that what you think? That he broke you into pieces?"

She shrugged. "Didn't he?"

He swiped his thumb over her cheek, and it came away wet. She had started crying again and hadn't realized it. Bloody hell, she was turning into the sort of woman she despised—a weakling with no control over her emotions.

"I do not believe that for a moment, and neither would Michael," he said. "He might have tried, but he did not succeed. God, Amelia, look how vibrant you are … how passionate and fiery and strong. If a man cannot see the beauty in that, he does not deserve you."

A sob welled in her throat as she realized her brother was right. But that did not assuage her fear or stop her from wanting to hide the ugly parts of herself from her husband.

"I do not fathom how it can be possible," she whispered hoarsely. "How did you do it, Simon? Open yourself up to Sophie without tearing yourself to pieces in the process? How did you survive it?"

He gave her a sad smile, wiping away another tear. "That's the thing, Amelia … I opened myself to her, fully knowing it would tear me apart. I did it willingly, even though at times it hurt so much, I did not think I could bear it."

When she frowned, his smile widened.

"But you see," he continued. "It was all right for me to be in pieces. Because Sophie put them back together. If you love Michael, and you know that he loves you, as well, you should trust him to do the same. You may be cracked and chipped when he's finished, but you'll be his masterpiece … his beautiful little mosaic, made up of all those bits of pain and love and fire. How could any man not be proud to call you his after that?"

She smiled and laughed, the sound tinged with the sob she'd been holding back. "When did you become a bloody poet, Simon?"

"Love does strange things to a man," he confessed. "But if anyone else asks, I am still the frightening, brooding Marquis of Ashton. One must keep one's reputation intact, after all."

Reaching up to cup his jaw, she nodded. "Your secret is safe with me. And I want to thank you, Simon, for being the first man to ever love me. For making me value myself enough to wait for the one man who could love me more than you do."

"I would argue that it isn't possible, but I would not wish to anger your husband," he joked. "I deserve no thanks for the woman you've become. You did it all on your own."

Kissing his forehead, she then rose, turning to run toward the door. Fear niggled in the back of her mind, but she pushed it aside.

For once, she would not let it rule her ... she would outrun it straight into Michael's arms.

"Where are you going?" Simon called out after her. "You haven't finished eating."

Pausing in the doorway, she turned back to him with a smile. "I am going to get my husband back."

# CHAPTER 18

$\mathcal{M}$ichael gripped the rough, wooden banister as he descended into the dark room his brother-in-law had referred to as a dungeon. When the note from Amelia had arrived at his inn, requesting his presence at Ashton House, he'd come running like a lovesick fool. Perhaps he *was* one. A fool for loving a woman as complicated as Amelia … for hoping for even a piece of her heart when he'd already given her every bit of his. A fool for coming back to her after she'd pushed him away, time after time.

Yet, as he found himself swallowed by darkness and faint lamplight, walking willingly into a room filled with implements of torture, he became hopeful. He had made his ultimatum; he'd taken a chance on coming to London to, once again, force Amelia's hand. This was it. If she wanted him, she would have to tell him and trust that he would not abuse her love for him.

He'd spent a miserable night in a hotel much nicer than the one he'd occupied on his previous trip to London. But he'd hardly noticed the finery surrounding him—finery he could now afford thanks to his wife and her dowry. Not when he missed her with an ache that could only be assuaged by her presence. He certainly hoped she intended to come home with him, because he did not wish to spend another night alone.

Reaching the bottom of the staircase, he found Amelia in the center of the room, dressed in her customary Mistress attire. Hair piled on top of her head with a few loose tendrils framing her face, white linen shirt covering her to the thighs, sinful black boots hugging her legs, and a matching corset cinching her waist.

Yet, as he approached, wondering what this could be about, he noticed her expression was not that of the Mistress. Instead of the imperious stare that could drop a man to his knees within seconds, she graced him with a warm smile.

"Thank you for coming," she said.

He glanced about the room, his curiosity piqued by what he saw. Hanging on the wall, ropes and other harnesses created for restraint hung alongside riding crops, whips, and floggers. A table boasting straps and buckles raised his eyebrows. In one corner of the room, the ominous St. Andrew's cross rested, the shackles attached to it glinting in the lamplight.

"Of course," he replied, trying to keep his voice light.

Skimming his hand over a table holding a collection of cock rings, nipple clamps, and other various tools of torture, he avoided her gaze. He couldn't bear to look her in the eye while she rejected him, if that proved to be her aim.

"Why are we here, in this room?" he asked.

"Because it was in this room that I first donned this costume," she said. "The persona of the Mistress."

That got his attention, causing his gaze to swivel back to her. "You and your brother both practice domination, do you not?"

She nodded. "It seems odd … both of us sharing this same predilection. It happened quite by chance. Simon began it, and created this dungeon without my knowledge. It wasn't until I eavesdropped on a guest he'd allowed to use it, that I realized what the room was for."

Remembering the ravishing widow, he nodded in understanding. "Lady Dane."

"Yes," she confirmed. "I watched her and Peter in this room and became transfixed. The way she controlled him, making him desire her enough to do whatever she asked … I wanted that power. I wanted to be her. By then, I had already realized I was not like other ladies. I had already given my maidenhead to a stable boy, for heaven's sake."

He raised his eyebrows in shock. Though, he supposed he should not be surprised. His wife was, as she'd said, different from any woman he'd ever known.

"She taught you well," he offered, uncertain still where this conversation might lead.

"She did," Amelia agreed. "I reveled in it … the powerful feeling of ruling over a man, of hurting him … of being able to look him in the eye and not feel fear."

And then, he understood. His facial muscles softened, and he experienced a twinge of sympathy for her.

"Your uncle," he stated. "He made you afraid."

Her eyes grew wide as she nodded, her lower lip trembling. To her credit, she kept herself together as she cleared her throat and carried on. He marveled at the display of inner strength.

"When I was a girl, Uncle Gregory was all I knew," she told him. "A man who never smiled at me or showed me affection. He hated us both, Simon and I, and resented our presence at Ashton Abbey because he'd hoped to someday inherit the marquisate. Simon's birth ruined that, and he hated me because of simple proximity. His rules reflected that resentment. We were not allowed to make noise. There could be no running, laughing, or raised voices. If we disturbed him, we were punished."

A bitter taste crept into his mouth, and his stomach roiled at what she implied. "How did he punish you?"

"He was very creative," she spat, derision curling her upper lip. "There were the beatings, but of course, that was only part of what he proved to be capable of. There was a closet ... a dark, tiny closet in our nursery he would force us into. Sometimes, we'd remain there for days, only able to keep track of the days by the number of times he brought us stale bread and water. Eventually, Simon began carving notches into the door with his fingernails to tally the days."

"Dear God," he exclaimed, the palms of his hands tingling as he itched to hit something, to strangle the life from someone—preferably the bastard who had done these things to her. Of course, that would be impossible given her uncle's present location in the Fitzwilliam family graveyard.

Amelia nodded as if to confirm that she was, in fact, telling the truth. "He made our lives Hell, though Simon did his best to protect me, to take the brunt of it. He truly did suffer the worst of my uncle's abuse."

She paused, taking a deep breath and lowering her eyes.

When she raised them again to meet his, he found tears glistening in the depths. She was reaching the limits of her control, and he wanted to take her in his arms, soothe her pain and take it on as his own. But she seemed to need to get this out, to lay all of her truths bare.

It was what he had wanted—what they both needed to move forward. So, he kept his hands by his sides and waited for her to continue.

"There were nights I thought he would kill Simon ... when he would come into his bedroom and ... and climb into his bed. I often slept with him because I was afraid of the dark. But when Uncle Gregory would come, he would hide me—under his bed, or in the armoire. 'Stay quiet, Amelia', he would say. 'Don't let him know you're here.'"

Michael felt as if he would be ill, but he remained silent and did his best not to let it show. He would be strong for Amelia, who needed to tell this story. No matter how unpalatable, he would listen to every word.

"His screams still haunt my dreams sometimes," she whispered, her face reddening as she trembled from trying to hold it all in, to keep from losing control. "I hear them and remember that I could not help him. I could only hide and listen while my brother was raped by that whoreson … night after night until he left for Cambridge."

Michael released the breath he'd been holding as she finally gave voice to what she'd been implying, what he'd known she'd been trying to convey. He had known the Fitzwilliam children had suffered, but sodomy and incest? It was unconscionable. Amelia had been right … he did not understand it. He did not understand how a man could harm a child that way.

Suddenly, he remembered the Whittles, and his jaw dropped in shock. "Oh, God … when we visited the tenants …"

"I truly thought Mr. Whittle intended to hurt John," she said, swiping at her eyes with the back of her hand. "And when I saw him getting into the bed, all I could see was my uncle climbing over Simon and pinning him down. I wasn't strong enough to save him … too young and too weak. I wasn't strong enough, and my brother suffered for it."

His control fled, and he crossed the distance between them, pulling her into his arms. She came willingly, collapsing against him and sobbing into his waistcoat.

"Shh," he crooned, stroking her hair and kissing her forehead tenderly. "You are not to blame for any of it. Your uncle was a vile, evil man, who delighted in tormenting others. You were only a scared little girl. What could you have done?"

She sniffed and burrowed closer to him, and the satisfaction of having her seek comfort in him swelled in his chest. He held her tighter, and it seemed to still her trembling. His hand stroked her back through the corset, and he thought of the scars the garment concealed, of her secret pain.

"What of you, Amelia? What did he do to you?"

Lifting her head to look at him, she bit her lower lip and took a deep breath before plunging ahead. "I had always preferred boys' clothing, you know. Because Simon was so slender before he was sent to university, I could wear many of his castoffs. My uncle hated it. He wanted me to know my place as a lady—one who could be bartered away with an advantageous marriage. I took countless thrashings for it, spent several nights in that accursed closet for dressing as I pleased. I suppose, one day, he decided he'd had enough. I needed to be taught a lesson."

Michael braced himself for what she would say next. It had all been so hard to take in … so difficult to bear. Yet, he had not lived through it, which surely proved much worse than simply hearing it.

"He cuffed me so hard on the side of the head, I almost fell unconscious," she whispered, her voice hoarse, her eyes growing glassy as if she relived every moment. "As I lay there, my head pounding, he took up a lamp and broke it, spilling the kerosene over me. He called me a whore and told me I would never make a good match for marriage, because there was something wrong with me. No man would ever want me, so what difference did it make if I was kept pretty for one?"

She paused, and he held his breath, his heart pounding so hard, he was surprised it did not leap right out of his chest.

"And then he struck a match," she whimpered, lowering her head.

He jerked in visceral reaction, tears springing to his eyes as he tried to fathom how terrified she must have been.

"Amelia," he whispered, one hot tear racing toward his jaw.

"I've never known such pain," she continued, her voice hollow. "It took four servants to put the fire out, and by then, the damage had been done. Simon was away at university, so our housekeeper, Mrs. Mounsey, took it upon herself to care for me and send for a physician. Uncle Gregory told the doctor it had been an accident … that I had knocked the lamp over and set myself on fire. I was afraid of what would happen if I told him otherwise."

Shuddering with anger and revulsion toward the man who had maimed his beautiful Amelia, he lifted her chin, swiping her tears away and kissing both her cheeks.

"My God," he whispered, his lips pressed to her forehead. "You were right, Amelia. I do not understand … I do not understand how you could overcome such odds. After all that was done to you, you emerged a strong, vivacious woman. The sort of woman others wish they could be, but could never be because they lack the courage. I cannot tell you how much I admire you for your bravery and strength. How much I love you for persevering through all of that."

She sobbed and lifted her hands to cover his, turning her head to kiss one of his palms.

"I was so afraid to let you see the scars … to let you see what I've kept hidden for so long. Even Simon does not know. I had recovered by the time he returned home, and I swore our servants to secrecy. After all he'd done to try to protect me from Uncle Gregory, it would kill him to know. He will think he failed me."

Michael nodded his understanding. "Your secret is safe with me. *You* are safe with me, Amelia. I loved you before, but knowing what I do now, I think I love you even more. I find myself feeling most unworthy to stand in the presence of such unwavering fortitude."

"And here I thought myself the unworthy one," she quipped, forcing a smile.

He could see she still wrestled with herself—and why shouldn't she? She had just revealed more to him than she ever had to anyone else. He felt honored, humbled.

"Your scars only serve to make you more beautiful," he assured her. "Your past has shaped you into the woman I love."

Bracing her hands upon his chest, she pushed him away, raising her hands to the ribbons of her corset.

"I wanted you to come down here, where it all began, with me wearing this, so you can watch me take it off," she said. "I want you to see me, Michael. I want to give you what I've withheld all this time, because I love you, and you have been so patient with me. I want you to know how grateful I am for that."

He placed a hand over hers, stilling her fingers before she could begin unlacing. "Not like this … not after I forced your hand. I do not want it out of obligation."

Smiling, she brushed his hand aside and gave the ribbon a tug. "This is not out of obligation, Michael. It is done in love. I am ready."

It killed him to keep his hands to himself when he wanted to undress her, help her out of her ensemble. Yet, he endured, realizing this was something she needed to do. He'd robbed her of it before by tearing her shirt off himself, so this time, he would be patient and allow her to have her moment.

The corset fell away, and her shirt loosened, wrinkled across her torso. With a bit of struggling that made him chuckle, she removed her boots, then her stockings, revealing her shapely calves and dainty feet. Then, she stood before him in only the white shirt, much like she had that day in the pasture, when he had begged her for more.

She gave him more now, slowly unbuttoning the shirt before pulling it off over her head. He sucked in a sharp breath at the sight of her, completely bared to him. Her nipples shrank and hardened as he stroked them with his gaze. His mouth watered at the sight of her smooth belly, which he could spend hours kissing and nibbling. Now, perhaps she would let him.

Amelia stood before him for a long while, allowing him to drink her in. He watched the fear war with desire and determination in her gaze—watched her arrive at the exact moment she decided to allow him to see the rest. Turning slowly, she put her back to him, exposing everything she'd kept hidden.

His heart ached at the sight of her scars, the marks clearly delineating themselves as burns now that he allowed himself closer inspection. The welts looked like white tongues of flame lashing from her lower back up toward her shoulder blades, angry and twisted.

Approaching her, he reached out to touch them, skimming his fingertips over the raised, contorted lines. She stiffened with a gasp, but relaxed when he continued, tracing the lines of her waist down to her hips, gripping them with both hands and pulling her against him. Bending his head, he kissed her shoulder, working his way toward her neck.

"So beautiful," he whispered in her ear. "My wife ... my love ... my Mistress."

Turning in his arms, she met his gaze and inclined his head. "I have used being a dominant as an outlet for my pain for so long ... I am not certain I can learn another way to do so."

He smiled, allowing his knuckles to skim the plane of her belly, wanting to explore that part of her body now that she would allow it.

"You do not have to," he assured her. "I can take your pain, Amelia. I want you to give it to me and let me carry it for you ... whenever you like, however you like."

Her smile was radiant as she nodded, relaxing even more in his hold as he went on touching her, exploring her, learning the parts of her she had barred him from in the past. Then, he sank to his knees before her, holding her gaze as he clasped his hands behind his back.

"What does my Mistress want from me?" he offered.

As she stroked his hair, then the line of his jaw, her smile faded away, desire and lust flaring in her eyes.

"I command you to make love to me, right now. I am yours to do with as you please. Make me yours, Mr. Darling."

He was on his feet in an instant and taking her into his arms, carrying her across the room to the empty restraint table. He did not need the buckles and straps to bind her—she'd already given him every part of her. She belonged to him.

Laying her on the table, he pulled her to the edge so that her legs hung off it, then stepped between them. He leaned over her, bracing his hands on either side of her, and kissed her. She returned his kiss eagerly, hungrily, opening herself to him in a way she never had. Gone was her control and restraint, and in its place a woman who just wanted to be loved lay before him, naked, spread, and his.

He kissed his way down her throat, pausing to flick his tongue over her beating pulse, to feel the force of her need pounding in her veins. His lips traveled down the center of her chest, and he cupped her breasts, plucking at her nipples until she cried out, arching her back in a silent plea for more. He obliged her, covering one with his mouth and teasing it with his tongue. She moaned when he suckled her, then sighed when he released it from his mouth, blowing a cool stream of air over the tight bud. He treated the other the same way before moving his attentions to the stretch of soft skin previously hidden from him.

Turning his head to rest his cheek against the soft plane of her belly, he inhaled her scent, nuzzling her and reveling in the feel of her against him. He smiled when she giggled, proving ticklish when his rough stubble caressed a sensitive spot. He rested a palm on her lower stomach, marveling at how his large hand appeared when splayed, covered her from hipbone to hipbone.

Reverently lowering his head, he kissed her just above her mons, realizing that soon, she might begin increasing with his child. The notion filled him with a sense of pride and possessiveness. Nothing would bring him more pleasure than watching her swell with the life inside her … a life he would plant there himself.

He took his time exploring the untouched terrain of her middle, nipping at her sensitive skin, smiling when she laughed. Then, he continued on, spreading her thighs and lowering his head between them. She sighed and moaned as he took her into his mouth ever so gently, teasing her silken inner flesh with slow, languorous tongue strokes. Before long, she was quivering and begging him for more, thrusting her hips up to urge him on.

He reached beneath her raised body to grip one of her buttocks, then gave it a swat to remind her that she'd given him control. She yelped and sank back to the table, quivering as if the blow had set off a reaction in her that heightened her pleasure. He had to admit, the sting of his palm sent a rush through him, causing him to want to do it again.

Standing up straight, he lifted her to her feet and turned her around, pushing her to lay her upper body on the table. He gave her another swat, this time on the opposite cheek. She groaned, raising her hips as if in invitation, her skin blushing pink with his handprint.

Lowering his body over hers, he kissed the back of her neck, working his way down her body, tracing his tongue over the ridges of her spine. He paused when he approached the mass of scars, worshipfully tracing one with his thumb. She whimpered, but he reached up to stroke her hair, to reassure her. She calmed, and he carried on, dragging his tongue over one of the raised marks, drawing a gasp from her.

"I love you," he whispered against her marred skin, so she would understand that he loved her because of the scars, and not in spite of them.

She sighed and squirmed as he went on kissing her, taking his time and paying homage to every burn mark his lips touched.

Then, when he could wait no longer, he turned her back over and opened his breeches, releasing his cock from his smallclothes. He took himself in hand and gazed down at her, her nudity in stark juxtaposition to him, fully clothed.

His priceless offering, his beautiful treasure.

She spread her legs and gazed down at his swollen member, clutched in his fist and straining toward her. He stroked himself and smirked when she made a sound of longing, biting her lower lip.

"Is this what you want?" he teased, stroking himself again. "Tell me, Amelia. Beg me for what you want."

"I want you, Michael," she whispered, her voice raspy and hoarse from both her tears and her desire. "Only you. Take me, Michael … give me your cock."

He surged into her with a groan, both her soft, warm body and her words contributing to the force of his need. Her moan echoed from the walls of the dark chamber as he grasped her waist and took up a steady rhythm inside her, pulling her forward to meet each of his thrusts. Her hips came off the table, and he held her up, pounding into her slick channel, his knees buckling from the overwhelming pleasure of claiming her, taking her, making her his.

"Michael," she moaned, his name a sweet note of music when whispered in passion. "My God, Michael … I love you."

Lowering his body back over hers, he took her lips, pumping into her faster and faster as climax began bearing down on him. He smothered her scream with his lips when she spent, his own muffled groans mingling with hers as he followed her, spilling inside her with a force that left him breathless.

Still braced over her until he could regain his strength, he lifted his head and gazed down at her. She watched him with parted lips, eyes wide with wonder, her chest heaving with heavy breath.

"I am going to have to do away with my safe word," she said.

He frowned. "Why?"

She smiled. "Because I have no need for one. I trust you, Michael. Besides … I do not think there is a thing you could do to me that I would not like … nothing you could do that I would want you to stop."

Glancing at their surroundings, he raised his eyebrows. "Perhaps we should build a room like this at Oakmoor … where we could put that to the test."

Laughing, she reached up to cup his face. "Whatever you want, my darling husband."

"Darling," he repeated with a chuckle. "It does have a different ring to it when you say it as opposed to someone else calling me by name."

She raised her head to kiss him, and in that act of affection, he felt every bit of her love for him.

"That is because I love you. It is a mere coincidence that your name happens to also be what you are to me … my darling Mr. Darling."

Straightening, he lifted her into his arms, still nestled inside her as she wrapped her limbs around him. "Submission has made you downright giddy. I ought to coerce you into it more often."

She scowled at him. "Enjoy it while it lasts, because the moment we return home, I will become your Mistress again. I warn you, I will be difficult to please. You had best obey or suffer the consequences."

Holding her close, he grinned. "Challenge accepted, Mistress … willingly and with relish."

# EPILOGUE

*A*melia glanced up from the papers arranged on her desk—the menu for two weeks' worth of meals at Oakmoor to be approved and returned to Cook, an inventory of the household linens, many of which needed replacing, as well as a list of preparations to be made for the house party, which would take place in just a few short days. She was exhausted, but such was the burden of duty. With the maintenance of Oakmoor to help oversee during the day, she found fulfillment in a way she never could have in London. Instead of the fast pace and temptation of the city, she now found peace in the tranquility of the countryside.

A knock on the door had interrupted her work, and she bid the person to enter. In truth, she was grateful for the distraction after an entire morning of poring over her work.

Lydia and Perdita materialized in the doorway, timidly peering into the study at her. She had been avoiding them, embarrassment causing her to shun their company. Her behavior had been abysmal, both at the Whittles' cottage, and the morning she had left Oakmoor and Michael.

Surely, they would want to take her to task for abandoning a member of their family. The Darlings were close knit, and she had done something to hurt one of them. It might not matter to them that after the christening of Joanna and Phineas, she and Michael had returned home together and had been inseparable ever since.

Standing to meet them, she lifted her chin, determined to take whatever censure they would dish out. It would be well-deserved, and once it was over, she would do her best to gain their trust again. She would show them all how much she loved Michael ... that she would never hurt him again.

To her surprise, Perdita gave her a friendly smile, while Lydia hugged her without preamble.

"Mother says we should not disturb you with so much to do to prepare for the house party," her sister-in-law said in that rapid-fire way of hers. "But I told her we have hardly seen you since your return from London, and we simply must stop in and see how you are getting on. After all, you might still be angry with Michael after your row and wish to talk to someone ... you know, someone who isn't Michael, in case you need to browbeat him."

"Child, calm yourself," Perdita admonished, giving her daughter a withering look that brought a smile to Amelia's face. The girl was so much like she had been at this age. "Amelia, we do not wish to disturb you. We only want to offer our services. Planning for a house party of this magnitude can be quite taxing, and we wanted you to know that we are here if you have a need."

Amelia frowned, truly puzzled by the behavior of these women. "You *want* to help me?"

Lydia giggled. "Of course we do, silly. Why wouldn't we?"

"Because I have not behaved as well as I ought," she said before she could lose her nerve. "And while I have made amends with Michael, I want you both to know how sorry I am for leaving. I would understand it if you both hated me, or regretted welcoming me into your family. I want you to know that I intend to make it up to you all. Whatever it takes to show you how sorry I am, I will do it."

Perdita gave her a sad smile as she came forward and took both of her hands. "My dear, no apologies are necessary. Whatever occurs between you and your husband … well, that is your affair, is it not? As your mother and sister, we are not here to castigate you or judge you. We are here to love and support you."

Tears threatened her eyes, but she held them back, determined this time to keep them at bay. She'd cried enough to last a lifetime, and was ready to go back to being the girl with the ready smile.

"I have never had a sister or a mother before," she confessed. "I did not know that this was the way things worked."

Lydia hugged her from one side, while Perdita embraced her from the other.

"Once a Darling, always a Darling," Perdita declared. "For better or for worse."

"Thank you," she murmured. "Thank you so much for accepting me."

"How could we not when Michael clearly loves you?" Perdita replied. "Now … I do believe it is time for you to quit for the day. Michael has requested your presence in his study."

A wide grin spread over her face as she realized what his summons must be about. She disengaged from the women's embraces and made for the door.

"I believe you are right," she said. "I shall go to him now."

They waved her off, and it was all she could do to keep from running as fast as she could to her husband's study. She managed to get there with her dignity intact, and entered the room to find it empty. However, she knew that Michael waited for her—in the secret chamber just on the other side of one of the bookcases. He'd assured her that no one else knew of the hidden room, and the only entrance was the one she would now open.

Finding the hidden switch to unlock the panel, she stood back as it opened to admit her between rows upon rows of books. Smiling, she stepped into the room Michael had begun transforming for her.

A dungeon fit for a Mistress.

He stood in the center, studying his latest handiwork—a St. Andrew's cross he'd crafted himself from oak wood. Shirt removed, covered in sweat, he seemed to have just finished. Her mouth watered at the sight of all that exposed skin and the powerful, rippling muscles beneath it.

Turning to her, he gestured toward the cross and beamed with pride. "Well? What do you think?"

Dodging the other odds and ends littering the unfinished room, she approached the cross. He had spent hours in Simon's dungeon, taking measurements and jotting down notes so he would be prepared to create their own little den of sin.

Running a hand over the wood he had smoothed and lacquered until it gleamed, she smiled. Iron shackles hung from the tops of the cross, and another set rested at the bottom.

"It is perfect," she declared. "You commoners have your uses."

He chuckled and swatted her arse, then pulled her back to rest against his front. "This commoner can curl your toes like no nobleman can … don't forget that."

"Hmm," she murmured as he began kissing her neck. "My toes are curling just thinking of you tethered to that cross, helpless at my fingertips."

Releasing her, he moved to a table neatly arranged with some of the implements Simon had given them—spare items he had not used. Taking up her black leather bullwhip, he extended it to her with a raised eyebrow.

"Your paintbrush, Mistress."

The leather kissed her palm as she accepted the whip, a tremor rolling through her as the excitement of playing with Michael, of engaging in this game of submission and domination, rippled through her.

"I am going to paint your back, Mr. Darling," she declared, giving the whip a flick and smiling when it cracked through the air. "What say you?"

Approaching the cross, he spread his arms so that she could shackle him. "I am your willing canvas, Mistress. Do your worst."

Placing the whip aside, she reached up to enclose his wrists in the shackles, lifting and spreading his arms. Then, she wrapped her arms around him, pressing her cheek against his back. She could hear his heart beating, feel his excitement as he waited for her to do what she did best—balancing pain and pleasure until he begged her for more.

She sank to her knees and relieved him of his boots and stockings, then stood once more. Pressing her breasts against his back, she reached around to cup the front of his breeches, finding his cock already full and thick. He groaned, thrusting into her hand. She bit him, sinking her teeth into the meaty flesh of his back, causing him to grunt and hiss from the pain. But he went still, understanding the admonishment and the clear instruction in her punishment. He was to stand still until she instructed otherwise.

Opening his breeches, she freed his cock and teased him, stroking his shaft and smearing him in his own wetness, then cupped his bollocks, pulling a groan from him. Dropping his breeches, she helped him step out of them, then proceeded to tether his ankles to the bottom of the cross.

Pressing herself to him again, she reveled in the feel of his naked body against her clothed one, the power of his muscles tamed and trapped for her pleasure. She trailed a fingertip down his spine, making him shudder, then kissed his shoulders, nipping and licking at him until he began to sigh and groan. She teased him with a few strokes of his cock, ensuring his desire had reached fever pitch before she returned to her whip.

Taking it in hand, she stood back and tested it a few times, flicking and swirling it through the air, letting him anticipate the first blow. He was magnificent, the muscles of his back and the ones blanketing his ribs swelling when he inhaled, then growing taut when he exhaled.

She let the first blow fall, aiming for a shoulder blade. He flinched from the light strike, no more than a sting. Having always enjoyed symmetry, she struck the opposite shoulder blade, creating a mirror image of the first pink mark she'd created on the other side. She drew out the encounter, enjoying every lash, reveling in his gasps and groans as she put more force behind each one, until the lines upon his back appeared not unlike wings.

Later, she would ease the pain with a soothing salve that would take away the redness and rejuvenate his muscles. But for now, she wanted him to feel that pain, to sink into that place where it mingled with pleasure. He was already there, she could see. His breaths came harsh and shallow, his body trembling as he stood on the precipice of perfect bliss.

"Your back is a masterpiece, Mr. Darling," she declared, setting the whip aside.

He winced when she touched him, trailing her fingertip over one of the lashes with the gentlest of touches. To him, it would feel euphoric, a comforting balm over the fiery sting.

"Thank you, Mistress," he panted. "Your touch is Heaven."

She gave him more, using her fingers to soothe the pain, stroking the red feathers streaked over his ribs, pressing her lips to them and laving them with her tongue. He trembled against the wood, but the shackles held him still for her, allowing her to play with him to her heart's content.

He gasped when she reached around to grab his cock again, pumping it in her fist until he was shaking and groaning, rattling the chains keeping him bound. If not for the cross, his limbs might have given out. Yet, he was forced to remain there, helpless in her hands as she pumped his cock until he spent with a roar, his seed staining her hand and the hard, wooden floor beneath him.

Satisfied, she rose to her feet with a smile. Finding a handkerchief in the pocket of her coat, she used it to clean her hand, then set it aside before pulling off the garment. Freeing him from the shackles, she took some of his weight onto her shoulders and helped ease him onto a nearby cushioned chaise longue—a piece of furniture she was grateful for now, with Michael sated and weak. He lay on his side, closing his eyes and enjoying his moment of tranquility, the calm following the storm of her torment.

Removing her cravat, she used it to dab the sweat from his brow, then located a jar of the balm she would use for his back. While he lay there, reveling in her attentiveness and closeness, she soothed him, massaging the salve into his skin. By the time she had finished, he'd begun falling asleep, his golden hair tumbling into his eyes, his lashes resting on his cheekbones.

"Thank you, Mistress," he murmured again before drifting off.

Kneeling before the chaise, she reached out to stroke his cheek, her love for him making her feel as if she might burst.

This man was literally willing to take her pain onto his back and carry it so she did not have to. He loved her despite her faults and the things she had done to hurt him. As a Mistress, she could not have asked for a better submissive … As a woman, she could not have asked for a better husband. She was not certain which part of her was more fortunate.

But then, by finding both the perfect submissive as well as perfect husband, there seemed no reason to separate the two any longer. She was both a lady and a dominant. A wife and a Mistress.

But, above all, she was Michael's, and Michael was hers. Nothing else mattered.

"No," she murmured, kissing his brow. "Thank *you*, my darling."

*Start the Scandalous Ballroom Encounters Series from the beginning with TWO free books!*

*Click here to download Masquerade from your favorite ebook retailer!*

*Continue Camden and Maggie's story with free copy of A Honeymoon Masquerade when you sign up for Victoria's newsletter. Click here to get your freebie!*

*A kiss neither will ever forget ... a forbidden attraction that can't be denied ...*

After a disastrous first Season, Lydia Darling abandons all hope of love and marriage. A simple country girl, she does not belong amongst the debutantes of the ton. Rather than rely on her family for the rest of her days, she chooses to find work as a governess, a position that allows her to hide away from the society that shunned her. However, she cannot seem to forget the mysterious stranger she encountered at a ball during her Season … a man whose kiss haunts her dreams. He never even told her his name, yet Lydia cannot forget the one man who made her crave his touch in a way no other has been able to since.

Sinclair Clayton thought he'd never see the young lady he kissed in a garden during a London ball four years ago … until she turns up on his doorstep applying for the position of governess to his young son. He finds his heart quickly ensnared by Lydia, the strength of their attraction growing more powerful the longer she remains in his home. The illegitimate son of a viscount, he's always stood on the fringes of society, never feeling as if he belongs. All that changes when he is in Lydia's presence, and with her becomes the place he knows he should be.

Yet, Sinclair's loveless marriage to a woman who has made his life a living hell from the moment he said 'I do' prevents them from being together. That does not stop them from wanting one another, despite how hard they fight to resist their visceral connection. Will the whims of fate ever allow them to spend their lives together, or are they doomed to long for each other while remaining apart?

# ABOUT THE AUTHOR

*Sexy heroes ... sassy heroines ... electrifying erotic romance.*
Victoria Vale has written over two dozen Romance and Young Adult novels under various pseudonyms. As a lover of erotic romance, she enjoys nothing more than a sexy hero paired with a sassy heroine, flavored with a dash of spice and lots of heat. A wife and mother of three, she enjoys reading (of course), cooking, sewing ... and other activities that aren't appropriate for inclusion in a biography.